A HAUNT FOR JACKALS

A Novel

BENJAMIN WESTBROOK

Visit Benjamin Westbrook's website at
www.benjaminwestbrook.com

Follow Benjamin Westbrook on Twitter: @BKWestbrook

A Haunt for Jackals

ISBN 978-0-9862136-3-2

For my God and my Family...
I'm nothing without you.

Prologue
(From the final chapter of *Infringement*)

Kevin approached the front door and, as he'd done twice before, called out, "Mrs. Parker, it's okay, it's Kevin Cameron."

Declan could hear him and cursed Kevin, beginning to think the message Kevin had sent was intended to be a trap. Kevin called out again, "Mrs. Parker...Mrs. Parker, it's Kevin Cameron," but nothing happened. He could hear or see no movement in the house.

Bleeker stepped from the car and turned his head in a slow scan of the very dimly-lit forest surrounding the house. Bleeker continued scanning the hillside and forest. Despite the creeping darkness, the sun hadn't completely fallen and a small amount of soft orange light still colored the lake and hillside. Declan began to worry that he would spot Evan and the others moving on the cliffside above. He kept an eye on Costello and the other agent, who had found Megan's dad's car and taken up positions at the back of the house, weapons raised.

As Declan turned back to Bleeker, he noticed Bleeker motion for Kevin to be quiet, but couldn't make out what was said, as Kevin walked back toward the car. Declan watched Bleeker's gaze focus on the hillside behind the house, on a rocky, well-wooded spot about forty feet from the cave entrance. Declan turned his attention to that spot as well, trying to make out any movement up there.

For a split second, he spotted something move through the thick evergreens, and immediately turned his eyes back to Bleeker, who then appeared to be talking to Kevin. Declan caught movement in his peripheral and turned back to see Costello and Jurickson entering the lake house from the rear door. About 10 seconds later, Costello appeared on the front porch and Declan heard him yell, "It's empty, but it doesn't look like they've been gone long!"

Upon hearing the house was empty, Bleeker looked squarely at Kevin. His face betrayed no thoughts whatsoever. His eyes still locked in on Kevin, Bleeker spoke calmly into his radio, "They're on foot, headed up the hillside directly behind the house. Crandon, bring the van up immediately. We need you three here. Costello, you and Jurickson head up after them. I spotted movement on the hillside about forty to fifty feet above the house."

"What do you want me to do?" Kevin asked.

Saying nothing, but with his eyes still locked onto Kevin, Bleeker simply raised his side arm and fired two quick rounds. Each hit Kevin squarely in the center of his chest. The bullets ripped through his heart, throwing Kevin onto the gravel.

"You've done enough already."

Declan jerked his eye away from the scope on the Remington as Kevin Cameron fell to the ground, dead. Without time to let the shock of Kevin's execution wash over him, he caught sight of the van's headlights coming down the road through the trees. Out of his peripheral vision, he saw Costello and Jurickson exit the rear door of the house and head toward the hillside.

"Damn," he said to himself. "Bleeker must have seen them up there."

Still standing near Kevin's body, Bleeker had turned to face the oncoming van. Declan's eyes flashed back and forth from Costello to Bleeker. He knew he couldn't let Costello and Jurickson get up into the forest, or he'd have no shot; however, he desperately wanted to take Bleeker first, thereby finally giving Bleeker what he deserved, eliminating command and, hopefully, causing confusion amongst the others.

Seeing Jurickson almost to the forest line, immediately followed by Costello, he quickly raised the Remington, lined up his shot through the scope, and fired one round, hitting Jurickson just above the right knee, which was precisely where he'd aimed. Jurickson fell screaming to the ground.

On hearing the shot, Costello hit the ground and Bleeker ran for cover behind Kevin's car. Declan quickly found Costello through the scope, lying flat on the ground, but still out in the open, aimed for the side of his exposed right leg, and fired. As with Jurickson, the bullet found its mark, and Costello screamed out that he was hit.

Evan and the others had heard Bleeker's two shots when they were still about twenty feet from the cave entrance. They'd stopped for a second and, unable to see anything, sprinted toward the cave. Evan had gathered everyone inside, when Declan's two shots rang through the forest.

"That was a rifle," Evan said nervously.

"Are you sure?" Michelle replied.

"I'm certain. It's a different sound than a handgun."

No sooner had Evan spoken, when another rifle shot filled the air. "There it is again. That's gotta be Declan. I should help."

"No," Michelle replied. "You have to get us to the plane. We don't know our way through this cave. You're not leaving us. I won't lose you again."

"You're right, my love, you're right," Evan said. "Okay, let's go. Everyone together." He flipped on the flashlight and hurried them along.

With Bleeker still hunkered down behind Kevin's car,

Declan fired a round at the side mirror just above his head, taking it out and keeping Bleeker pinned down. Watching the van's headlights growing larger, Declan waited for the van to come into view, then took aim at the front driver's-side tire, squeezing off two rounds. The second round blew out the tire, causing the driver to lose control. The van hurled off the gravel road and smashed sideways into the heavy evergreen trees lining the road about twenty-five feet from Kevin's car.

Declan was unable to get a sight on anyone inside the van. He scanned back to the car to see if Bleeker had popped his head up, but saw nothing. A few seconds later, an agent stumbled out of the van carrying a rifle and, keeping low and zigzagging, tried to make his way to Bleeker. Declan lined up his shot and fired again, hitting the agent just above the knee. The agent fell to the gravel, writhing in pain.

––––––––––––––––––

Bleeker took out his phone and dialed 911, "I'm FBI and we're under fire. I'm pinned down and I have men down. I need anyone and everyone you can get out here and I need them now!"

––––––––––––––––––

Evan and the family could see the plane on the landing strip just about ten yards away. Evan's mom ran ahead and when Tom Langham saw her emerge from the forest, he fired up the engines. The plane was fueled and cleared for takeoff. After starting her up, Tom came out onto the tarmac and met Mrs. Parker, saying, "Is everyone okay? I could hear gunshots out there."

"We're fine, but Declan isn't with us. We need to wait for him."

"I'll do what I can ma'am, but I gave him my word

I'd get you all safely out of here, with or without him. Please climb aboard."

A few seconds later, Jessica, Michelle, Charlotte, Evan and Will arrived. Tom helped them all into the plane.

"We have to wait for Declan," Evan shouted.

"I'll wait for a few minutes, but I've promised to get you all to safety."

"Just wait, he'll be here. We can't leave him, I don't care what you've promised."

"Trust me, I don't want to take off without Declan any more than you do, but the objective of this mission was clear. We'll wait a few more minutes. That's the best I can do."

———————————————

Declan continued firing rounds, keeping Bleeker and the agents in the van pinned down. They tried to return fire, but in the darkness, couldn't get a solid location on Declan. Each time he'd fire, he'd zigzag a bit further up the hillside, slowly making his way back toward the cave entrance.

Nearing the edge of his range, Declan heard sirens in the distance and assumed, correctly, that Bleeker had radioed for back up. Finally, he put the Remington on his shoulder and hurried up the hillside toward the cave entrance, at once thankful and annoyed that he hadn't heard or seen the plane takeoff yet.

As he finally reached the cave, red and blue flashing lights could be seen outside the house below. Declan watched for a few seconds, unable to tell whether they were police or Homeland, but he was able to make out three squad cars and an ambulance. More sirens could be heard in the distance, and spotlights had begun scanning the forest and hillsides surrounding the house.

Taking the first step into the dark of the cave, he finally heard the jet overhead and looked up to see its lights flashing as it sped off against the stars in the newly black night sky. Watching Tom's plane bank slightly and begin the journey south, Declan breathed in deeply, relieved beyond measure that his family was onboard and safe.

Looking up to the stars in the sky, too numerous to count, for the first time in years Declan remembered something his dad had told him as a boy when visiting the lake house in summers gone by. Quoting Psalm 147, Verse 4, his Dad had said of God, "He determines the number of stars in the sky and calls them each by name."

Standing between the red and blue lights flashing below and the innumerable stars glistening above, the true number and names of which were known only to the God who had created them, Declan was at peace, for he knew with absolute certainty that he was anything but alone. The Lord was with him, and would deliver him safely back to Megan and the rest of his family. He didn't know how, or when, but just as his dad had done before taking his final breath, Declan kissed his closed hand three times, made the sign of the cross, and headed into the darkness with his faith and trust in God alone.

PART I

"[6] Do not be anxious about anything, but in every situation, by prayer and petition, with thanksgiving, present your requests to God. [7] And the peace of God, which transcends all understanding, will guard your hearts and your minds in Christ Jesus."

Philippians 4:6-7

Chapter 1

The sun set in a blaze of red, yellow and orange, dazzling and glittering off the surface of Lake Pontchartrain. The scene seemed to Declan Parker as if God had reached down through the heavens and touched the lake with a whisper, lighting it up with a glorious display of color dancing atop the wavy water. The splendor of the lake at sunset reminded Declan of the Urubamba Valley in Peru, his new home, and his wife, Megan.

He could see her there, sitting in the quiet garden outside their hacienda, overlooking the lush green valley below, and he desperately wanted to be next to her again, to look once more into her eyes, and know, finally, he was home. The warm gulf breeze pressed against Declan's scruffy bearded cheeks, and, along with the image of Megan in his mind's eye, breathed life into his worn and thinning frame as the pickup truck sped along the interstate toward New Orleans proper.

Declan took another bite from the apple his benefactors in the truck's cab had given to him, along with the ride, when he'd hooked up with them earlier that day at a truck stop near Brooksville, Mississippi. He hadn't asked their names and they hadn't asked his, but with Tom Langham scheduled to pick him up in less than 36 hours, Declan had been desperate for a ride after eight straight days of walking the backcountry roads.

The journey south from his family's lake house in the Midwest had been more difficult than Declan had anticipated. Initially, he'd spent nearly four days after his family escaped John Bleeker's capture hiding in the network of caves within the hillsides around the lake house. He'd gone into the cave system, alone, with only a couple of energy bars, and a bottle of water. Unfortunately, finding more food in the small country towns he'd traveled through had grown more difficult with each day, as the protests, civil unrest, and resulting martial law had negatively impacted the supply chain drastically in the less-populated regions of the country. Declan had spent a substantial number of days hungry and, at certain points, had resorted to eating what roadkill he came across and any insects or small game he could catch and kill. The troubles he'd faced, and witnessed others facing, had forged Declan's new-found faith in God like iron in a blue fire. He'd quickly discovered that, by relying only on himself, he'd likely never reach New Orleans. So, instead of depending on his own limited strength and resources, he'd depended on God, and, finally, home and Megan were within reach.

The slight tartness of the apple tickled his tongue and, coupled with the reality that, after nearly thirty days of walking and very-occasionally hitching, he was finally within spitting distance of New Orleans, reinvigorated Declan. He savored the burst of flavor, the tartness, that flooded his senses with each bite of the apple, and the aching in his feet and back, the general exhaustion that had accompanied him since he'd been on the run, dissipated, if only temporarily. Soon, very soon, Declan would be holding Megan again, and every last inch of him ached for her.

"Please, Lord, see me back home. Please get me back to her," he prayed, as he had ever since escaping into the darkness of the cave in the woods above his family's lake house nearly a month earlier.

The pickup truck hit a bump in the road, jostling Declan slightly in the rear, and he leaned back against the cab, and closed his eyes, relishing the warm air as it brushed against his face. He began to lose himself in his thoughts as the truck sped across the highway, its driver anxious to get to where he was going, and off the road, before the national curfew took effect just after sunset.

The next time Declan opened his eyes was when he felt the truck come to a stop and a voice say through the cab's back window, "We'll let you off at St. Charles Street, okay?"

"What?" Declan replied.

"We'll let you off at St. Charles & Louisiana."

"That's great. Whatever works for you guys."

The passenger slid the back window closed again and the truck continued through a green traffic light. Declan pulled his backpack close and unzipped the main compartment, making sure his Bible and the few other possessions he had were all inside. The sun was almost fully set and, with the settling darkness, the streets in the Garden District were nearly empty, but for a few other cars and a handful of people hurrying to get whatever it was they needed before the sunset to sunrise curfew began.

Declan looked around and took in the general disarray of the neighborhood. He'd been to New Orleans previously, a few years earlier, and remembered it differently. He didn't sense the same laissez faire vibe in the air he had before. Everything looked closed up and the people who were still out appeared to him focused on finding trouble or getting to wherever they were going as quickly as they could.

As they approached the intersection of St. Charles Street and Louisiana Avenue, the truck began to slow again. When it came to a stop, Declan noticed the reflection of a flashing blue light in a window to his left. Instinctively he slumped low in the truck bed, pulled a blanket over himself, and tucked up against the sidewall on the driver's side.

"You know it's a just few minutes before curfew?" he heard a voice say.

"I do," the driver replied. "We're almost home."

"Where are you coming from?" a Homeland trooper asked.

"Drove back home from seeing family in Tennessee."

"Let me see your ID's."

"Why?" the driver asked. "I told you, we're almost home and it's not curfew yet. If you hadn't stopped us, we'd already be there."

"Step out of the truck and let me see your ID's," the trooper repeated.

"This is ridiculous."

"Get out of the truck."

Declan's mind was racing. He'd only heard one trooper's voice, but that didn't mean there wasn't another, or even a few more, nearby, likely covering the situation from their cruiser. The "Lone Ranger", his dad's 9 mm, was tucked away in his backpack, but he didn't want to use it, and doubted he could get to it anyway without the trooper noticing his movement. It was only a matter of time, likely seconds, before the trooper, or another trooper, would check the truck bed and discover him there. Declan heard, and felt, both of the truck's doors open. He had to have a plan, and quickly.

"You, on the passenger side, slowly step around to the driver's side of the truck," another voice called out.

"So there are at least two," Declan thought. Suddenly, a gunshot rang through the air and Declan heard the passenger groan and fall to the pavement next to the truck.

"What the hell did you shoot him for?" the driver screamed. "He didn't do nothin'."

"Put your hands in the air and kneel on the ground! Now!"

"He didn't do nothin'! Neither did I! Damn you! We were just on our way home!"

"Hands in the air now," the Homeland trooper yelled again.

Declan couldn't wait any longer. He grabbed his backpack tightly and slowly rolled into position near the passenger sidewall. In a flash, he sprang up and over the truck bed, taking the trooper off guard, and sprinted for cover near a building on the corner.

His feet felt heavy at first, still stiff, but as the first gunshot burst out behind him, Declan's adrenaline kicked in and he barreled toward the building. More gunshots cracked the air in succession behind him, but he kept running, keeping tucked, as fast as he could. He could hear the rounds whiz by on either side of him, and thought, as he was within a few feet of the building, that he'd made it to the safety of cover; however, just as the thought formed, Declan felt a burning sensation rip through his right arm. The pain was sudden and intense, but he kept going and finally turned the corner, taking cover on the opposite side.

Declan looked down at his arm and quickly saw that his sleeve was covered in blood. A rush of lightheadedness pulsed through his head, exactly as it had on Christmas Eve, the only other time he'd been shot, but unlike that night, Declan fought off the sensation of drowsiness and tried to focus his thoughts. The Homeland trooper would assuredly be chasing him.

Trying his best to ignore the searing pain, he quickly unzipped his backpack with his good arm, and pulled out his 9mm. Closing his eyes to gather himself and catch his breath, Declan listened for the troopers' footsteps. At first, he could only hear the blood pulsing through his veins and arteries, but a few seconds later, after quieting his mind, Declan heard one of the troopers approaching from the left. He laid on his stomach in the shadow of the wall, and waited, until the footsteps grew louder. When he saw the trooper's shadow fall across his view, Declan steadied his finger on the trigger and aimed for where the trooper's next footstep would land. A second later, the trooper's boot came into view and Declan squeezed the trigger. The round exploded out the chamber of the 9mm and ripped through the trooper's boot, dropping him instantly to the ground. Declan jumped to his feet and ran away from the writhing trooper into the darkness toward Carondelet Street.

Chapter 2

John Bleeker looked up from his computer screen when he heard the light knock on his partially-open door.

"Come in," he said.

The aide stepped into Bleeker's tiny West Wing office and stood silently in front of the desk, waiting for Bleeker to look up from his monitor again.

"So, what is it?" Bleeker asked.

"Sir, I've been running checks for privately owned aircraft registrations and have come up with something I think you'll find interesting."

"Go on," Bleeker said, leaning back in his chair.

"I've found three registered to Neary Capital Management, which is the firm owned by Megan Neary's father. One of the planes is a Gulfstream G500, which has a range of roughly 5,000 nautical miles. The other two are much shorter range planes."

"So the G500 could fly international."

"Easily. In fact, that's what it's designed for."

"Anything else?"

"Yes. Aviation records show Neary's G500 flying from Potomac Airfield, with a brief stop in Dallas and then onto Cusco, Peru on the night Declan Parker and Megan Neary disappeared from the hospital."

"Peru?"

"Yes, sir. That's not all though. The G500 was also registered as leaving Cusco and flying to Oklahoma City on the day Declan Parker and his family absconded. It returned to Cusco the following morning."

"Has it left since then?"

"Not that I've seen, sir. I didn't see any flight registrations subsequent to that date."

"So the Parkers headed to Peru?"

"It appears that way, at least initially; however, I suspect they're still there. I also performed some background and records checks to see if there was an obvious connection to Peru."

"And?"

"Megan Neary's mother was originally Peruvian. Her family, specifically her brother, still own substantial property in and around Cusco."

"That is interesting."

"I thought so too, sir."

"Keep a status check on the G500. I want to know the moment it leaves Cusco again. In fact, keep an eye on any private flights leaving Cusco. Coordinate with the Peruvian authorities."

"I already have access to their flight registration system, sir."

"Thank you, Paul. That'll be all for now, and, please, close my door on your way out."

Once the door was closed, Bleeker took out his secure smartphone and called Special Agent in Charge Costello at Bleeker's former FBI field office in the Midwest.

"Costello here."

"It's Bleeker. Are you up and about yet?

"Yeah, unlike Jurickson, I was fortunate that Declan didn't do any significant damage."

"Good, because I have a new lead on Parker."

"What is it?"

"It seems his family may be in Peru, near, Cusco. I want you to pick someone from our select list of agents, and get down there right away."

"Do you think Declan is down there too?"

"No, I think he's still in the U.S., but I'm not sure for how much longer."

"I'll make arrangements for us to leave tonight."

"Good. I'll send over the particulars, as well as a special memento for you to leave when the job is done."

"What is the job?"

"I want anyone you find down there permanently eliminated."

Chapter 3

"Do you have everything you need?" Declan's older brother, Dr. Evan Parker, asked as his good friend, Jessica Ehlers, stepped from the small car.

"Yep, I'm all good."

"And you know the plan?" Megan asked, stepping out beside her. "Tom'll be coming into the Landmark Aviation Terminal."

"Don't worry. I know the plan and I have the cell phone and Tom's mobile number."

Megan smiled and gave Jessica a genuinely warm embrace. "Take care of yourself. It's worse in the States now than it was when you left. Keep as low a profile as possible, and if anything goes wrong with Tom's pickup, you and Declan get to D.C. right away. Louis Martino has made arrangements to get you and Declan Israeli passports and to get you out with the Prime Minister's entourage at the end of the week, so you'll only have four days if you can't get back with Tom."

"Like I said, don't worry. We'll be back before you know it."

Megan took out an envelope containing a letter to her husband and handed it to Jessica. "Will you please give this to Declan for me?"

"Of course," Jessica replied, putting the envelope into her coat pocket.

"See you in a few days," Megan replied. "God speed."

Jessica looked over to Evan, who stood next to her on the sidewalk outside the terminal at the Astete International Airport in Cusco, Peru. "See you soon," she said.

"I wish I was going instead of you," he replied.

"I know, but you'd be picked up by Homeland before you ever got outside the airport. Nobody is looking for me."

"Just take care of yourself."

"I'll be fine. No worries."

"I'm serious," Evan replied. "I want to see you back here day after tomorrow. Be extra careful and don't underestimate the conditions and challenges back in the States."

"Don't worry, Evan. I promise, I'll be careful."

Jessica gave Evan a long and heartfelt hug, and a quick kiss on his cheek. She had so many emotions running through her, about going back to the U.S., about her mission, and about Evan. While Jessica knew that Evan's love for her was totally platonic, she couldn't help the attraction she felt towards him and, a substantial part of her was happy to put some distance between them, and Evan's family (whom she both adored and often found herself resenting), if only for a couple days. Hopefully, the time alone would give her a chance to sort out her head. Smiling one last time at Evan, Jessica slung her backpack over one shoulder, and walked into the airport to catch the last commercial flight of the evening to Lima.

"See you in a few days," she said, turning back to Evan and Megan, before disappearing into the terminal.

Chapter 4

Declan slunk low amid the shadows of the Garden District, desperately looking for a place to hide. The pain in his arm had grown more intense, as had the urge to close his eyes and sleep. The feeling of fatigue was almost overwhelming as Declan struggled to keep his balance, strategically looping around southeast, into the heavily residential areas between St. Charles Street and Magazine Street. Except for the Homeland vehicles and New Orleans Police cars which were tirelessly looking for him, the streets were empty, as the sun had long since set and curfew had begun.

The night was quiet, and a moderate breeze swept through the solitary streets. Declan ducked among the houses, careful to stay out of the glare of any street lights or passing headlights. He'd come too far, and gotten too close to being picked up by Tom Langham, to get caught. It was unfortunate that he'd had to use the Lone Ranger on that trooper, but it couldn't be helped. The important thing, Declan knew, was to get off the streets until the curfew lifted in the morning, get himself situated and somehow take care of the wound, and then to make his way to Lakefront Airport to meet Tom.

His right arm was throbbing, and clearly needed attention. The pain continued to grow more intense with each minute, and Declan felt himself becoming groggy. From time to time, his vision would blur and he became somewhat disoriented and Declan knew, without looking, that he had lost a good amount of blood.

As he was crossing from the shadows of one house to the next, Declan noticed a partially-open side door leading into a single-car garage. He quickly slipped inside and closed and locked the door behind him.

There was a black Honda Accord parked in the tiny garage, along with a mountain bike and various small cardboard moving boxes. Looking against the wall, Declan spotted a bulk package of bottled waters, which still had about a dozen full bottles of water. He grabbed two of the plastic bottles and tucked down behind the car, on the opposite side from the door. Declan marveled at how comforting the hard concrete floor of the garage felt beneath him, and how good it felt to be off of his feet. Opening both bottles, he quickly drank most of the water from one, which helped steady his vision a bit. Then, Declan grabbed his backpack, and removed a relatively-clean long-sleeve t-shirt from inside. He stripped off the blood-stained button up shirt he'd been wearing, ripped a small strip from it and doused the cloth with the water.

The wet cloth felt good against the wound, although it still burned. Finally being able to get a good look at the wound confirmed that he'd lost a substantial amount of blood, but the bullet appeared to have gone in-and-out, and, most importantly, it appeared not to have done any damage to any major veins or arteries. He ripped another, longer, strip of cloth from one of the cleaner sections of his old shirt, and wrapped it around the wound, pressing it firmly against the two-sided wound, and tying it as tightly as he could with one arm. Finally, Declan put the long-sleeve t-shirt on and leaned back against the garage wall, taking a big swig from the water bottle. He could still hear the sirens outside, and looked down at his watch to see that it was only a little after 9:00 P.M.

"Lord, I thank you for bringing me here to New Orleans, just one step from home," Declan whispered. "I simply ask that you provide for my needs, as you have to this point, and see me home to Megan. In the name of Jesus Christ, through Whom all things are possible, I pray. Amen."

Desperate for a moment of rest, Declan finally let his eyes close. The rush of exhaustion that followed overwhelmed him, and despite trying, he simply couldn't open his eyes again. His mind tried to push them open, tried to fight off his body's urge to sleep. The sirens outside, which had filled his ears seconds before, slowly faded into the background and Megan's face appeared in front of him.

"Come home, babe," she said to him. "I'm waiting for you."

"I'm coming," he whispered back. "Don't worry, Megan. I'll be home tomorrow, just like I promised."

Chapter 5

By midnight, the sirens and flashing lights had left the otherwise generally quiet and calm Garden District. Luke Williams had finally finished packing up the last of his things and, relatively confident that it was safe to venture outside, headed out the back door of the small house he'd lived in during his last three years at Tulane University. Balancing a box of plates and glasses in one hand, with the other hand, Luke tried to turn the handle to the side door of the garage.

"I didn't think I locked this," he said to himself, setting the box down on the ground and taking out his keys. A few seconds later, after finding the right key, Luke finally opened the door and, not wanting to draw attention to the fact that he was out well after curfew, gently placed the box down on the hood of his black Honda in the dark. He walked slowly to the trunk, opened it, and stood for a moment trying to determine what he could move in the already packed trunk, to make room for the box.

As Luke pondered the most efficient packing arrangement, he began to pick up on an unexpected sound. The sound was subtle, but close. He stood stone-still in front of the trunk, and held his breath. The sound became more audible and clear. A chill ran up Luke's spine as he realized that he was listening to someone else breathing. Their breath was deep, rhythmic, and horrifying.

The light from inside the trunk slightly illuminated the garage, but not enough for Luke to see anything too clearly. From what he could tell, whoever was breathing seemed to be in front of him, up near the front of the Honda. Not knowing what else to do, Luke asked softly, "What do you want? I have food inside and some money, and I'll give it to you."

His query was simply answered with more breathing. Still standing like a statue by the trunk, Luke waited for a minute or two, but whomever was in the garage with him said nothing. He listened more closely to the breathing and finally it occurred to Luke that the person may be sleeping.

Slowly, he stepped away from the trunk, being sure to leave it open so as to provide some light. He quietly stepped to the side of the Honda and looked up toward the front of the car. In the very dim light, Luke could see the two empty water bottles and Declan's backpack sitting on the ground next to his feet. Luke cautiously stepped toward Declan, becoming more convinced that the person breathing was either asleep or injured. As he reached the front of the car, Luke could finally see Declan lying against the garage wall. The dim light allowed him to make out Declan's facial features, and that he was shivering. Luke could also see the, by then, bloody shirt sleeve covering Declan's right arm.

Chapter 6

One of the few exceptions to the federally imposed curfew involved air transportation. In an effort to maintain some semblance of normalcy with respect to commerce and business in the larger cities, the President had carved out a curfew exemption for commercial air traffic; however, all passengers were required to be either on a plane in transit or locked down inside the airport during curfew hours.

Louis Martino, Co-Founder and Editor of The Free Voice, an independent online news magazine, had taken advantage of this exception, along with other business travelers, to catch a red-eye flight from Chicago to New York City. After spending a week in the hospital recovering from a late night visit by some of the agents from John Bleeker's "select list", Louis was on the mend. Louis had found himself on Bleeker's hit list due to the series of articles he'd written about Declan and his innocence in the Christmas Eve massacres. The three broken ribs Louis had suffered at the hands of Bleeker's guys were still tender, but overall he was close to one hundred percent again. He was happy to get out of Chicago and desperately anxious to cover the Israeli Prime Minister's imminent address to the United Nations, and join his convoy for a quick stop in Washington, D.C., then, finally, on to Jerusalem.

Speculation was rampant that a coalition led by Russia was on the verge of attacking the Israelis as a reprisal for Israel's sound defeat of its Islamic neighbors and its use of a nuclear weapon, and resulting destruction of Damascus, roughly six weeks earlier. The Russians were publically furious about the attack and the claimed casualties of Russian military personnel who had been in and around Damascus. That was the stated justification; however, as with most things in the world, and particularly in the world of politics, Russia's true motivation was somewhat more complicated and hovered somewhere closer to Russia's interest in co-opting the vast natural gas fields that belonged to the Israelis.

The Russian President also saw an opportunity to take advantage of a substantial decrease in global influence by the United States, due to the ongoing civil strife and military crackdown in the U.S. after the passage of the Firearms Protection Act, also known by opponents as the Infringement Act. Regardless, Israel had become the center of international news and Louis knew that wasn't going to change anytime soon. He'd planned on an extended stay in Jerusalem and had made arrangements with his friend, and former college roommate, Adam Benjamin, for just such a stay.

The plane landed shortly after sunrise. After clearing the three different TSA checkpoints, and showing his identification, yet again, to a Homeland trooper upon exiting the airport, Louis grabbed a taxi from LaGuardia to the Four Seasons Hotel in Manhattan, where he found Adam Benjamin in the opulent lobby drinking a cup of coffee.

"Louis, my friend, you made it."

"I did," Louis responded, gently embracing Adam.

"How are you feeling?"

"I'm better. Not perfect yet, but better."

"Good. You'll be welcome in Israel."

"Thank you, Adam. I'm looking forward to it. Were you able to get the things I asked you about together?"

"Of course. I've booked you a room here at the Four Seasons for the next two nights under my name. Here's your room key and your press credentials. These credentials will allow you the highest access, along with the senior Israeli press corps. The other documents we discussed are already in the safe in your room. The combo is 7711."

"Thanks, Adam. I owe you big time. When are you headed over to the U.N.?"

"Not until tomorrow, about an hour before the Prime Minister's address. He's taking meetings here at the hotel today and will be giving a brief statement to the press at one o'clock this afternoon. I have you down for that already."

"Excellent. Anyone who stands out?"

"No, not really. A few U.N. delegates, most of whom will, I'm sure, ask him not to address the General Assembly. Last night we received a request for a meeting from Raffaele Firenze, the newly-appointed President of the European Commission. That one could be interesting. The P.M. is scheduled to meet with him last."

"Firenze was the E.U. parliament member who opposed hardcore economic sanctions against Israel a few years ago when settlement building in East Jerusalem was a big issue, right?"

"One in the same," Adam answered. "That was when he served as the Chair for the Parliament Foreign Affairs Committee. He's quickly climbed the power ladder, but has generally been considered a friend, or at least friendlier."

"Cool. I'll be ready."

"Why don't you go up to your room and freshen up, and I'll see you around 12:45? We can grab a quick bite to eat here at the hotel after the Prime Minister's statement and catch up."

"Sounds good. See you then."

Louis took the elevator up to his room, and went straight to the safe. He keyed in 7711 and found a small manila envelope inside. Opening the envelope, Louis removed three authentic Israeli passports, one with his photo and the name Michael Pressman, one with Declan Parker's photo and the name Stephen Aaronson, and a third with Jessica Ehlers photo and the name Adina Hartmann.

Chapter 7

Declan felt the frigid air burning his lungs as he breathed it in slowly, peering ahead through the darkness. As he stepped closer, he could hear David Stanton breathing up ahead. Suddenly, Stanton looked up and straight at Declan as the two men came within ten feet of one another. A smile flashed across Stanton's face and Declan raised his weapon, taking aim at David Stanton, who had gone back to the work of loading his rifles.

"Freeze," Declan yelled.

He heard Stanton, who was still looking down, laugh in response, but realized that what he heard wasn't Stanton's laugh, but someone else's. Declan stepped closer, focusing on his target and called out again, "Drop the weapon and put your hands up, Stanton!"

In a flash, Stanton's head jerked up, an AR-15 still in his hands. Declan began to squeeze the trigger of his weapon, but, suddenly, instead of having David Stanton in his sights, Declan saw John Bleeker there. Declan's hesitation allowed Bleeker to fire first. The blast from the AR-15 snapped Declan from his sleep and he woke with a start, jerking his head backward and hitting it against the garage wall.

"Ow," Declan said, groggily rubbing the back of his head. "That one was intense."

Still trying to regain his composure, Declan pushed off a flannel blanket, leaned over, picked up another water bottle, and took a drink. He was so caught up in his nightmare, which was at least the fifth or sixth such dream he'd had since stopping David Stanton from murdering a church full of people on Christmas Eve, only to later be framed by John Bleeker as Stanton's accomplice, that Declan didn't initially notice the blanket that he'd been under or the young man standing silently at the end of the black Honda a few feet from him. When he finally did see the young man, Declan became startled.

"It's okay," Luke said, as Declan scrambled to his feet. "It's okay. You were shot and bleeding pretty badly."

Declan looked the young man over. He was athletic looking and appeared to be about 6'2" tall. Judging from his face, Declan guessed he was maybe twenty-one or twenty-two years old. What struck Declan immediately was the sense of genuineness and caring in Luke's brown eyes, which showed through his tousled light-red hair.

"You seemed to be having a pretty bad dream," Luke said. "I can help you. My name's Luke, Luke Williams."

Although he wasn't sure exactly why, Declan felt as though he could trust Luke, who'd clearly had enough time to call the authorities if he'd wanted to, but instead had gotten Declan a blanket and appeared to want to help. It was something in his eyes, something in the tone of his voice. Luke exuded a palpable sense of calm, of peacefulness.

"I, uh…my arm, I was shot last night."

"I know. You'd lost a good amount of blood when I found you in here. You had passed out. I was able to stitch your arm up, get it cleaned, and get a proper bandage on it without you ever waking up. I thought for sure the stitches would wake you up, but they didn't."

Declan looked down at his arm. The sleeve of his shirt had been cut off and the wound had been wrapped in actual bandages. Overall, the arm felt drastically better.

"Is that what all the noise was about last night?" Luke asked. "Were they looking for you?"

"Yeah. Homeland troopers stopped a truck I was riding in just before curfew, and shot one of the passengers. Maybe both of them. I made a run for it and got hit in the arm. I didn't think it was that bad last night. I tried to clean it and wrap it, but I guess it was worse than I thought."

"It should be okay now. It's been disinfected and the bullet passed through."

"I feels much better than it did last night. Thank you."

"I'm happy to help," Luke replied. "Do you live

nearby?"

"No, I'm not from New Orleans. Is this your garage?"

"Just until tomorrow morning. I'm renting the house. I was anyway. The lease is up and I'm headed to St. Simons Island, Georgia tomorrow. That's where my family is living now."

"Are you from here?"

"No, I grew up in St. Louis. I was just down here for college. I graduated from Tulane in December and was supposed to start medical school at Emory in the fall."

"Clearly you have a talent for healing," Declan said, looking down at his right arm again. "That's a good school."

"One of the best. I was really looking forward to it, but with the protests, martial law, and all that's going on, everything with school has been put on hold, at least temporarily I hope. So, was New Orleans your final destination, or are you headed elsewhere?"

"No, I'm just meeting a friend here and moving on."

"Well, if you're hungry you can come into the house. With all the blood you've lost, you could definitely use some food and water. Both my roommates moved out already, so there's no one else there."

"I'm famished."

"Then let's get you something to eat."

"Alright."

Luke led Declan out the side door of the garage and quickly into the house. The inside of the house was pretty empty, with a few packed boxes stacked in one corner of the tiny dining room.

"Sorry, there's no furniture left. My roommates owned most of the living room and dining room stuff and almost all of my stuff is packed. I do still have food and plenty of water and even a soda or two."

"No worries," Declan replied, taking in the Spartan-like qualities of the house. It looked like three college kids had lived in it, and reminded Declan of his own college house.

Luke laid out bread, packaged deli turkey, sliced cheese, and mayonnaise and mustard. "Here, help yourself. With the food shortages and prices lately, I've been kind of limited, but one of the grocery stores nearby has started getting more stuff in the last week or so. For a while it was basically pasta, peanut butter and water. Seems like things are starting to normalize a bit, at least in some ways. The crime has gotten a lot worse down here, even during the day in some parts of the city, but it looks like people are going into work again and running errands and such."

"This is the first big city I've seen in almost a month," Declan replied as he began making himself a sandwich. "I've mainly been traveling the country roads."

"What are things like in the more rural areas?"

"Horrible. The smaller towns have been hit hard by the interruptions in the supply chain and the huge price increases on what items they do get in. Gas, if you can even find it, is upwards of twenty bucks a gallon. Bread, again if you can find it, will cost five or six bucks a loaf."

"That's a couple dollars more than it has been here. What about the government presence? Is there still fighting with the protesters?"

"I don't know what they're saying on the news, but it's still going on. There are a lot of holdouts in the country. Many of them are close to starving, and many more are being arrested or killed, but however normal things are beginning to look in the bigger cities, this thing is a long way from over."

Declan took a bite of his sandwich, enjoying the full flavor of the turkey and mustard together. "Thank you for this," he said to Luke. "I know food isn't cheap. I can pay you for it."

"No, please, don't worry about it. It's cool, really."

"Thanks. So, if Emory is on hold, why are you leaving for St. Simons now?"

"It's better to be near family these days, strength in

numbers. For a few weeks after the protests began, the looting in the city was almost out of control. For a good week or so, my friends and I pretty much stayed indoors. It got to the point where we were eating once a day to reserve the food we had, because it just wasn't safe to go out. People were being attacked in broad daylight and the police and Homeland troopers weren't doing anything in that regard. My sister left Atlanta, where she and one of my cousins were living, and went to our parents' house on St. Simons. She said Atlanta was crazy. When prices skyrocketed and the supply chains stopped working, the place went nuts. People were getting beaten up and stabbed over canned food and bottled water. It was pretty much the same here. I don't have any family down here and most of my college friends have gone back home. My roommates left a couple weeks ago."

"I agree with you about being near family," Declan replied, as he thought about how crazy it was that everything Luke had just talked about was a direct, albeit orchestrated, result of David Stanton's thwarted plan to commit the largest mass-shooting in history on Christmas Eve.

"Where's yours?"

"They're all out of the country."

"Is that where you're trying to get?"

"Yes. My wife, my mom, and my brother and his family are all together. They got out shortly after everything went crazy with the protests and martial law."

"When's the last time you saw them?"

"Just about a month now. What about you, when did you see your family last?"

"At Christmas. Everyone was down here for my graduation, then we spent Christmas at my parents' house on St. Simons. I left St. Simon's the morning of December 26th, just after the Infringement Act passed, to come back here and get packed up, but then the protests started, people started getting rounded up and arrested, and martial law was declared. I was basically stuck here. This is really the first chance I feel like it's safe enough to make the trip. My parents have been worried to death about me being here alone. My dad tried to get here last week to drive back with me, but Homeland wouldn't let him board the plane. He was able to get me enough cash to cover gas for the trip."

"Why couldn't he board the plane?"

"They didn't give him an explanation, they just told him his file showed that he wasn't air travel eligible, whatever that means."

"Well, I pray that you get back to them safely."

"Thank you. I pray the same for you. Can I ask you a question?"

"Sure, you can ask it."

"It's been bothering me since I saw you in the garage, but I've had this feeling that I know you from somewhere. Then, just a minute ago when I was talking about Christmas, I realized where I'd seen you. You're the FBI Agent who's wanted in connection with the Christmas Eve murders. You're Declan Parker, aren't you?"

Declan sat silently.

"It's okay. I read The Free Voice and my parents instilled a healthy dose of skepticism about the government and what we hear and read in the mainstream media in my sister and I. 'Critical thinking' is what they always used to hammer home. I've read all of Louis Martino's articles on the Christmas Eve shootings and your innocence. I know you don't know me at all, and probably aren't used to trusting people lately, but I'm happy to do whatever I can to help you."

"Thank you," Declan replied with a touch of hesitation and confusion. "I appreciate it. This sandwich and your medical handy-work are already more helpful than you know."

"Well, if there's anything else I can do, I'm in. At least until I leave tomorrow morning."

While Declan sensed that he could trust Luke, that maybe Luke was someone God had put in his path to help him on his journey back to his family, he was reluctant to fully do so. "Thanks," Declan repeated.

Chapter 8

Jessica Ehlers' plane landed at Louis Armstrong New Orleans International Airport shortly after noon. She passed through customs without issue and, after being grilled by a Homeland trooper about her reason for being in New Orleans, hopped in a taxi and headed for the French Quarter.

A little past one o'clock in the afternoon, Jessica stepped out of the cab onto Royal Street. She was surprised by the heavy Homeland presence on the streets, particularly in the Quarter, where, during the short course of her drive, she'd seen four or five different instances of Homeland troopers stopping people on the street. "Is it still pretty easy to get cabs around here?" she asked the driver.

"Sure, it's usually not a problem before curfew. It's impossible after curfew, and I wouldn't advise walking around after five o'clock or so. Everything except the hotel bars are dead down here after curfew now. The only people out on the streets are feds and people looking for trouble. Your best bet is probably to head to the cab stand at one of the hotels well before curfew."

"Will do. Thanks."

As she made her way slowly along Royal Street, Jessica took in the sights and sounds of the Quarter, which she thought, except for the numerous and conspicuous Homeland and military troops, looked largely like it had the last time she was there a few years earlier. She wandered the narrow picturesque street, taking in all the history surrounding her and imagining what life in New Orleans would have been like in the early-1800's.

Jessica could see herself in the past, living in what seemed to her, a simpler time. She loved the old buildings, the character of the streets, and, most of all, the gas lamps. She inhaled the sumptuous smells of the French Quarter. During the day, the streets, while not exactly bustling, had lots of activity. Many of the restaurants appeared to be open and doing business to one degree or another, with the aroma of gumbo and andouille sausage making its way out to the street. Most of the shops were also open, but none seemed particularly busy.

As Jessica made her way through Pirate Alley and into Jackson Square, she caught a whiff of what she knew to be beignets, and decided to walk over to Café du Monde. Crossing the square, a voice called behind her, "Excuse me, ma'am."

Jessica turned to see two Homeland troopers following her. Instantly, her defenses went up and her face became stoic. The troopers wore the same heavy black military fatigues as the trooper who had raped her in Dallas on the first night of protests after the Firearms Protection Act, or the Infringement Act, as it was widely known, had been passed.

"Sorry, ma'am," one of the troopers said, approaching her. "But, I need to see your identification."

"Why?" Jessica asked. "Curfew isn't in effect."

"It's just procedure. Please, your I.D."

Jessica handed her passport to the trooper, who appeared to be no more than a year or two older than her, if that. The trooper looked the passport over carefully, took out a small notepad and pen, and began scribbling something on the small sheet of paper, while his partner stood a few feet away, looking around the square.

"Why are you in New Orleans, Ms. Ehlers?" the trooper asked politely, handing the passport back.

"I'm just passing through on my way home. I leave tonight."

"Where's home?"

"Denton, Texas."

"Well, if you find yourself in town longer than expected, give me a call," the trooper said, reaching out toward Jessica with the small piece of paper in his hand.

"I won't," Jessica replied flatly, not reaching out to take the piece of paper.

The trooper's face went a bit flush and he quickly

stuffed the piece of paper, which had his name and phone number written on it, into one of the many pockets on his fatigues.

"Is that all?" Jessica asked. "Can I go?"

"No," the trooper replied in a much less friendly tone than before. "I need to search your backpack."

Knowing there was nothing in her backpack but a couple changes of clothes, some deodorant, toothbrush, small toothpaste, and a couple books, Jessica handed it over, staring the trooper down the entire time. His partner seemed to be getting bored as the trooper rummaged through the backpack, slowly removing each item, including Jessica's extra clothes and her toothbrush, and simply dropping them onto the pavement until he'd emptied the backpack.

"Here," the trooper said, handing the empty backpack to Jessica. "Keep yourself out of trouble while you're here."

The troopers left Jessica standing in the middle of Jackson Square, an empty backpack in her hands and its contents littering the pavement at her feet. Jessica watched as they headed toward Decatur Street, quickly picked up her belongings, and, fuming, went straight to the Omni Royal Orleans Hotel, as originally planned, to wait for a few hours until it was time to take another taxi over to Lakefront Airport.

———————————

"Está claro para el despegue," the voice from the tower came over Tom Langham's headset.

"Gracias," he replied.

With final clearance from the tower in Cusco, Tom throttled the Gulfstream G-500 forward, quickly increasing speed as the plane sped down the runway and finally glided easily into the air and up above the tall majestic mountains surrounding Cusco. Once clear of the city, Tom banked the plane northwest and headed toward the United States for what he hoped would be the last time.

"Sir," Paul said, catching John Bleeker as he exited a security briefing with the White House Chief of Staff.

"What is it, Paul?"

"The Gulfstream has left Cusco, sir. Approximately one hour ago."

"Destination?"

"The filed flight plan said Houston."

"Get one of the planes ready for us, Paul. I'd like to leave within the hour."

"To Houston?"

"I'm not sure about that yet."

"What are you thinking?"

"It just seems too easy."

"Do you think the Gulfstream is headed somewhere other than Houston?"

"Maybe. Do these planes have GPS identification that can be tracked?"

"I believe at least some do."

"Find out and meet me at my car in twenty minutes. Also, this is probably a longshot, but the car with the Texas plates we found parked behind the Parker family lake house the day they escaped, get me the name of the registrant again."

"Will do."

"Special Agent Costello?" a man asked as Costello and Special Agent McCall stepped out of the airport in Cusco.

"Yes, and this is Agent McCall."

"It's good to meet you both. I'm Ryan Hewson, with the consulate here in Cusco. Welcome to Peru. Our car is just over here."

"Excellent," Costello responded.

"I have the information on Megan Neary's uncle, Ignacio Velarde Diaz, which your office requested. He's a prominent and respected businessman in the area. His family is an old-money Peruvian family which has owned large plots of land for hundreds of years, and still has a number of influential contacts throughout Peru."

"Do you have a present address?"

"Of course," Ryan said as they reached the car. "I have a file for each of you to review back at the consulate. The file should have all the intel you need. Would you like to go to the consulate now, or stop at your hotel first?"

"Let's go straight to the consulate," Costello responded.

Chapter 9

"*²⁵'Therefore I tell you, do not worry about your life, what you will eat or drink; or about your body, what you will wear. Is not life more than food, and the body more than clothes? ²⁶ Look at the birds of the air; they do not sow or reap or store away in barns, and yet your heavenly Father feeds them. Are you not much more valuable than they? ²⁷ Can any one of you by worrying add a single hour to your life?'*

²⁸ 'And why do you worry about clothes? See how the flowers of the field grow. They do not labor or spin. ²⁹ Yet I tell you that not even Solomon in all his splendor was dressed like one of these. ³⁰ If that is how God clothes the grass of the field, which is here today and tomorrow is thrown into the fire, will He not much more clothe you—you of little faith? ³¹ So do not worry, saying, 'What shall we eat?' or 'What shall we drink?' or 'What shall we wear?' ³² For the pagans run after all these things, and your heavenly Father knows that you need them. ³³ But seek first His kingdom and His righteousness, and all these things will be given to you as well. ³⁴ Therefore do not worry about tomorrow, for tomorrow will worry about itself. Each day has enough trouble of its own.'"

Declan let the words of Jesus from Matthew Chapter 6 sink in as he closed his Bible and looked down gratefully at the clean shirt and jeans Luke had given him. For only the second time in a month, Declan had been able to take a hot shower and get himself cleaned up, and he felt like a new man. Moreover, his right arm felt a hundred times better than it had the night before. He looked at his thin pale hands and wrists, thinking that he must have lost twenty pounds since leaving Peru.

Declan's mind wandered, for a moment, back to the cave and the hunger which had filled his entire body as he waited for the opportunity to leave. Bleeker's men had combed the hillsides for days, looking for any sign of Declan. Many times, they'd ventured into the vast network of caves. In order to stay hidden, Declan had been forced deeper and deeper into the depths and darkness, to a point he was unfamiliar with and became lost. On his third day in the caves, hopelessly lost and not having seen light from any source other than his flashlight, Declan had almost lost hope. He hadn't had water in over twenty-four hours and was so hungry that he had resorted to eating whatever small insects he could catch.

As Declan stood, hunched over, desperate for a way out, he'd heard a whisper bounce over the stone walls which surrounded him. The words were, simply, "Trust Me." Declan recalled the peacefulness that filled his body when the voice spoke again, from slightly further down the dark narrow passage, "Trust Me." Declan followed the whisper and, an hour later, he had emerged from the network of caves onto a forested hillside bathed in moonlight. From that point forward, Declan's faith was cemented.

Looking again at the clean clothes Luke had given him, Declan said, "Your Word always holds true, Lord. Thank you for putting Luke in my path. I pray that you give me guidance and wisdom, Lord, and that my faith in You and Your promises remains unfailing, regardless of the road ahead. Please, Lord, get me home to Megan and my family tonight."

The thought of Megan, of finally holding his wife in his arms again, of her smell and the familiar softness of her touch brought a smile to Declan's face. He looked at his watch, which read 2:37 P.M., and began thinking about how to get to Lakefront Airport. If Tom was on schedule, he'd be there, refueled and ready for takeoff, at 7:00 P.M. Sunset was approximately 7:15 P.M., so Declan and Tom should be in the air well before the curfew went into effect.

Declan stood up from where he was sitting on the floor and walked into the kitchen, where Luke was packing a few last items into a small moving box.

When he saw Declan come into the kitchen, Luke asked, "Are you feeling better?"

"Much better, thank you. It's amazing what a shower and clean clothes will do. Thank you again."

"No problem. You do look a lot better. You'd fit right in on campus now."

"That's definitely better than looking like a hobo, like I did this morning."

"How does the arm feel?" Luke asked.

"Amazingly better. I don't know your secret, but you definitely have a gift."

"No secret, really. Just prayer and faith that God will do what He's promised. Like Jesus said of healing in Mark 9:23, 'Everything is possible for one who believes.'"

Declan was somewhat surprised by Luke's answer and paused for a moment. It truly seemed that God had put Luke, a fellow Christian, in Declan's life for at least one reason, if not many.

"I'm not entirely familiar with that verse."

"It's one of my favorites. I've had an interest in the power of faith in healing for a long time now. God truly can do anything, heal any ailment, if we just believe."

"Luke," Declan began, "in light of what you've just said about prayer and faith, I take it you're a Christian."

"I am, and even more so lately."

"So am I. I've just recently rediscovered my faith."

"There's nothing like crisis to remind us how much we need God."

"Very true. It's just too bad that's often what it takes though."

"Sad, but true," Luke replied.

"I hope this doesn't sound too strange, but I've given

this a lot of prayer and feel as though I can trust you, like you and I were put in each other's paths for a reason."

"It doesn't sound strange at all."

"Good, because earlier you offered your help. If that offer still stands, I may need some."

"Absolutely. I'll do whatever I can."

"I'm meeting my friend at Lakefront Airport tonight. He's supposed to pick me up there and fly me back to my family in South America. Is Lakefront nearby, like within walking distance?"

"No, you can't walk there. It's on Lake Pontchatrain. Definitely too far to walk from here and probably not safe anyway. I can drive you there though."

"I don't want to put you in any danger, and I don't think that I am. I mean, I don't think anyone knows I'm here in New Orleans, but if you would just drop me off there, it would be an immense help."

"Definitely. It's the right thing to do and I'm not afraid. What time do you need to be there?"

"I'm thinking about 6:00. That'll give me time to scope everything out and time for you to get back before curfew."

"That works. We'll leave here at 5:15, which should be plenty of time."

"Thank you, Luke. I mean it, thank you."

Chapter 10

John Bleeker sat silently in his seat on the small plane, looking down over the, in his view, terminally-bleak and monotonous brown landscape passing below. He sighed, took a sip of the steaming cup of green tea in his hand, and looked over to Paul, who was seated across from him, his face buried in his laptop.

"Well, do you have anything yet, Paul?"

"We haven't picked up a GPS signal on the Gulfstream, so it either isn't equipped with one, or more likely, the pilot has disabled it."

"What about the vehicle we found at the lake house?"

"It was registered to a James Allen Ehlers of Denton, Texas. I haven't come up with anything on him, or his wife yet, but I'm cross-checking the detainee registration records for the federal facility in Fort Worth that Evan Parker was sent to for any Ehlers now."

"And?"

"Wait…it looks like there was a Jessica Ehlers registered there. She was brought into the facility in late December and appears to still be unaccounted for after the escape. Her driver's license listed the same address as James Allen Ehlers."

"It's a huge longshot, but run her through the system for any travel in the past three weeks."

"I'm already on it."

Bleeker sat back and took another sip from his tea, trying to determine his next step. The Gulfstream picking Declan Parker up in Houston made perfect sense, but it just seemed too easy, particularly given that flight plans were not set in stone. Naming the final destination seemed almost like an intentional telegraph, a misdirection. But, maybe it wasn't.

"Sir, you're not going to believe this," Paul said with obvious excitement.

"What?"

"Jessica Ehlers arrived back in the states from Peru this morning."

"Where?"

"New Orleans."

Bleeker sat up quickly and put on a headset and microphone that was connected to the cockpit. "Pilot, change of course. We're headed to New Orleans, not Houston."

"Yes, sir," the pilot replied.

"Pilot, where do private flights typically fly into New Orleans?"

"Generally, Lakefront Airport, sir."

"Excellent. Put us down at Lakefront as quickly as possible."

"Yes, sir. I can have you on the ground in forty-five minutes."

"Paul," Bleeker said, "I want select plainclothes agents at all New Orleans area airports, particularly Lakefront, right away."

Even Special Agent Costello was overwhelmed by the beauty of the Sacred Valley as the SUV sped along the main road, parallel to the Urubamba River. A few miles after passing through the small town of Urubamba, Ryan Hewson pulled the SUV over and stopped in a small dirt pull-off across from a gated dirt road.

"That's the road," Hewson advised, pointing across the road. "Ignacio Diaz owns all the land on that hillside, thousands of acres. That dirt road winds up the hillside and runs to the various haciendas. Our intel says there are three, a main hacienda and two separate smaller guest houses. You'll find various satellite photos of each in your briefs."

"Any security that we know about?"

"We don't know specifically, but aside from at the main hacienda, I doubt it, and even there it's probably nothing overly high tech. There are definitely dogs, and lots of them, but generally there's not much need for substantial security measures in the area."

"In this sat photo, the road looks to be a few miles long," Costello replied.

"It's 3.3 miles to the main hacienda, if you follow the road."

"That's not bad," McCall replied.

"No, but keep in mind, it's almost all uphill on the way in."

"Alright," said Costello. "Take us to the hotel and we'll come back tonight."

Chapter 11

"So tonight's the night," Megan's older brother, Timothy, said to her, holding his 18-month-old daughter, Eliza, in one hand and a half-full pisco sour in the other.

"As long as everything goes to plan," Megan replied.

"It'll all be fine, sis. Declan will be home tonight, and you two can finally get started with married life."

"Thanks, Timmy. That's what I keep hoping for. Here, let me hold this little princess," Megan said, taking Eliza and giving her a big loving squeeze.

"She's definitely a princess," Tim replied. "Diana says this little angel has me wrapped around her pudgy little finger."

"As she should," Megan answered. "The ability to wrap their daddies around their fingers is a gift all daughters are born with. It's part of the female DNA."

"I don't doubt that."

As Atau continued laying a series of decadent Peruvian dishes on the table, including Megan's favorites, ceviche and causa, her young nephew, Will Parker, came shooting across the garden lawn, followed by her other nephew, Aiden Neary, each brandishing a glowing green replica Jedi lightsaber. Evan's wife, Michelle Parker, called after her son, "Will, slow down, honey."

"They have a ton of energy this afternoon," Megan said to Michelle.

"Every day," Michelle replied. "I can't keep up with him anymore. At least Charlotte will still sit still once in a while. With Will, if he's awake, he's in motion."

"Won't Will be seven soon?" Tim asked.

"In two weeks," Michelle answered. "It's hard to believe. It goes by so fast."

Soon, the rest of the family showed up in the garden overlooking the Urubamba Valley below. Evan Parker emerged from the house with four-year-old Charlotte, who had clearly just woken up from a rare nap. Megan's oldest brother, John, had walked up from the lower hacienda he, his wife, Sara, and their youngest son, Ryan, who was Aiden's two-year-old baby brother, shared with Tim's family.

Mrs. Parker, Declan's mom, sat under a eucalyptus tree talking with Megan's mom, each drinking a glass of wine from Ignacio's private collection. Evan, Mr. Neary, and Tim started talking about certain professional sports resuming and what they'd heard and read about conditions back home in the United States. The atmosphere was jovial, festive, and thankful. Ignacio had planned multiple evenings of festivities, pulling out all the stops in terms of food and drinks, to celebrate Declan and Jessica's return home and, more generally, the immense gift of life he and his newly-extended family were fortunate enough to enjoy in the Sacred Valley.

As the family was ready to sit down to eat, Megan's dad stood up. "I'd like to say something," he began. "As we all know, circumstances none us could ever have anticipated in our own country brought us together here in the beautiful Andes. Conditions in the United States have been devolving for some time, our freedoms being slowly diminished over the years, often handed over in exchange for the promise of security. We've witnessed many of our rights, our human rights, being reclassified as privileges. Even with that gradual decline, with the seemingly isolated incidences of civil unrest we'd witnessed over the years, I don't think any of us saw the midnight passage of the Firearms Protection Act, and the subsequent protests, riots, gun confiscations, arrests, martial law, and general chaos that followed it, on the horizon. It's a mournful day for the U.S.A., which, from everything I've seen and read, truly has become a haunt for jackals. I, as I'm sure we all are, am thankful for being blessed with the resources to escape the chaos back home, and I'm particularly thankful for the selfless hospitality of our host, my kind and generous brother-in-law, Ignacio. We have something special here, amid all this natural beauty, and that's our family. Family is one of the greatest treasures one can possess, particularly in times like these. Later tonight, when Declan, Jessica and Tom return home, we'll have our whole family back together again and safe in this place of refuge we've been blessed with. So, let's raise our glasses to family."

"To family," everyone exclaimed together.

A few minutes after four o'clock, a taxi dropped Jessica Ehlers off outside the terminal for Landmark Aviation, a private operator at Lakefront Airport. She took a look around and walked inside. The building's interior was well-appointed, even luxurious, Jessica thought as she took in the plush furniture and modern streamlined decor.

"Good afternoon," an attractive older woman sitting at the concierge desk said with a heavy southern accent.

"Hello."

"How can I help you today?"

"I'm, um, meeting a plane here later. I wanted to make sure I got here before curfew."

"Are you meeting Tom's plane, honey?"

"Tom?"

"It's okay, Tom and I are old friends. He told me he's coming in on an express turn-around and to expect you and a young man. 'The Inca Kola Pickup' is what he said. I've set aside a room where you can wait. I'm Barbara Lemley."

"It's nice to meet you, Ms. Lemley," Jessica replied, relaxing as she heard Ms. Lemley use the mission's name. "Tom told me to look for you when I got here."

"It's nice to meet you too. Please, follow me and I'll show you to the lounge where you can wait."

Jessica followed Barbara upstairs to a private room, which had a comfortable black-leather sofa, flat-screen television, a small refrigerator, a private restroom with a shower, and windows looking out past the runway onto Lake

Pontchartrain.

"Here you go, honey. Make yourself at home."

"Thanks. I'll need to go out and keep an eye out for my friend."

"Come and go as you please. There are plenty of beverages in the fridge there, and I'll have some food brought up. Unfortunately, we don't have as much as we typically do, but I'll have something put together for you."

"Thank you."

Barbara left and Jessica stepped over to the window and looked out over the tarmac to the lake. She wanted to sit down on the sofa and relax, maybe even try to get a quick power nap, but she couldn't even bring herself to stand still. Her nerves were all tied up in knots and she just wanted to get onto Tom's plane with Declan and get back to Peru.

She put her backpack on the sofa and decided to take a look around the terminal. The second floor featured a number of other private rooms and lounges, all of which were empty. Overall, the terminal seemed pretty dead. As Jessica walked toward the stairs, to head back down to the main floor, she heard Barbara say, "Good afternoon, gentlemen. How can I help you today?"

"Are you expecting any arrivals this evening?"

Jessica stopped in her tracks and listened, making sure to stay hidden upstairs.

"I don't have any arrivals scheduled for this evening, but I do have a charter from San Francisco scheduled to arrive a few minutes before six. Are you gentlemen looking for a charter or something?"

"No, ma'am," one of the men responded. "Thank you."

"Of course."

The men left the terminal, and Jessica ran quickly to one of the rooms that had windows facing out to the parking lot. A few seconds later, she spotted the two men, one wearing jeans and a short-sleeve polo shirt and the other wearing khakis and an oxford shirt, walking toward a silver sedan parked outside.

She nervously watched as they got into the car and simply sat there. After ten minutes, the men were still sitting in the car.

She heard Barbara ask down the hall, "Where'd you go, hon?"

"I'm in here."

Barbara came into the room and saw what Jessica was looking at. "I've been watching them too. Apparently, they're at all the FBO terminals and the main terminal."

"Who are they?"

"My friend over at the main terminal says they're FBI."

Jessica's face went ghostly white. "This isn't good. I've got to call off Tom and stop Declan from coming."

She rushed back to her private room, with Barbara following her, and grabbed her backpack. Quickly pulling out the smartphone, she sent a text to Tom which read, "Abort. Feds are all over the airport. Confirm?"

The Gulfstream was cruising north over the Gulf of Mexico, within about an hour and a half of New Orleans, when Tom felt his phone vibrate. He picked it up and, reading Jessica's text, yelled, "Dammit! Dammit! Dammit!"

Reluctantly, he typed back, "Confirmed. Aborting. Get yourselves where you need to be."

Chapter 12

As the pilot had promised, Bleeker and Paul were on the ground at Lakefront Airport within forty-five minutes. An unmarked silver Ford SUV was parked on the tarmac about twenty feet from where their plane came to a stop. Bleeker stepped out of the plane and breathed in the warm breeze blowing across Lake Ponchartrain as he hurried to the SUV, with Paul following quickly behind him.

Once in the passenger seat, Bleeker closed the door. "What's the status?"

"We have agents stationed at the main terminal and outside all the FBO terminals," the agent sitting in the driver's seat answered. "We've set up a command center in the security room at the main terminal. We have video surveillance of the entire airport from there. According to the various FBO's, there's only one more flight expected in today and it's coming from San Francisco around 18:00."

"Nothing international?"

"No, sir."

"Which FBO is the San Francisco plane coming into?"

"Landmark Aviation."

"Paul, check the FAA database for info on that plane immediately."

"I'm on it," Paul replied, again tapping away at his laptop keys.

"Keep everyone in place and keep the profile low. I don't want any units placed outside the airport grounds and I don't want any vehicles or agents visible from outside. Declan Parker is no idiot. If he suspects there's any extraordinary law enforcement presence, he'll disappear before getting close to the airport. I don't want any checkpoints for traffic in or out or anything out of the norm."

"Understood."

"Has the Ehlers girl's photo been circulated to our people?"

"Yes, sir, and so far there's no sign of her."

"Fine. Now take me to the command center."

———————————

Jessica's watch read 5:24. She sat in a darkened office on the upstairs floor of the Landmark terminal. Her fingers rapped nervously against the arms of the chair and her eyes flashed back and forth from the two agents still parked outside to her watch. Jessica's heart felt like it was going to beat out of her chest as she tried to figure out how to find Declan before he got to the airport.

Calming her breathing somewhat, and getting her pulse more under control, she closed her eyes and leaned back in the chair. Could she call him? Tom had given her the number to the cell phone he'd given Declan when he'd dropped him off a month earlier, but warned her that it may not even have a charge and against using it unless it was an absolute emergency. Her fingers began to dial the number, but stopped on the sixth digit when she realized how stupid that was given the chance the feds were tracking cell transmissions from the airport.

Putting her head in her hands, Jessica let out an exasperated sigh. "I've just got to calm down and think. Just think, Jessica."

———————————

"Where are you supposed to meet the plane?" Luke asked as he drove his Honda east along Stars and Stripes Blvd.

"There," Declan replied, pointing to the Landmark Aviation terminal off to their left a ways. "Here, turn off here."

Luke turned right onto Downman Road, and drove under a train overpass.

"Go down a bit further and turn around at that

intersection. Let's park under the overpass for a minute."

Luke drove south a few seconds more, then did a U-turn at Hayne Blvd., and finally parked on the side of Downman under the overpass, facing Lakefront Airport.

"That's the place," Declan said. "It's tough to get a good look, but it seems okay, at least from here."

Declan looked up the embankment supporting the overpass, and saw a relatively hidden space at the top that looked big enough for him to fit into without being seen from the road. His thought was to hide up there and watch the Landmark terminal, to try and determine whether it was safe to approach. It would likely be difficult to see much of anything over the walls surrounding the airport, but it was better than nothing.

"Okay, Luke, this where you can drop me off."

"Wait, I can't drop you off here."

"I'll be okay. I can't just drive up to the airport. I have to scope out what I can first, and this looks like a good place to begin. I can try and watch the terminal from up there, and if everything looks okay, slowly move forward."

Luke looked up the embankment. "Yeah, maybe, but what can you really tell by watching from there? Especially with the concrete wall around the airport. If there are Homeland troopers inside, or behind the terminal, you won't see them from here."

"Well, I don't have a much better option at the moment."

"I do."

"What?"

"Let me go check it out."

"No way. You've done enough already."

"It's not that big a deal. Nobody is looking for me. Nobody even knows who I am. Cars go in and out of the airport all the time. There's probably a ton of them parked outside the main terminal now. I can go inside and check everything out. It's the only way you'll know for sure."

Declan thought for a second. He was reluctant to

involve Luke further, but his options were extremely limited and Tom was scheduled to arrive soon. He couldn't walk in blind.

"Okay," Declan replied. "Check it out. When you go in, there should be a woman named Barb at the front desk. If there's anyone else inside, just ask her for directions to one of the other terminals and leave. If not, ask her if the Inca Kola pickup is still on schedule."

"Inca Kola pickup?"

"She'll know what you're talking about, and, as long as you say that, she'll know you're one of the good guys."

"Will do."

Declan hopped out of the car, but before closing the door said, "And be careful, Luke. Trust your gut. If something doesn't look right or feel right, it probably isn't."

"I will."

Declan closed the door and darted up the embankment with his backpack, quickly tucking himself into the nook at the top and watching as the Honda drove away toward the airport.

Chapter 13

"Sir," Paul said to Bleeker, "the FAA confirmed the flight origination and plane make on the 18:00 arrival, and it's not our Gulfstream. It's a Cessna Citation, registered to an individual in Palo Alto, California with no connection to Neary or any Neary entity."

"Fine," replied Bleeker, not looking up from the various security monitors.

"So it's…"

"There," Bleeker interrupted Paul, pointing to the black Honda one of the airport security cameras had picked up. "All units, a black Honda, looks like an Accord, has just entered the airport grounds and is proceeding west along Walter Beech Street. Get your eyes on."

Bleeker followed the car intently on the security monitor as it drove slowly toward the Landmark terminal, and eventually came to a stop outside. "Who's at Landmark?" he asked.

"Unit Four, sir."

"Unit Four, can you get a make on the plates?"

"It's a Louisiana plate, William, David, Larry, 374."

"Paul, run the plates," Bleeker commanded.

Paul hammered quickly at his keyboard.

"It looks like a young male, Caucasian, auburn hair, sir," said Unit Four over the radio. "Should we intercept?"

"No, stand down. That's not Declan Parker. Paul, do you have a registration yet?"

"The car is registered to Luke Christopher Williams, age 22. He has a New Orleans address and…hold on, I'm cross-checking….no criminal record or associations in any of our databases. Looks like he just graduated from Tulane."

"Do we have a unit inside the Landmark terminal?" Bleeker asked.

"No, sir. We don't have units inside any of the FBO terminals."

"Fine. Mr. Williams has no obvious connection to

Parker, so let's stand back for the time being. Unit Four, keep your eyes open."

———————————

Luke stepped through the doors and into the quiet terminal building. He quickly scanned the downstairs and, seeing only a lady who appeared to be in her sixties sitting at the concierge desk, made his way toward her.

"How can I help you, hon?" Barbara asked.

"I'm looking for Barb."

"Well, you've found her. What's your name?"

"Luke Williams."

"What can I do for you, Luke Williams?"

"I, uh…I'm checking to see if the Inca Kola pickup is still on schedule."

Barb's expression changed noticeably and she replied, "No, I'm sorry to say the Inca Kola pickup has been cancelled."

"Cancelled?"

"Yes, it won't be coming in today or any other day."

"I see. Alright, well, thank you," Luke said as he turned toward the doors.

"Wait, what are you going to tell them if they stop you outside? The whole airport is crawling with federal agents. I'm sure they saw you come in here."

"I, uh…I'm not sure. I'll tell them I was looking for directions."

"Good. Tell them you're trying to find Southern University. I actually have had people come in here looking for it."

"Okay, thank you."

"Luke, is *he* with you?"

Luke nodded affirmatively and answered, "Nearby."

"Tell him that Jessica is here with a Plan B."

"Jessica?"

"He'll know her."

47

Barbara started quickly scribbling down directions to Southern University on a scrap of paper and handed the paper to Luke, saying, "Here, this'll help your story if you're stopped."

"Thank you."

"Where are you taking him?"

"Back to my house for the night, I guess."

"Write down your cell number and address?"

"Why?"

"Because I'm going to get Jessica to you."

"How are you going to do that?"

"I have an idea. Keep your cell on. If my plan works, I'll be calling you soon."

John Bleeker again intently watched the black Honda proceed across the video monitor.

"Should we stop him, sir?"

Hesitating a few seconds, Bleeker finally responded, "No, let him go."

"Unit Eleven," the Command Agent spoke into the radio, "Let the Honda pass, copy?"

"Copy," Unit Eleven retorted.

"Instead," Bleeker began calmly, "I want two plainclothes units outside his house within the next five minutes."

Chapter 14

As the Cessna, inbound from San Francisco, made its final descent into Lakefront, Barbara rifled through a desk drawer, looking for the credentials of one of Landmark's female drivers. Finding a close match, one with a driver in her early-twenties, she grabbed the credentials and one of the Landmark jackets the drivers wear when chauffeuring clients, and hustled upstairs to the office where Jessica was hiding out.

"Here, you need to pull your hair back in a really tight bun, and do makeup like this," Barbara said, showing the ID photo to Jessica. "As you can see, Kim goes heavy on the eyes and lips. You can use my makeup bag."

"Why, what's going on?"

"I'm getting you to Declan. You're going to be our driver to the Quarter."

Jumping up, Jessica replied, "You know where Declan is?"

"No, but I know where he's going to be. He sent a young man in, someone named Luke, to check things out. I gave him the bad news, but I got Luke's address and cell number so I can get you to Declan. You've got to hurry though, and get ready. You need to look like Kim Hanlon, one of our drivers."

Declan simply put his head in his hands as Luke told him the bad news about Tom's pickup being cancelled. He so desperately longed to hold Megan again, to see his family again, that he was unable to hide his immense disappointment. He had been within hours of finally being home again, of seeing his wife again, of feeling the touch of her lips against his own and inhaling every ounce of her essence.

All at once, the blood pulsing through his veins and

arteries carried dejection, anger, failure, and hopelessness, to the point where he could only stare blankly at the passenger-side floorboard of Luke's Honda. He sensed that Luke was still talking, but heard nothing, until he thought he heard Luke say "Jessica."

"What did you say?"

"Which part?" Luke asked.

"Did you say Jessica?"

"Yes, Barb said to tell you that Jessica is here and that she has a Plan B."

"What Plan B?"

"I don't know. I gave Barb my address and cell number and she just said that she'd get Jessica to us."

Declan sat silently for a moment, trying to decipher and digest everything that had just transpired. Tom had never said anything to him about a backup plan. What could such a plan possibly entail? Without Tom and the Gulfstream, there was no way out of the States and back to Peru. He certainly couldn't just book a commercial flight and stroll into the airport. How did Jessica even get to New Orleans if Tom hadn't brought her?

His mind full of questions, for the first time in over a month, for the first time since that whisper in the caves had led him back out to the light, Declan's faith began to waver. How could this failure possibly work into God's plan for him? How could being stuck in the United States a moment longer, still apart from Megan and his family, be a good thing?

Declan leaned back in the passenger seat and closed his eyes. He visualized all the ground he'd covered to get to New Orleans, all the cold nights sleeping outside and the all the days without anything decent to eat. He'd endured it all, and trusted God along the way without wavering, because he could see the light at the end of the tunnel. The thought of finally boarding Tom's plane in New Orleans had kept him going and, for the first time, that motivation, that finish line had simply vanished.

As he was on the verge of tears, with anger seething just beneath the surface of his skin, Declan recalled Jeremiah 29:11, a verse he'd read only days before: "'For I know the plans I have for you,' declares the Lord, 'plans to prosper you and not to harm you, plans to give you hope and a future.'"

Declan focused on those words, "*I know* the plans I have for you." Declan remembered the numerous times on his journey when God had provided, when, to Declan at least, there had appeared no hope of relief, and, slowly, his rage subsided, and his faith steadily regained its place in the forefront of his mind. Deep down, Declan knew who the whisper in the cave had come from. He knew, somehow, everything would work out for good. Opening his eyes and taking in a slow deep breath, Declan said to Luke, "Okay, we'd better get out of here. You need to get home before curfew and I need to figure out what to do next."

"You're coming back with me. That's where we're supposed to meet Jessica."

"I don't think that's a good idea."

"Why?"

"If the airport really was under surveillance, they would have seen you go in. At the very least, they'd have run your plates and gotten your name and address. You may have come up clean, but now you're known to have been in an area where they suspected me to be, and if John Bleeker is involved, he'll trust no one and take no chances. Taking me back to your house just isn't a good idea. Look Luke, I know you want to help, and you've been a huge help. In all likelihood, without you going into Landmark just now, I'd already be finished, but I can't let you keep doing this. You need to get on the road early tomorrow morning and get back to your family, and I need to find out what Plan B is and how to make it work."

"Well, Barb is supposed to call my phone soon. Let's at least stick together until she does. That's the only way we'll be able to coordinate getting you and Jessica together."

"Agreed. But after that, you're moving on and getting out of harm's way."

Chapter 15

Bleeker paced back and forth through the temporary command center, constantly checking the various security monitors and radio communications, but nothing came. There was no sign of Jessica Ehlers, no incoming Gulfstream, and no Declan Parker. He watched as the Cessna inbound from San Francisco landed and taxied to the Landmark Aviation terminal, and felt an odd mix of anger and disappointment dance within himself. Bleeker had been so sure, certain, that Lakefront was going to be Declan's attempted departure point. Why else would Jessica Ehlers have come to New Orleans if not to somehow facilitate his escape?

Suddenly, in a flash, for the first time a different answer to that question struck him and John Bleeker realized, with perfect clarity, that he'd, in fact, been duped. His light-blue eyes lit up and a smile began to creep ever-so-slowly across his face. He sat down in a plush leather chair and leaned back, letting himself fall into its coolness. The smile on his face morphed into an enormous grin, reminiscent of the Cheshire Cat, and, without warning, a deep laugh burst forth from him.

"Are you okay, sir?" Paul asked.

Bleeker just continued to laugh, unable to do anything else at the thought of his monumental folly.

"Sir?" Paul repeated.

"Don't you see it, Paul?"

"See what?"

"The girl, Jessica Ehlers. It was brilliant really."

"I'm not following," Paul replied.

"Neither did I, which is precisely why we're sitting here looking like idiots in New Orleans. The decoy was never Houston, it was the girl. Jessica Ehlers coming to New Orleans, flying commercial even. She's the decoy. She's the telegraph. Declan Parker is nowhere near here."

Suddenly the thought hit Paul too. "So he planned to

leave through Houston all along."

"Maybe, maybe not," Bleeker responded, still smiling. "Either way, he was never leaving through New Orleans. They telegraphed Houston, probably knowing we'd look deeper, and that if we did, we'd find Jessica's travel plans, which would lead us right here. Like I said, brilliant."

"So,…"

"So, nothing. It's over. That Gulfstream has, in all likelihood, already picked Parker up somewhere else and he is, as we speak, headed back to Peru and laughing all the way there. For all we know, Jessica Ehlers is with them. She could have landed in New Orleans and left immediately, heading to Houston or wherever the real departure point was located."

"Well, we have men in Peru."

"Yes we do, and I want them to leave Parker something special to come home to. I want the job done tonight."

A voice came over Bleeker's radio, "Unit Four here, sir. We have five leaving the Landmark facility. Two females, both appear to be Landmark employees, and three males. Copy?"

"Copy, Unit Four," Bleeker replied. "Let them go. It's over. This op is off. Copy?"

"Copy, sir."

Bleeker sat back in the chair again and took a deep breath. "Call all units off. It's over. We'll stay here tonight, Paul. We can head back to D.C. in the morning. At least we can get a good dinner out of this trip."

Chapter 16

Luke's cell phone rang as the Honda headed toward the Garden District. "Hello," he answered.

"Luke, it's Barb."

"What's the plan?"

"Jessica is at the Hotel Monteleone in the Quarter. She's in Room 514, which is booked under Landmark Aviation. Can you get him there?"

"Absolutely. We're just a few minutes away."

"God speed," Barb replied, and hung up.

Luke brought the Honda to a stop, and began to turn around.

"What?" Declan asked.

"Jessica's in Room 514 at the Hotel Monteleone. Barb booked it under Landmark. She wants me to take you there."

"Perfect. Let's go. It's not long before curfew."

Luke hurried toward the French Quarter. Traffic was diminishing quickly as the day ticked closer to sunset and it only took a few minutes to reach the ancient narrow streets of the Quarter. As they passed The Court of Two Sisters restaurant, Declan thought about the last time he'd been there, with Megan about a year after they'd started dating. He remembered the Dixie jazz band they'd listened to during brunch and watching Megan try on too many hats to count at some crazy hat shop she'd found as they walked through the Quarter. Declan missed her with the same intensity and longing he'd had as a boy when his dad died. Whatever it took, however long it took, he would get back to her.

The Honda stopped in front of the historic Hotel Monteleone. "Here we are," Luke said.

Declan unbuckled his seatbelt and looked Luke in the eyes. "Thank you, Luke. I mean it. You've been an immense help and, more importantly, you've been a friend. I won't forget it."

"Thanks. I just wish I could do more. What will you

and Jessica do next?"

"I'm not sure yet. I guess I need to see what Plan B is, and we'll go from there, but, regardless, I know everything will work out for the best. I just have to remember that I'm not the one driving this train. I'm just along for the ride."

"He is faithful."

"Yes, He certainly is. Now, you'd better get going. I don't want you to take a chance on being out after curfew. It's not safe and I've already put you in harm's way enough for one day. God bless you, Luke."

"And you."

Declan stepped out of the Honda, closed the passenger door, and walked quickly into the hotel. Luke watched as he hurried inside, put the car in drive, and headed home.

Chapter 17

A gentle wind whispered through the drowsy moon-lit eucalyptus trees surrounding the hacienda in which Megan's brothers and their families were staying. Agents Costello and McCall, with night-vision goggles on, crept along silently toward the house, keeping cover in the dark shadows of the forest. They moved deftly among the trees, systematically edging closer and closer to the smallest of Ignacio's three haciendas.

When they were within twenty feet, Costello motioned for McCall to stop and silently pointed to an open window. McCall acknowledged his assent with a nod and the two snaked forward quickly, like a pair of ninjas, until they arrived below the open window.

Once beneath the window, they crouched low against the wall and simply listened, only to hear the breeze continue to rustle through the plentiful eucalyptus trees. Costello nodded to McCall, and each simultaneously attached a suppressor to his 9mm Glock. Once finished, each assassin nodded affirmatively and Costello slid slowly up the wall, bringing his shoulders level with the bottom of the open window.

He peered quickly through the window, finding the kitchen. Still hearing no movement inside, Costello slid a cutting tool from his pocket and quickly cut around the edges of the screen, which he discarded quietly on the ground outside. After handing his weapon to McCall, with a swift fluid motion Costello was up, through the open window, and inside the kitchen, barely making a sound. McCall handed both weapons to Costello and, a few seconds later, he too was silently inside.

Without hesitation, each moved swiftly through the house, first encountering the room where Megan's brother, Timothy, and his wife were sleeping. A few seconds later, their first victims tallied, Costello entered the room across the hall, where Timothy's infant daughter slept. Then, he and

McCall moved down the hall, to the room where Megan's other brother, John, slept with his family. They moved methodically and, with neither their pulses increasing nor their breaths deepening, Costello and McCall simultaneously added four more bodies to their night's work. No thoughts crossed their minds when it came time to pull the triggers. Each simply placed the cold metal suppressors within an inch of the intended target's head, fired, and moved on, without giving any consideration to the dreams they were forever eliminating.

They moved swiftly through the rest of the spacious hacienda, verifying that it was clear. After taking the lives of two young men, two young women, and three small children in less than two minutes, the assassins were back outside and looking up the hillside to the lone light shining through the trees from the next hacienda.

———————————

Declan rolled over in bed, his feet tangled with Megan's beneath the supple, soft, white linens. He felt her bare feet, her toes, gently touching his own and her touch sparked an urge in him to wake her up. He ran his hand softly along his wife's back, carefully outlining her angelic contour, watching her face through the darkness for any small sign that she was emerging from her slumber, but her eyes remained closed and her breathing peacefully rhythmic. Unsatisfied, Declan brought his hand up to her face, first softly caressing her forehead, then her cheeks, and, finally, her lips.

"Wake up," he whispered softly. "Wake up, Megan."

———————————

Unsure of everything but that she had very distinctly heard her husband's voice, Megan jolted awake. She sat up on the sofa and looked at her watch, disappointed that she had fallen asleep, even for such a short time. It was nearly 1:00 A.M. Atau should be outside any moment with the car to drive her to Cusco to meet Tom Langham's plane and, finally, Declan. She longed to see him again, to feel herself in his arms, to run her fingers through his hair, and to finally truly laugh again.

"Are you ready?" Evan Parker whispered as he walked quietly into the living room.

"Yeah, I'm ready. I must have nodded off. Are you still coming with?"

"Absolutely. Michelle and the kiddos are asleep. I couldn't sleep if I tried."

"That's what I thought too. C'mon, Atau should be outside."

Megan and her brother-in-law made their way outside to find Atau and her Uncle Ignacio standing by the car, speaking to one another in Spanish.

"Uncle Ignacio, what are you doing up?" Megan asked.

"I couldn't sleep my dear niece, so I'm going to drive you and Evan to the airport to meet the plane."

"You don't have to do that."

"I want to," Ignacio replied getting into the driver's seat. "Now, let's be off."

Megan and Evan got into the running car, Ignacio flipped on the headlights, and they were off along the dirt road, heading quickly down the mountainside toward the town of Urubamba below.

———————————

Costello and McCall watched from the cover of the trees about thirty feet from the second hacienda as the car passed. "Could you see anyone inside?" McCall asked.

"No, I couldn't make out who it was," Costello whispered.

"What do you want to do?"

59

"Clear the house. We won't get another chance. This is it and if we don't get Megan Neary or the Parkers tonight, there'll be hell to pay with Bleeker."

Chapter 18

Atau finished his prep work for what would be a celebratory morning breakfast and tidied up in the kitchen. Ignacio's favorite dog, Tambo, a Peruvian Inca Orchid (a dark hairless breed of Incan origin) lay nearby, next to the kitchen door. As Atau was putting the last of the dishes away, Tambo raised his slumbering head. His long pointed ears stood straight up and he began barking.

"Silencio," Atau commanded, but Tambo barked again and hurried outside through his small dog door. Once outside, the dog's bark became vigorous and violent. Atau went toward the door leading outside but stopped when he heard Tambo whimper and then, silence. His hands shaking, Atau bolted the kitchen door, at first fearing that an animal of some sort was outside. He picked up a kitchen knife and headed out into the main room of the hacienda, listening for any sounds throughout the house.

Costello stepped over the strange-looking dead dog and hurried toward the opposite side of the hacienda, looking for another point of entry. McCall had made his way toward the solid wooden main gate. It seemed heavy and probably well-fortified on the other side.

On the opposite side of the hacienda, Costello found an open window. He looked inside to see what appeared to be a woman sleeping in a double bed set in the middle of a small room. He raised his Glock, took aim, and began to squeeze the trigger as the woman rolled over. The round sprinted out of the chamber and hit Declan's mom in the back, jolting her awake with a blood-curdling scream that pierced the night. Costello quickly fired another round which found its intended target, and Mrs. Parker fell back against her pillow, dead, but the element of surprise had been compromised, and Costello rushed quickly through the window.

Mrs. Parker's scream, and the ensuing silence, made Atau shudder violently. Evan's wife, Michelle Parker, burst from her room in a panic, finding Atau in the hall.

"What was that?"

"It came from Senora Parker's room," Atau responded, clearly shaken. "I think an intruder."

"Atau, go get my children and take them up to the main house. Hurry."

Atau ran to the children's room and picked them both up from their beds. Carrying Will and Charlotte, one in each arm, he hurried back out to the hall.

"What's going on?" Will asked, still partially in the haze of sleep, as he slipped from Atau's arm onto his feet.

Suddenly the door from Mrs. Parker's bedroom swung open and Costello emerged, spotting the group in the hallway.

"Run!" Michelle screamed. "Run!"

Still holding Charlotte, who was just beginning to wake up, Atau grabbed Will by the arm and darted as fast as he could back to the kitchen. Hoping to give her children some time to escape, instinctively, Michelle rushed Costello. Unshaken, Costello raised his 9mm and meticulously fired three tight rounds, taking Michelle down in the hallway within five feet of him.

He stepped over Michelle's lifeless body and hurried after Atau and the kids.

Atau quickly pushed the refrigerator in front of the kitchen door and ran over to the frantic children.

"Shhh…shhh, it is okay," he said. "Will, take your sister and go hide in the forest. Do not come out, no matter what. Understand?"

"But, where's my mom?" he asked.

"I'll protect her. You must go now and keep quiet. Find a place to hide and wait there."

Atau kissed the children on the heads and pushed them out the door, "Silencio…silencio."

The children hurried off into the darkness and cover of the dense eucalyptus trees, and as Atau went to close the kitchen door again, a bullet ripped through his chest and he fell to the floor.

"The house is clear," McCall said, coming into the kitchen.

"Good," Costello replied, taking an FBI identification badge, the memento Bleeker had sent, out of his pocket. "I need to leave this, and then we'll move on to the main house."

"What about the two children?"

"Forget about them for now. They'll be cold and scared out there. They won't last long."

Costello made his way back to Mrs. Parker's bedroom, stepping over Michelle's lifeless body in the hallway. Once inside the bedroom, he maneuvered Mrs. Parker's body on the bed, such that she was lying on her back, her head on her pillow again and her eyes still open. Costello folded her hands gently together on her stomach and placed the memento, the identification badge that had belonged to Declan's mentor and friend at the Bureau, Kevin Cameron, in her hands where it would clearly be seen by anyone who would find the body.

Satisfied with the scene he'd created, Costello smiled, then he and McCall headed back out into the night and further up the mountainside toward the main hacienda.

Chapter 19

Despite his exhaustion, Tom Langham brought the Gulfstream down to the tarmac in Cusco like a feather drifting onto a pillow. After taxiing to the hangar and completing his post-flight checklist, he checked in with the hangar supervisor and asked that the plane be refueled by morning.

Shortly before 2:00 A.M., Tom had made his way through customs and had begun the walk he'd been dreading since responding to Jessica's text: the walk to the airport exit, where he knew he'd find Megan and Evan anxiously anticipating Declan's long-awaited arrival. With each step toward the exit doors, Tom's face grew a bit more ashen and his stomach a bit more nauseous.

As the doors came within view, so did Megan and upon seeing Tom walking toward her alone, Tom witnessed the excitement rush from her face like water down a drain. Tears began to pour from Megan's eyes and, unable to watch the woman he'd known since she was but a little girl breakdown completely, Tom ran toward Megan, his heart breaking for her all the while.

Megan threw herself into Tom's arms and balled against his chest. "It's okay," he whispered to her. "It's okay, he's gonna be home soon. It's all going to be okay."

As Tom stood holding Megan, he looked up to make eye contact with Evan, who was also clearly concerned and struggling to keep his composure. Ignacio approached Tom slowly and said, "Welcome home."

"Thanks," Tom replied.

Pulling herself up from Tom's chest, Megan looked into his eyes and asked, "What happened? Where's Declan?"

"I'm not sure. When I was a little over an hour away, Jessica texted and told me to abort, that feds were all over the airport. I hated to do it, but I had to turn the plane around and come back. I couldn't land."

"Was Declan there? Is he safe?"

"I don't know. I haven't received anything from Jessica since her text. I wish I could tell you something different, but I just don't know. I'll call Barb in the morning."

On the verge of tears again, Megan thought about what had woken her up earlier, Declan's voice, as clearly as if he had been sitting next to her on the sofa. That thought, the clearest recollection of his voice, gave her an unexpected sense of peace. "He's okay," she said, looking at Tom and Evan. "I don't know why I know that, but I do. He and Jessica are okay."

"I feel the same way," Evan responded.

"I suggest we get going," Ignacio interjected. "I don't know that any of us, except possibly Tom, can sleep, but let's get going."

After easily overcoming the security system at the main hacienda, Costello and McCall made short work of disposing of Megan's sleeping parents, the three in-house staff employed by Ignacio, and four more of Ignacio's prize dogs. They cleared the main hacienda in less than three minutes, again thinking nothing of the lives they stole along the way, and headed back down the mountainside to meet Ryan Hewson for their ride to the hotel in Cusco.

"What about the car that left?" McCall asked. "I didn't see Ignacio Diaz, Megan Neary, or Evan Parker in any of the houses."

"They were obviously the ones in the car."

"Why do you think they left in the middle of the night?"

"Not sure. Clearly they weren't trying to escape or they would have alerted and taken their families."

"What about the Parker children?"

"They're still hiding out somewhere in these woods, I suspect," Costello replied. "We'll let them be. I've had more than my fill of killing children tonight."

"Agreed."

"Bleeker wanted us to send a message to Declan Parker. I think we've accomplished that."

"I thought that message included taking out Megan Neary and Evan Parker," McCall said.

Costello stopped and looked at McCall. "As far as Bleeker is concerned, that message has been sent. Are we on the same page?"

"Entirely."

"Will," Charlotte whispered.

"Shhh," Will cautioned, putting his index finger up to his mouth, which his little sister mimicked. The two young children sat about thirty feet from the second hacienda, tucked well inside a large bush, listening as the two men talked. Charlotte took her brother's hand and squeezed it three times in succession, which was the sign their mom had taught them for saying "I love you." Feeling his little sister's three squeezes, Will responded with three of his own and the two sat in their footy pj's, shivering in the dark night, listening to the voices of Costello and McCall trail off into the distance.

Chapter 20

As everyone knew they'd be unable to sleep, and
Tom was famished, Ignacio had driven the group to a quiet
little restaurant in Cusco that was open early, before making
their way back home. Megan thought about Declan the
entire way back, her eyes taking in the wondrous landscapes
so prevalent in that region of the Peruvian Andes and her
mind envisioned Declan riding next to her, his hand
interlocked with her own.

The sun rose over the mountainsides and began to
sprinkle its earliest purest morning rays on the floor of the
valley, as Ignacio turned onto the dirt road leading up the
mountainside to the haciendas. As the car wound up the
road, he caught sight of his prized purebred Great Pyrenees,
Manco, named after Manco Capac, the first Incan King and
founder of Cusco.

"Manco should not be out," Ignacio said. "He was in
the house when I left." Ignacio stopped the car, stepped out
and called Manco, who came to him straight away. Manco
licked Ignacio's hand and nuzzled his nose against his
owner's leg. Ignacio stroked the dog's cold, soft, white fur,
and turned to the car. "I'll walk back up with Manco. Can
one of you drive the rest of the way?"

"Sure," Evan answered, getting out of the backseat.
"I'll drive us up. Is he okay? It looks like there's something
on his side, toward the back."

Ignacio knelt down next to the dog and saw, quite
clearly, something dark caked in Manco's fur on one side.
He ran his hand over the substance and said with great
surprise, "It's blood. This is blood."

Evan went over and took a closer look. Manco didn't
seem to be in any pain and Evan couldn't see any sort of
injury. "He looks fine. It looks like he either rolled or sat in
blood."

"Something's wrong," Ignacio said. "We'd better get
up to the house."

Evan and Ignacio hurried back to the car and started quickly up the mountainside, Manco doing his best to keep up running behind the car. They drove quickly past the first hacienda and, as they were about to pass the second on their way to the main hacienda, Megan called out, "Wait, the kitchen door is wide open!"

Ignacio slammed on the brakes and each of the four jumped out of the car.

Will heard the car doors close and opened his eyes. His little sister was sleeping cuddled up next to him, both still completely covered by the large leafy bush they'd taken refuge in. He crept forward slowly and peered through the plush green leaves to see Megan and his dad standing about thirty feet away, outside the hacienda. Will jumped up and screamed, "Daddy!"

Evan heard his son calling for him and turned around to see Will emerging from the forest. Evan ran toward him, "Will, what are you doing out here? Where are your mom, Charlotte and Nan?"

"Charlotte's with me. A man came into the house last night and Atau made us hide in the woods. He said..."

"What do you mean a man came into the house?"

"I don't know. Mom woke us up and I saw a man come out of Nan's room and mom told us to run. Later, while we were hiding, I heard two men talking. They said your name and Aunt Megan's name."

Evan turned and sprinted into the hacienda through the open kitchen door and immediately tripped over Atau's body. "Oh my God," he shouted. "Oh, God!"

Ignacio, who had followed him inside, saw Atau as well, and looked back to Megan, who was about to come inside. "Go to the children, Megan."

"Why, what is it?"

"Atau is dead. Keep the children outside."

Megan's face went white and a look of panic flashed in her eyes. She ran toward Will and asked him to show her where Charlotte was. Evan jumped to his feet and, with Ignacio and Tom right behind him, ran through the kitchen, through the main living room and, finally, into the hallway leading to the bedrooms, where he saw his wife, Michelle, crumpled in a bloody heap on the floor. Evan dropped down next to her and lifted Michelle into his arms, holding her and weeping uncontrollably.

Ignacio and Tom stopped, looking at one another, but not entirely sure what to do. "I should go check the lower house," Tom said.

"Should I come with you?"

"No, stay with Evan. I'll be okay."

Tom darted out the main door and back down the dirt road, as Megan emerged from the forest with Will and Charlotte and put them both in the backseat of the car, where it was warmer. Ignacio felt it best to let Evan grieve in peace, so he checked the rest of the house and found Mrs. Parker dead in her bed. Ignacio gently closed her eyes, removed Kevin Cameron's FBI credentials from her hands, and placed a clean blanket over her body.

"My mom?" Evan asked as Ignacio emerged from the bedroom.

"She's gone, Evan. I'm so very very sorry."

Evan just buried his face in his wife's hair, unable to let her go. Ignacio left him there, allowing Evan his privacy, and went back outside to the car. He saw Tom walking back up the road from the lower hacienda.

"What happened?" Megan asked. "What's going on in there?"

Ignacio looked at her dejectedly and replied, "They are all muerto."

Megan looked at him in total disbelief. "What do you

mean?"

Ignacio pulled her aside, away from the car and out of earshot from the children. "They were all shot. Atau, Michelle, and Mrs. Parker. They were assassinated. I found this in Mrs. Parker's hands."

Megan looked at the credentials and said, "This is Kevin Cameron's."

"Who is Kevin Cameron?" Ignacio asked.

"He was Declan's friend at the FBI. Kevin was the one who warned Declan and I about John Bleeker, and told us to get out of the States."

"So he helped you?"

"Yes. This doesn't make any sense," Megan replied. "Kevin wouldn't have done something like this."

Ignacio caught sight of Tom, who was within ten feet, and Tom simply nodded affirmatively. Megan caught the nod and, knowing where he had been, burst into tears at the thought of what had happened to her brothers and their families.

"I should check the main hacienda," Ignacio said to Tom. "Wait here, I'll be back."

Tom held Megan as Ignacio headed up a shortcut trail through the forest.

Chapter 21

As Declan Parker rolled from his right side to his left on the firm carpeted floor, he felt a slight twinge in his back. He opened his eyes to see that it was shortly after 6:00 A.M., and heard the sound of the shower running in the bathroom. Sitting up, he took out the note Megan had sent with Jessica again, and placed it just under his nose, taking in the unmistakable, almost intoxicating, scent of Megan's perfume. The note said, simply, "See you tonight. Love, Your Wife."

Taking one more whiff, Declan put the note away and, pulling himself up from the floor, he looked over to the bed to see it empty. He unwrapped the bandage on his right arm and, to his amazement, the gunshot wound looked to be almost completely healed. Declan sat amazed by what appeared to him to be nothing short of a miracle.

"Thank you, Lord. Thank you. Really, nothing is impossible for one who believes, and I believe. I definitely believe."

As Declan finished removing the old bandage, his thoughts turned immediately to how he and Jessica would be able to get to Washington D.C. within the next three days. He and Jessica had spent a few hours the night before going over the new plan, which was, in essence, to get themselves to Washington D.C. as quickly as possible so they could meet up with Louis Martino and depart the United States with the Israeli Prime Minister's delegation.

If he'd done his part, Louis would have already obtained valid Israeli passports for them and would have made arrangements to get them on the flight. While Declan wished that he was already back in the Urubamba Valley with Megan and his family, it seemed to him that God had provided another way home. Declan just had to get there, which, given the general conditions in the U.S. and their inability to simply book a flight or a train, was easier said than done.

"I know the plans I have for you," Declan repeated to himself, citing Jeremiah 29:11. "I'm glad You know, because I have absolutely no idea."

Declan stood up and stretched, then turned on the TV, the first time he'd done so in over a month. The news was filled with coverage about how conditions were improving and how the dangerous extremist elements in the country were slowly being rounded up and subdued. CNN had a clever piece about how the United States had already become safer, citing the total absence of any mass-shootings since Christmas Eve, and credited the passage of the Firearms Protection Act and the swift federal government action to quell dissent with this better safer America.

There was also a story about the Israeli Prime Minister's imminent address to the United Nations in response to the draconian sanctions resolution aimed at Israel that had moved at record speed through the general body and was to be presented to the Security Council later that day, after the P.M. had an opportunity to plead Israel's case. According to CNN's United Nations correspondent, the Israelis were completely isolated, without a friend in the U.N., including the United States, which was also expected to vote in favor of the sanctions.

The buzzing from John Bleeker's iPhone roused him from his sleep. He drowsily reached over to the nightstand and answered the call, saying simply, "What?"

"It's Costello. Sorry to call so early."

"If you were so sorry, you wouldn't have actually called, Costello. What is it?"

"It's done."

"Good, because New Orleans was a bust and I suspect Parker will be back there shortly, if he isn't already."

"Do you want us to wait for him?"

"No. If you've done your job well, living will be

substantially more miserable for Parker than dying would."

"I promise that he definitely won't be enjoying a joyful homecoming."

"I'm glad to hear it."

"We'll fly back today."

"Excellent. Come to D.C. when you get back. I'll want a full briefing then."

"Will do."

"Good work, Costello."

"Thank you, sir."

––––––––––

An overwhelming urge for a good hot cup of espresso came over Declan, so he threw on his shoes and turned off the TV. Knocking on the bathroom door lightly, he said, "Jessica, I'm going downstairs to get an espresso. Do you want anything?"

"I'll take one too, thanks," Jessica called back through the closed door. "I should be ready to head out in the next twenty minutes or so."

"Cool. I've been thinking about it, and I think the best way to get to D.C. is to try and rent a car and drive it."

"Unfortunately, I think you're right."

"I should be back up in a bit."

"Okay."

Declan grabbed one of the room keys and stepped out into the hallway, heading toward the elevators.

––––––––––

"Paul," Bleeker said into his iPhone, "Are you ready?"

"Yes, sir."

"Well, I'm not. I'll meet you downstairs in about 30 or 40 minutes and we'll head over to Lakefront. Our car should be outside soon."

"Okay. Sir, I wanted to let you know that the Gulfstream arrived back in Cusco early this morning."

"Not surprisingly. Any trace of Jessica Ehlers?"

"No, sir, nothing."

"Thank you, Paul."

Sipping his espresso as he walked through the Monteleone's ornate lobby, Declan thought back to all the mornings he'd stopped for espresso on his way into work and to his former life. Despite being just a few months removed from that life, it seemed like ages had passed. The country, the world for that matter, had changed so drastically and quickly. It was as if the world was spinning out of control, although Declan knew that wasn't the case. He didn't understand nearly as much about God's prophecies as his mom and Evan did, but he'd read enough of his Bible over the past month to know, without a doubt, that God did have a plan and that plan was being revealed, piece by piece, just as He'd said it would.

A twinge of depression bearing the unfamiliar tint of failure was annoyingly present in the forefront of John Bleeker's thoughts as he finished tying his navy-blue-and-white polka-dot tie. The capture of Declan Parker had been, as Bleeker had to finally admit to himself, a complete failure, and John Bleeker simply did not fail. His entire life had been about winning, regardless of the game and irrespective of the means. He was first in his class at prep school, the winningest pitcher in school history, and class president (in a class replete with future leaders). At Yale, Bleeker had been in the top 3% of his class and, like his father and grandfather before him, had been selected to Skull and Bones, the elite of elite Yale institutions.

John Bleeker had been bred for achievement, his pedigree was of the highest order and failure was simply not a consideration or factor in his life. And yet, as he stood looking back at himself in the mirror, he had to acknowledge, when it came to Declan Parker, who was really an average nobody, just some kid from the Midwest, Bleeker was by all accounts a failure, and that was entirely unacceptable.

As Declan turned into the hall from the elevator, he took another sip of espresso and savored its full flavor. His thoughts on the journey ahead, Declan barely noticed a room door open to his left a few feet ahead of him. A man in a gray pinstripe suit carrying a brown leather weekend bag began to emerge, and, out of habit, Declan said, "Good morning."

With the door still open, the man turned to return the greeting. Face to face, the two made eye contact and, without thinking, Declan tossed both cups of steaming espresso at the man and rushed at him, arms outstretched. He tackled the man in the doorway, shoving him violently back into the room before the door closed.

The man's back and head slammed hard into a wall, as Declan followed, hurrying the hotel room door closed behind them. Regaining his composure somewhat, the man reached for the handgun holstered under his coat, but Declan was on top of him again, grabbing him by the wet coffee-stained lapels of his coat, and shoving him forcefully into the wall again. With one hand on the man's shoulder, Declan delivered a succession of three quick punches to his gut, knocking the air from the man and dropping him to the ground.

The man's helplessness didn't prompt Declan to let up, instead he dropped down on top of him, pinning his shoulders to the ground with his knees and delivered two hard punches to the nose. The second punch apparently broke the man's nose, as blood began to spurt forth. With blood pouring from his nose, and pain shooting throughout his body, John Bleeker, yelled, "Damn you, Parker! You're a dead man, just like the rest of your family!"

Furious, Declan grabbed Bleeker by the hair and violently slammed his head against the tiled floor, until Bleeker went unconscious. Declan reached under Bleeker's coat, un-holstered his pistol, and pointed the weapon at Bleeker's head. His rage and base instincts urged him to pull the trigger, to take revenge against his former boss for framing him in the David Stanton affair and putting him on the run. Declan wanted to end John Bleeker's pathetic life then and there, but as his finger hovered against the trigger, he could see his dad saying, "Back off, Declan. Think about what you're doing. This isn't who you are. This isn't who you were meant to be. You're better than this, you're better than him."

Still aiming the pistol at Bleeker's temple, Declan slowly steadied himself and regained control of his breath. The sound of a gunshot would surely echo through the whole floor, if not the entire hotel and security would be on the scene in no time. His thoughts turned again to Megan, and how she must be feeling. Declan had given her his word that he'd return, and he wouldn't be proven a liar. Besides, Declan knew right from wrong, and taking Bleeker's life under those circumstances, whatever harm he'd caused Declan, was clearly wrong.

Declan stuffed the pistol into his jeans, got up, and pulled Bleeker's unconscious body over to a chair next to the bed. After dragging Bleeker up into a limp sitting position in the armchair, Declan ripped the sheets from the bed and used them to create makeshift restraints, securing Bleeker to the chair.

Satisfied that Bleeker was sufficiently bound, Declan rummaged through Bleeker's coat pockets, found his iPhone, and put it into his back pocket. He then hurried into the bathroom and grabbed a hand towel. After that, he removed the leather shoulder strap from Bleeker's weekend bag.

"You know they're all gone," Bleeker mumbled weakly. "They're all dead, Parker. Your whole family is dead and it's your fault."

"Shut up," Declan replied and quickly stuffed the hand-towel into Bleeker's mouth, gagging him, and secured the makeshift gag with the leather strap, tying it very tightly into a triple knot behind Bleeker's head.

Bleeker jerked against his restraints, to no avail, as Declan hurried back out into the hall, and hung the "Do Not Disturb" sign on the door. He tossed Bleeker's phone and gun into a trashcan by the elevators and rushed back to his own room.

Hurrying inside, he exclaimed, "We've got to go, now!"

Concern spread across Jessica's face as she asked, "What's up? Why are you bleeding?"

"I'm not. I just ran into Bleeker."

Jessica grabbed her backpack and Declan his, and the two rushed out of the room, quickly taking the stairs down to the hotel lobby.

"Let's walk over to the Omni to rent the car," Declan said.

"Okay."

As they hurried out the lobby doors onto Royal Street, they heard a voice, "Declan!"

Declan and Jessica turned to see Luke walking toward the hotel entrance. "Luke, what are you doing here?" Declan asked.

"I couldn't leave without making sure you two had a plan and were okay."

"Sorry to ask, but can you give us a quick lift to a rental car place?"

"Of course, but why do you need to rent a car?"

"We need to get to D.C. in the next few days. A car is the only way."

"Ride with me to St. Simons. We should be there by

the end of the day and can figure out the rest of the trip from there. It's a lot closer to D.C. than New Orleans is."

Without hesitating, Declan replied, "Okay, let's go."

PART II

"[34] Therefore do not worry about tomorrow, for tomorrow will worry about itself. Each day has enough trouble of its own."

Matthew 6:34

Chapter 22

Evan Parker held his children tightly, one in each arm, in the back row of Ignacio's passenger van, as it wound up the mountain roads from the Sacred Valley toward Cusco. Silence hung like a heavy tapestry over the van, each of its inhabitants quietly trying to digest what had happened to their families and loved ones. Evan had lost his wife and his mother, but was enormously thankful to be holding his beautiful children (who had, themselves, lost their mom). Tom Langham had lost his best friend in Megan's dad, and, Megan and Ignacio had lost everyone in their families, save one another and Declan.

The sadness in the van was immense and palpable, and no one spoke even one word until they were almost to the airport in Cusco, when, finally, Will looked at his dad and asked, "Will we get to see mom and Mimi again in Heaven?"

Without hesitation, Evan replied, "Yes, absolutely."

"But will we have to die too? I mean, to see them again."

"No, not necessarily."

"But they had to die to go to Heaven. I want to see them, but I don't want to die too, daddy."

"Well, not everyone will have to die to get to Heaven," Evan began. "One day, Jesus is going to come. He's going to appear in the sky with a loud shout and a trumpet, and in an instant, in the blink of an eye, all who believe in Him will be taken from the Earth to Heaven."

"Without dying?"

"Without dying. In a flash, we'll be in Heaven and we'll be like Him, perfect. No more pain, no more sickness, no more death."

"I think I'd like to do that, daddy," Will responded.

"So would I," added Megan. "How do you know about this, Evan? Is it in the Bible somewhere?"

"In a few places, but my favorite description comes

from Paul's first letter to the Thessalonians. It's in Chapter 4, Verses 15 through 17."

"Maybe we'll all be so lucky," Megan replied.

"I pray for just that every day," Evan answered.

Once they'd finally arrived at the airport, Ignacio pulled the van up to the curb and hopped out, heading to the back to start unloading the luggage. A porter came over with a luggage cart. Ignacio handed the porter one hundred Peruvian Sols, and instructed him in Spanish as to where to take the luggage.

"Are you going to park the van?" Megan asked her uncle.

"No, my love, I'm going back home," Ignacio replied with a smile. "This is my home, this is where I belong."

Megan shuddered at the thought of leaving her uncle. "But…"

"Please, my dear niece. I can't come with you. I belong here. I'm going home to give our loved ones their proper burials. You, on the other hand, need to go to Israel to meet your husband, the father of that beautiful little baby growing inside you, and to keep you all safe."

Megan looked surprised. She'd not told anyone she was pregnant and it was too early for her to be showing. "How did you know?"

"I've known you since you were a baby yourself. I suspected last week, when you began to glow even more than usual and you stopped taking wine with dinner."

"I just found out last week," Megan responded with a smile. "I'm going to miss you."

"And I you. Go to Israel, stay safe and come back home when the time is right. I'll always be here and you, Declan and your beautiful child will forever have a place here."

Megan squeezed her uncle tightly, not wanting to let him go, but knowing it was time. She kissed him on his cheek and said, "I love you."

"I love you."

With the luggage all loaded, Ignacio said his goodbyes to Tom, Evan and the children. He promised Evan that he would give Michelle and Mrs. Parker proper burials and erect headstones on their graves, and swore the Parkers and Tom would always have a home in the Andes.

"Goodbye, Ignacio," Evan said.

"Huq p'unchaykama," Ignacio replied in Quechua (which translates into, "Until another day").

As the group headed through the doors into the airport, Megan looked back at Ignacio still standing on the sidewalk outside, and waved one final time. Ignacio, with tears in his eyes, blew his niece a kiss and, a few seconds later, she was gone, on her way to the Gulfstream and, ultimately, Jerusalem.

———————

Louis Martino stood against a wall in the press section, eagerly awaiting the Israeli Prime Minister's address to the General Assembly of the United Nations. As he waited, a man in a dark suit caught his attention. Not recognizing the man out of uniform, it took Louis a few seconds to realize who it was before he walked over to him, saying, "Sgt. Ya'alon, it's Louis Martino."

"It's good to see you again, Mr. Martino."

"You too. What are you doing here?"

"I've been temporarily assigned as additional security for the Prime Minister."

"So you're working?"

"I am. May we catch up later?"

"Absolutely. I'm actually traveling with your group to D.C. later this evening."

"I know. I saw your name on the press roster and hoped we'd have a chance to speak."

Louis left Ya'alon to his work and prepared to take notes on the speech as the Prime Minister approached the podium. Even before the P.M. could reach the podium, the delegates in the General Assembly broke out into a loud chorus of boos.

Outwardly unfazed, the Prime Minister began, "Colleagues, please...", but even with the microphone, he was shouted down by the body of diplomats. Again, he began, "Indulge me a moment to make our case...", but, as before, the P.M.'s words were barely audible over the growing verbal disdain coming from the delegates. Louis didn't know most of the words, but quickly recognized that it was a chorus of obscenities being hurled at the P.M. in a world of different languages.

Despite it all, the Prime Minister held his ground at the podium, determined to be heard. He stood silently, taking the verbal abuse and looking out over the body of diplomats, patiently waiting out their venom. As the P.M. stood, an object Louis couldn't make out was hurled from the assembly floor toward the podium. Even though it missed the Prime Minister by four feet, his security team ran quickly toward him. Suddenly, another projectile was lobbed at the P.M. and Louis recognized the second thrown object as a black wingtip. The shoe was quickly followed by another, which smacked against the podium as the Prime Minister's security detail reached him and, surrounding him, rushed him out of the General Assembly chambers.

Chapter 23

His nose reset and bandaged, John Bleeker moved slowly toward the black SUV, his sore body aching a bit more with each step. After slowly ascending into the SUV, Bleeker sat in the passenger seat and relaxed for a second, pleased to have the weight off his legs. His head ached, and there was a consistent dull throbbing pain in his back, but the worst pain of all for Bleeker was the abject humiliation he felt at being bested yet again by Declan Parker. Bleeker couldn't understand why Declan hadn't killed him when he'd had the chance. In his mind, Declan's hesitation equated to weakness, and Bleeker vowed to make Declan pay for his unwanted act of mercy.

The fact that it had been Paul who'd rescued him, witnessing him bleeding and helplessly tied to a chair, only compounded Bleeker's shame and embarrassment. This game he and Declan had been playing, the back and forth since Declan had stumbled onto David Stanton's Christmas Eve plans, was over. John Bleeker was no longer playing. He was no longer simply content to capture and arrest Declan Parker, but was intent on destroying him and everyone he loved. The operation was to take a significant turn and would no longer be about capturing Declan, but killing him. Bleeker would only use men he trusted completely, men who'd follow any order he gave without hesitation or question, and his orders would be to leave a trail of bodies leading to Declan.

Paul, himself cognizant of the awkward circumstances in which he'd found his boss, quietly entered the SUV and sat behind Bleeker in the backseat, careful not to ask his boss how he was feeling. The driver was about to enter when Bleeker waved him off, so he and Paul could speak privately.

"So, what's the status?" Bleeker asked.

"I've checked all the hotel security footage, and it shows Parker and Jessica Ehlers leaving the hotel together.

They spoke with someone outside, but the camera angle didn't allow for us to identify him. I suspect it was a taxi driver, but we can't confirm that. They left the Monteleone two hours and six minutes before I came to your room, so…"

"So," Bleeker interrupted, "They had a good head start and we have no idea what direction they were headed or how they were getting there."

"True. So far, there are no records of them purchasing plane, train, or bus tickets. There's also no record of either renting a car, so there is a chance they're still in New Orleans, possibly waiting it out somewhere."

"What about the room they stayed in?"

"It was booked under Landmark Aviation. A desk clerk on duty last night said Jessica Ehlers came in with Barbara Lemley, who is the concierge at Landmark. Apparently, Jessica was dressed as a Landmark driver. The original Landmark reservation was for three rooms, but Ms. Lemley added a fourth upon arrival. That's the one Ehlers and Parker stayed in last night. Barbara Lemley signed for all of the rooms."

"Okay, we'll bring Barbara Lemley in, but, Paul, we're taking this operation covert. From this point forward, I'm only using select personnel. Understood?"

"Yes."

"Here's a list of three such agents here in New Orleans. Get Agent Neal on the phone and have him pick up Barbara Lemley."

"Yes, sir"

"Have the other two meet us at this location in the next twenty minutes."

"Yes, sir."

"Finally, and this is very important, none of this goes on the record. Any record. I don't want Jessica Ehlers put on any lists, into any databases, or popping up on any radars. I want any info you've compiled on the Gulfstream and Neary erased from any and all of our databases. It stays strictly on your desktop. The same goes for information about Lemley, Ehlers, and anyone else we come across in this. Clear?"

"Crystal."

"Declan Parker is mine and mine alone, as is anyone who is helping him. We will find him and we'll ruin anyone in our path. This is personal."

"I understand, sir."

Bleeker thought for a moment. "So, it looks like maybe we actually were correct about Lakefront being Parker's planned departure point. We know the Gulfstream left Peru bound for the U.S. We know Jessica Ehlers was in New Orleans, and after our arrival at Lakefront the Gulfstream turned around and went back to Peru. Jessica and Parker met up last night and left together this morning."

"Correct," Paul replied.

"Then it would appear that, even though we didn't know it at the time, we eliminated Parker's preferred departure plan and he either has a fallback plan, or, he's improvising. Either way, he's still in the U.S."

"Sir, I just received an alert from the Peruvian air authority. It seems the Gulfstream has left Cusco again."

"Really?"

"Yes, but the flight plan indicates that it's headed to Fortaleza, Brazil."

"Brazil?"

"Yes, sir."

"Check in with the Brazilians at the estimated arrival time and let's see if it actually gets there."

"Yes, sir."

"And, you're driving, Paul. Tell the driver to get another ride and take us to the address I just gave you. I'm ready to have a little chat with Ms. Lemley."

Chapter 24

"Where are we?" Declan asked as the Honda sped along Interstate 10 at nearly 80 miles an hour.

"We're about 30 miles east of Pensacola," Luke replied.

"Wow, I didn't know what a lead foot you had, Luke."

"I like to get where I'm going. I must get it from my dad. When my sister and I were kids, whenever we'd drive somewhere for vacation, he hated stopping. It was all about getting there in the shortest time possible. My sister says that one year, when I was three and she was six, we drove from St. Louis to Colorado and our dad put a little training toilet in the back of the car, so we didn't have to stop at a gas station to go to the bathroom. We'd just pull off to the side of the road. My dad still says the stops lasted less than two minutes, and we made it to Denver in under twelve hours."

Laughing aloud, Jessica said, "I hope you don't have a training toilet in the back."

"No," Luke replied with a somewhat embarrassed smile. "You don't have to worry about that."

"Good, that could get a bit awkward."

Luke, who was normally not one to be shy, couldn't help his nervousness around Jessica. He didn't like the strange awkwardness he felt around her, but realized there was really nothing he could do about it. Jessica was, quite simply, the most beautiful girl he'd ever been within a few feet of and Luke had been attracted to her from the moment he had seen her with Declan outside the Hotel Monteleone.

"I'm going to try and close my eyes for a bit, if that's cool," Declan said from the backseat. Just let me know if either of you need the training toilet."

"Funny," Luke responded.

As Declan leaned back and closed his eyes, a slightly uncomfortable silence filled the car. Luke wanted to say something to Jessica, but had no idea where to start and couldn't find the right words. Jessica too wanted to talk to Luke, but wasn't quite sure what to say either.

"Um…," they both stammered simultaneously.

"Sorry," Luke said. "Please, you go first."

Jessica smiled at him, which calmed Luke's nerves a bit. "So, Declan told me you were planning to go to medical school."

"Yeah, I was accepted to Emory for med school."

"Wow, that's a great school. I was a nursing student before everything happened. I was about to start my last semester."

"That's cool. Which field were you interested in?"

"I wanted to do something with pediatrics. I still do actually. I'm hoping that, at some point, everything kind of goes back to normal and I can finish my last semester somewhere. What about you? Why'd you want to be a doctor?"

"I guess because I spent so much of my early life as a patient. See, I was diagnosed with leukemia when I was three."

"Oh, wow. That had to have been tough."

"It was a lot of time at the hospital, lots of IV's, or pokes as my parents say I used to call them. I don't remember all of it, but I've been in remission ever since I got out of the hospital the first time, after induction."

"That's awesome."

"Yeah, so that's why I want to be a doctor. I'd like to go into pediatric oncology and do what I can to help kids who are going through what I went through."

Jessica found herself immensely impressed by Luke. He reminded her somewhat of her own dad and, in many ways, of Evan Parker, who was also a doctor. He seemed to share their qualities of gentleness and a caring spirit. "Well, I bet you'll be one of the best pediatric oncologists ever."

"I hope so. I know enough about what it feels like to be the one with cancer. Hopefully, I can take that experience and let it be used for something good, something positive.

Whenever I'd get stressed about something, like a big exam, my parents would always say, 'You've already survived cancer, Luke, so there really shouldn't be too much else in life that'll rattle you.'"

"They make a good point."

"Yeah, it really helps put things in perspective," Luke replied. "What about you? Where are you from?"

"The Dallas-Ft. Worth area, Denton specifically."

"Is your family still there?"

Jessica hesitated. She hated talking about her family, but she liked Luke and trusted him. "No, my parents were killed right after the Infringement Act was passed. I'm not certain, but I think Homeland troopers came to confiscate my dad's rifles. I found them at our house with Evan, that's Declan's older brother."

"I'm really sorry to hear that. It has to be difficult."

"It's life, I guess. I have an older brother, Aiden, but we got separated during the protests in Dallas and I haven't seen him since. I like to think he's still alive, but...," Jessica's voice trailed off.

"I'll say a prayer for you both, that you'll find one another."

"Thanks. You sound like Evan."

"Is that a good thing or a bad thing?"

"It's good. Evan is great. He's a doctor. He's back with his family in Peru."

"How'd you get hooked up with Declan and Evan?"

"Evan was placed in the same federal detention center I was after the protests started. There was an uprising and we escaped together. Initially, my plan was to go home, but when we found my parents there, I went on with Evan to find his family and that's where we found Declan. He'd come back to the States from Peru to rescue his family. Well, *we* all got out, but Declan got stuck here."

"So that's why you came back? That's why he was getting picked up in New Orleans?"

"Yep. The original plan was to fly him out, but as

you can see, it was a bust. Somehow John Bleeker, who used to be Declan's superior at the FBI, found out about it. We were just lucky Declan ran into you."

"I read in one of Louis Martino's articles that Declan is really the one who killed David Stanton on Christmas Eve and that Bleeker took the credit and framed him as being Stanton's accomplice when he wouldn't go with the official narrative."

"That's my understanding," Jessica answered. "Megan, Declan's wife, told me everything that had happened while I was in Peru. Bleeker and his bosses apparently knew about what Stanton and the other guy in Alabama were planning, and let them do it so the government could get a strong rationale and support to get the Infringement Act passed and start confiscating guns."

"That's crazy."

"I know, but even with Declan messing things up with Stanton, it seems to have worked. The nut job in Alabama was able to kill a bunch of people, and the Act passed. So, now we're on to Plan B to get back to Peru."

"So what's Plan B?"

"We're supposed to fly out with the Israeli Prime Minister's delegation from D.C. One of our contacts obtained Israeli passports for us. We're meeting Louis Martino there and flying to Israel. From Israel, we'll get back to Peru."

"You certainly don't lead a dull life, Jessica."

"No, I don't, but I don't think I'd mind dull for a while."

"Well, you never know. God has a plan for all of us and maybe His plan for you will end up dull."

Jessica laughed aloud. "I never thought I'd say this, but I kind of hope you're right."

Chapter 25

"So, Mrs. Lemley, are you ready to tell me what I want to know about Declan Parker and Jessica Ehlers?"

"Mr. Bleeker, I've already told you that I don't know anything."

"Yes, indeed you have; however, for whatever reason, maybe it's the fact that *you* booked their hotel room last night, I simply don't believe you. What's more, I get the distinct impression that you don't think I'm serious, and that's a notion I intend to dispel right now." Bleeker turned to one of the other men in the room and said, "We've wasted enough time here. Bring him in."

A moment later, two men stepped into the room with Barbara Lemley's husband of thirty-six years handcuffed between them. Upon seeing him, she exclaimed, "Stan!"

"What's going on, Barb?" her husband asked.

"Yes, Barb, what is going on?" Bleeker chimed in, but Barbara, with tears beginning to run down her cheeks, remained silent. Stan Lemley stood opposite Barbara, against a taupe wall, thoroughly confused.

"So, Barb, here's how this is going to go. You're going to tell me what I want to know, in detail, or I'm going to begin putting bullets into your husband. Shall we begin?"

Barb nodded affirmatively, saying, "Okay."

"Let's start with something simple. How do you know Jessica Ehlers?"

"She…she came into the terminal late yesterday afternoon."

"Why?"

"They were supposed to pick her up with Declan."

"Who's they?"

"Tom Langham."

"Bert Neary's personal pilot?"

"Correct."

"But Tom Langham never arrived. Why not?"

"Federal agents came into the terminal asking about

arriving flights," Barb answered, tears still trickling down her cheeks. "Jessica heard them and called Tom off, so he turned around."

"So Jessica Ehlers was at the terminal the whole time agents were at the airport?"

"Yes."

"And you helped Jessica get to the Hotel Monteleone and booked her and Declan Parker a room?"

"Yes."

"Where'd they go this morning?"

"I don't know."

Bleeker turned slowly toward and Stan Lemley, raised his sidearm and fired one round, intentionally missing just to his left. Barbara screamed and began balling as Stan also began to cry, shivering in terror.

"Do you see now, Mrs. Lemley, that I'm not screwing around? I promise you, the next shot I fire will go straight through your husband's forehead. Now, where were they going? Was there an alternate plan?"

"All I know…," Barb stopped, trying to get control of her sobbing. "All I know is that Jessica had a Plan B."

"What was Plan B?"

"I swear, I don't know. She never told me and I never asked."

"Did you ever see Declan Parker?"

"No, he never came to the airport and wasn't at the Monteleone when I dropped off Jessica."

"Where was he?"

"I'm not sure. I don't know."

Getting in Barb's face, Bleeker asked, "Why did you call Luke Williams yesterday evening?"

"I, I don't know who that is."

Bleeker turned again, raised his pistol and fired another round which hit Stan Lemley in the left thigh. Barb screamed again as Stan fell to the floor, moaning aloud.

Bleeker yelled at Barbara, "Do you think that I haven't already run your cell phone records, Mrs. Lemley?

You called his cell phone shortly after checking Jessica into the Monteleone, but you don't know who he is? Do I look stupid?"

"I don't think you're stupid," Barb replied, sobbing.

"Clearly you do," Bleeker retorted, turning again to Stan and raising his weapon.

"No, please!"

"Last chance, Barb!"

"Declan was with Luke. Luke was the one who was going to drive him to the hotel."

Bleeker turned back to Barbara and lowered his pistol. For about ten seconds, he simply stared at her, watching her body heave up and down with each sob. Finally, he asked, "How did Luke and Declan meet?"

"I have no idea. Luke came into the terminal to see if everything was okay and I told him the mission was off. He left, but I got his cell number first, because I was going to try to get Jessica to Declan. When I called, Luke said he'd take Declan to the hotel. That's all I know. I've had no contact with anyone after I dropped Jessica off. I don't know what Plan B was and I don't know where they went."

"Was Tom Langham coming back for them?"

"I don't know. That's the truth."

"I believe you, Barb. I do. I only have one other question for you, then you and Stan may head off into the wild blue yonder together. Why? Why did you help them?"

"It was the right thing to do."

"Aiding two criminals was the right thing to do?"

"Mr. Bleeker, the only criminal I see in all of this is you."

Bleeker smiled and stepped out of the room with the two other men, leaving Barbara and Stan alone together, Stan in agony and both in tears. In another room across the hallway, Bleeker found Paul, who had been listening in.

"Have we picked up Luke Williams yet?"

"Neal is on it. He left as soon as she mentioned Williams. Should be there in a few minutes. It isn't far."

"Fine, come get me when Neal calls in."

Bleeker stepped out into the hallway. He could hear the tearful confused conversation taking place between the Lemleys and smiled at the thought of poor clueless Stan Lemley lying in there with a bullet hole in his leg and absolutely no idea why. "Poor schmuck," Bleeker said to himself.

A few minutes later, Paul came out into the hall and said, "The place was empty. It looks like he moved. There was nothing in the house. Neal spoke to the owner, Luke's landlord, and he said the lease was up and Luke and his roommates had all moved back home."

"Where's he from?"

"St. Louis. I have an address. Should we get someone over there?"

"No, not yet. How long is the drive from here to St. Louis?"

"Approximately ten hours."

"If he left this morning, that would mean he'd be about four hours away from St. Louis by now."

"Roughly," Paul replied. "Do you think it was Luke Williams who met Declan and Jessica outside the hotel this morning?"

"I do, and it would appear there's a good chance they are headed to St. Louis, which is, I suspect, Tom Langham's actual final destination. Let's get the Williams' house under surveillance. Use a select team, three or four men we absolutely trust. Again, I want this kept under wraps. Nothing on the record. Finally, contact Costello and tell him to get up there with Agent McCall. They should almost be back from Peru."

"Will do."

"Call ahead and get the plane fired up. Have Neal meet us at the plane. I want to leave as soon as we get to Lakefront."

"Understood."

"And, Paul, have you been monitoring Louis

Martino's email accounts?"

"Yes, sir."

"Anything?"

"No, nothing. Louis Martino is apparently in New York covering the Israeli Prime Minister's address to the U.N. There's been no contact with anyone related to Declan Parker."

"Fine. Keep an eye on Martino."

"Yes, sir."

"Is there anything else?" Bleeker asked, seeing there was something on the tip of Paul's tongue.

"What about the Lemleys? Should we release them?"

"No," Bleeker replied. "Have the men take them home and kill them. Kill them both. I want it to look like an execution and I want a tip leaked to the local and national news outlets. We're going to send a message to Parker and his friends that anyone who helps him is going to end up dead."

Chapter 26

Louis Martino was still unable to believe the scene he'd witnessed unfold in the U.N. General Assembly chamber as he boarded the Prime Minister's plane with the other members of the Israeli press corps. He'd been a journalist for just over six years, since starting The Free Voice as a small online publication while still in college. Admittedly, his career was still young, but Louis had covered lots of political events in his relatively short time, and never had he witnessed such a spectacle amongst supposedly-civilized diplomats.

The disdain, the outright hatred, he'd witnessed directed to the Israeli P.M., and therefore toward Israel, had been shocking. It wasn't as though the verbal assailants had been a common enraged mob, although it felt that way. The assault came from some of the world's foremost and most respected diplomats and leaders, and it hadn't been limited to Arab nations. Louis had watched delegates from various European Union, Pacific, and South American nations booing and yelling as vehemently as those from Iran, Jordan, Egypt, and Syria. Louis had paid close attention to the delegation from the United States as well, and while they hadn't joined in the verbal assault, they certainly hadn't done anything to try and quell the outburst.

In fact, the only person he'd seen trying to calm or restrain the venom was Raffaele Firenze, the President of the European Commission, whom the Israeli P.M. had met with the day before. From what Adam Benjamin had told Louis about that meeting, Firenze was inwardly sympathetic to the Israeli position, but could not say so officially or publicly. With respect to the pending U.N. resolution, Firenze wasn't in favor, but his hands were tied.

Louis sat in an empty row, looking out the window as the plane rose into the perfectly blue sky and wondered what lay ahead for Israel. The P.M. was scheduled to meet with the President and various congressional leaders over the coming two days, but to what avail? The sanctions resolution was certain to pass the Security Council, as the President had already stated the U.S. wouldn't exercise its veto, and may actually vote in favor of the measure. Israel, it seemed, was completely isolated and reviled by the nations of the world.

————————

Declan awoke to see a road sign saying it was only another 55 miles to Jacksonville, Florida. Rubbing his eyes, he looked to the front and saw Jessica sleeping in the passenger seat.

"She's been out for a little over an hour," Luke said quietly.

"How long was I out?"

"A few hours. We're less than two hours from St. Simons now."

"And no trouble so far."

"No. I've seen a few National Guard or Army trucks along the highway, but nothing else. No stops or checkpoints."

"Hmm. I wonder if Bleeker has put it together yet. I'm sure someone found him hours ago. Knowing Bleeker and his ego though, I bet he hasn't made the info public."

"Why wouldn't he? I mean, if he wants to catch you?"

"You just said it. *He* wants to be the one to catch me, especially after what happened this morning. He won't go public with any information he has, if he has any, because he won't want some local cop or Homeland trooper at a checkpoint to luck into stopping us and take credit for the arrest."

"What did happen back there this morning?" Luke asked.

"We turned out to be in the same hotel, on the same floor even, as Bleeker. He and I ran into each other in the hallway and, needless to say, it wasn't pretty."

"You and Bleeker seem to have quite a bit of history."

"He's my former boss and, I believe, one of the architects of the two planned Christmas Eve massacres. I know, at the very least, he knew what David Stanton was planning and let it happen. Even to the point of shooting me when I tried to stop Stanton. I'm not certain about his involvement or knowledge of the other plan, the concert shooting in Alabama that night, but I suspect he knew about it. Bleeker was on the same security clearance list as the FBI Director, Homeland Director, and the White House Chief of Staff."

"So Louis Martino's articles about the Stanton affair are true? It really was a plan by the federal government?"

"I think it's more accurate to say that Stanton and the other wack job in Alabama had plans, which certain government officials knew about and did nothing to stop in order to further an agenda."

"What agenda?"

"Control. We've been seeing it for years, decades even. The people in power have an agenda, which is ultimately about control. Control over people, control over resources, control over wealth. Instead of blatantly taking away freedoms, which is an essential part of obtaining more control, they either create or, in many cases utilize, events to further their plans. Have you ever heard the expressions, 'Out of Chaos Comes Order' or 'Big Crisis = Big Change'?"

"Not really."

"Well, that's what we have here, as explained to me by John Bleeker himself. The powers that be have been pushing for gun control for decades, for disarming the populace, which makes them less able to fight change or the loss of other freedoms. Instead of just coming out and taking people's weapons, like the Nazi's did, they use circumstances, crises, to get the people, out of fear, to *ask* for the change. It happens little by little, over time, until, finally, you get the Christmas Eve shootings and the passage of the Firearms Protection Act."

"So the Christmas Eve shootings were about gun control?"

"They were about disarming the population. Certain high level officials knew ahead of time, based upon the mountains of data being collected on U.S. citizens by the NSA and Homeland, what David Stanton and the other guy in Alabama were planning to do. Instead of stopping them, those officials monitored them and let them move forward with their plans, knowing that once the massacres occurred, a substantial portion of the population, scared and shocked, would *ask* for stricter gun control measures so nothing like that could ever happen again. The people would essentially ask the government to disarm them in the name of security. We saw it after 9-11, after the Oklahoma City bombing, after Columbine, Aurora, and Sandy Hook, and after the Boston Marathon bombing. We saw it after Ferguson and Baltimore in the form of militarized police units. The only problem, the only hitch if you will, with David Stanton is that I stumbled right into the middle of it."

"And you were the one who stopped him?"

"Yes, I was. I'd been watching him and went to his apartment on Christmas Eve. I suspected him of killing two people, a young couple, a few nights prior. Turns out I was right. While I was at his apartment, I saw Megan, now my wife, on a live feed to his laptop from the church."

"Wow. How crazy is that?"

"Very. I now see it as God putting me in the right place at the right time."

"Absolutely," Luke agreed. "That's the way I feel about this morning. I was actually about to leave and get on the road, but something, God I believe, told me to go to the hotel first. I didn't totally understand why, but now I do. It's amazing how, when you trust God and follow His lead, even though you may not see it at first, eventually the picture becomes clear and everything makes sense."

"I couldn't agree more and, I for one, and I'm sure Jessica would agree, am glad He led you back to the hotel. We have one shot left to get out of here, for me to get back to Megan and my family. I can't fail this time."

"What about Jessica?" Luke asked. "She said her parents died after the protests started and she doesn't know where her brother is. Does she have any family down in Peru?"

"No. In truth, this is only the second time I've seen her. She left with my brother and the rest of my family when they all escaped to Peru. I really don't know her all that well, but I trust her. Evan trusts her, and Megan must trust Jessica to send her up here to help."

"We talked while you were asleep. She seems like…," Luke stopped himself, somewhat embarrassed.

"Like what?"

"She seems pretty amazing, that's all."

"I think she probably is. I know, from the brief conversation I had with Evan, that she's had a tough road since the protests."

"That's the impression I got too. She was going into her final semester of nursing school, and she said she'd really like to finish, but doesn't see how that's possible. I'd love to see her be able to do that. She seems like she'd be great with kids. I mean, she wants to go into pediatric nursing, that's why I said that."

Declan laughed gently. Luke was clearly smitten with Jessica, and who could blame him. She was intelligent, resourceful, beautiful, and trustworthy, with a subtle undercurrent of vulnerability. There was a lot to like about her.

"Don't worry, Luke. I understand. What's going on up ahead?"

"I'm not sure. It looks like cars are all getting over into the right lane."

Luke proceeded forward, following the other cars into the right lane. Traffic slowed down and the Honda inched closer to whatever was causing the backup.

"Can you see anything yet?" Declan asked.

Looking ahead, Luke finally spotted the issue.

"There's two Homeland cruisers up there. It looks like a checkpoint. What should I do?"

"Don't panic," Declan replied. "I have an alias passport and it's legit. Let's just see how this plays out."

As the Honda finally came to the checkpoint, one of the Homeland troopers approached the car, saying, "Good afternoon."

"Hello," Luke replied.

"Where are you headed?"

"To St. Simon's Island, sir. My family is there."

Jessica stirred awake in the front seat, and quickly realizing what was happening, instinctively hid her concern.

"I just need to take a look at each of your ID's."

"Oh, of course," Luke replied. He dug his drivers' license out of his wallet, and Declan and Jessica handed over their passports.

The trooper quickly ran each through a mobile device, cross-checking everyone with various security databases. When he was finished, he handed back the ID's and said, "Okay, you're all clear. Drive safely."

"Thank you, sir. Have a good day," Luke responded, and put the Honda in drive.

As they moved past the checkpoint, each breathed a huge sigh of relief. "What just happened?" Jessica asked. "I thought we were dead."

"Me too," said Luke, still shaking a bit.

"It seems I'm right. Bleeker hasn't put out any alerts or bulletins on us. He's keeping everything under wraps."

"Why would he do that?" Jessica asked.

"Either because he still wants to capture and arrest me himself, or he's planning something much worse and doesn't want anyone else to know about it."

"May I sit here for a few minutes, Mr. Martino?"

Louis turned from watching the clouds pass through the window, to see Sgt. Ya'alon standing next to the seat beside him. "Of course, and, please, call me Louis. I think we've been through enough together to warrant familiar terms."

"I agree. My first name is Ariel," Ya'alon said, sitting down. "How have you been, I mean, since you left Israel?"

"Honestly, not well. I still have nightmares sometimes about what we saw, about all the dead in and around Damascus. Some nights, I can hear their screams. I see the flash of light, the heat searing through their bodies, turning them to ash in an instant. It's all so clear."

"As do I. I think that's something one cannot ever forget. I know it had to happen, but still, I am haunted by it."

"Haunted is a good word, Ariel." The two sat silently for a moment, each reflecting on what they had witnessed the evening Israel had been left with no choice but to unleash a nuclear warhead on Damascus, until Louis, in an effort to break the silence and change the subject, said, "So, today at the U.N., that was unexpected. I mean, I knew the P.M. wouldn't be popular, but I sure didn't expect that."

"Yes, as the prophet Zechariah foretold, it would seem we are indeed increasingly alone in the world. I just didn't think I'd see it happen in my lifetime."

"You mentioned the prophets when we were in Nazareth too, when we saw the bomb wipe out Damascus."

"Yes," Ya'alon answered. "That was the fulfillment of one of Isaiah's prophecies."

"So, I take it you believe in the Bible? That you're a Christian?"

"No, not a Christian. I'm a religious Jew, but not a Messianic Jew, as those of us who believe our Messiah was Jesus and that He's already come, are called. I'm still looking, awaiting the arrival of our Messiah."

"And you think He's coming soon?"

"Very soon," Ya'alon replied with a smile.

Chapter 27

"Well?" Bleeker asked one of the agents who had been watching the Williams' home in St. Louis.

"No movement at all. I took a look around and the place looks empty."

John Bleeker took in the surrounding scene. The Williams' house was a large two-story with crisp white siding. It sat on a spacious lot, likely close to one-third of an acre, on a scenic street in a quiet, upper-middle-class neighborhood. "Okay, we sit tight for the time being. If they are headed this way, they could be arriving within the hour. Paul, what have you found out about the family? Any other properties?"

"Looks like Luke's sister, Hope, is renting a place in Atlanta. There's a house on St. Simon's Island, which is also in Georgia, that's titled in a trust that appears to be connected to the Williams family."

"Fine. We sit back and wait. Something tells me Parker and Jessica Ehlers are traveling with Luke Williams, whether it's here, Atlanta or St. Simon's Island. We're a couple hours from curfew, so wherever they're going, they'll be locked down there until morning. Costello..."

"Yes, sir."

"Take one of the planes and check out the condo in Atlanta. See if it's occupied."

"Will do."

"McCall, you fly down to St. Simon's and do the same."

"I'm on it."

"If either of you find anything, don't move on it until we get there."

———————

Luke's shoulders were tight and he was beginning to fade slightly as the Honda cruised over the F.J. Torras

Causeway and the final stretch to St. Simon's Island. Declan and Jessica had rolled their windows down and were both enjoying the saltiness of the ocean-tinged air blowing against their faces.

As the car exited the causeway and picked up Demere Road east toward the beach, Declan tried to focus on the present, and not worry too much about how the remaining 650 miles to Washington D.C. would be covered. As much as he tried to deny it, a vague uneasy feeling had settled deep within. The drive to St. Simons had been almost too easy. He knew Bleeker well and, therefore, knew that Bleeker wouldn't just let him go, particularly after being humiliated back in New Orleans.

A few minutes later, the Honda stopped in a driveway outside a large two-story house with an inviting wraparound front porch in the East Beach neighborhood, less than a block from the ocean. No sooner than the engine had turned off than Luke's family came rushing outside to greet him. Declan immediately noticed the look of surprise on their faces when they saw that Luke had brought two guests, but their welcome was warm nonetheless.

"Mom, dad, Hope, Caroline" Luke said, still hugging his mom. "This is Declan Parker and Jessica Ehlers."

"Why does that name sound familiar?" Mr. Williams asked.

"He's the one Louis Martino has been writing about, dad," Hope replied.

"Your son was gracious enough to help us out of a jam back in New Orleans," Declan said. "I hope we're not imposing, and I promise we won't stay long."

"Please, everyone come inside," Mrs. Williams said. "You're welcome to stay as long as you need to."

The group headed inside the house, Luke and his older sister, Hope, arm-in-arm.

"So, Declan and Jessica," Luke's dad said, "I'm Chris Williams and this is my wife, Nicole."

"It's a pleasure," Declan and Jessica replied.

"This is Luke's sister, Hope, and their cousin, Caroline. Hope and Caroline were sharing a condo in Atlanta until recently. Hope works with marine mammals and is, was, working on her doctorate. Finally, this is a good friend of mine from back home in St. Louis, Edward Vanek."

"Hello," Declan said, greeting everyone. "Again, Mr. Williams, I really hope we're not putting you out. When Hope mentioned Louis Martino's articles, I could see that you knew who I am and, I'm sure you know what I'm accused of."

"We do, but we've also read The Free Voice and are convinced of your innocence. It's an honor to have you in our home and, yes, I do understand the risks that come along with you."

"Well, we only plan to stay tonight, if that's not a problem."

"That's fine. We'd like to help in any way we can. There's food for everyone and plenty of room for each of you."

"This may sound strange," Jessica said, "But I'd love to see the beach. Is it close?"

"Just down the block," Luke answered. "I'd, uh, be happy to walk down there with you if you'd like."

Jessica smiled at Luke and replied, "That would be great."

"We'll be right back, mom," Luke said.

As they were walking toward the door, the cell phone Tom Langham had given Jessica rang in her backpack. She hurried to open one of the pockets and answer it. "Hello."

"Jessica, it's Megan," said the voice on the other end.

Chapter 28

The joy in each of their hearts poured through their voices as Megan and Declan spoke for the first time since he'd left Peru. Stepping out onto the back porch, tears streamed down Declan's cheeks as he heard his wife's voice. "Declan, oh thank God you're okay."

"I'm okay. I miss you like crazy, but I'm fine. How are you?"

"I'm fine. I think about seeing you again, holding you again, every five seconds."

"Me too. I love you, Megan. I love you so much."

"I love you too. Just a little longer and we'll be together again."

"I know. We're going to get to D.C. tomorrow somehow and meet up with Louis."

"Where are you now?"

"It's a long story, but we're on St. Simon's Island, in Georgia. It's just about a 10 hour drive to D.C. from here. We'll get to Louis, go with him to Israel and catch the first flight back to Peru."

"Babe, I'm going to be waiting for you in Jerusalem."

"You are? That's amazing. How?"

"We're on our way there with Tom now."

"Is everyone coming?"

Megan hesitated, not wanting to tell Declan about what had happened. She didn't want him to lose focus, but, at the same time, she couldn't lie to him. "Declan, there's something…no, not everyone is coming. Something happened…somehow they found out about us being at Uncle Ignacio's."

"What do you mean? What happened? Who found you?"

Megan steadied herself, "I'm not sure, but based on what they did and what they left, it must have been Bleeker, or someone working with him. They killed…," she stopped, trying to choke back her tears, but to no avail.

"They killed who, Megan?"

"They killed my whole family. Everyone but Uncle Ignacio. They also killed your mom and Michelle."

Declan tried to fight back his own tears, which came slowly, as he said nothing. His legs weakened at the thought of his mom, Michelle and Megan's family all being murdered, and he wobbled, grasping at a nearby wall to maintain his balance.

"Babe, I'm so sorry to have to tell you. I didn't want to, not now. I'm sorry."

Declan remained speechless. So many thoughts swirled through his mind at once that it was overwhelming. He was furious with Bleeker, whom he knew was responsible, he was immensely saddened by the loss of his mom and the others, and he was grateful for Megan's escape.

"Declan, are you still there?"

"What about Evan and the kids?"

"They're all fine. They're with me. Evan and I went with Uncle Ignacio to meet you and Tom at the airport. They must have come after we left. Will said Atau saved him and Charlotte, getting them out of the house and telling them to hide in the woods."

"Did Atau die too?"

"Yes. They got everyone except Tom, Evan, Will, Charlotte, Uncle Ignacio and me. We found them all when we got back the next morning."

"How were they killed?"

"They were all shot, most in the head execution style. And..."

"What?"

"They left something," Megan answered.

"What?"

"Kevin Cameron's ID badge. I'm not sure if he was one of the one's there, but it was strange."

"He wasn't."

"How do you know?"

"Kevin's dead," Declan replied. "I saw Bleeker shoot

him at point-blank range the night my family and Jessica escaped. Where was the badge?"

"It was left in your mom's hands, intentionally placed there."

As Megan spoke, Declan was struck with a realization, as if a voice were telling him something he'd already known but had tried to bury deep down. In that moment, his anger became focused on one man, and he knew that it would never end until John Bleeker was gone. As long as Bleeker lived, he'd chase Declan, wherever he went, and he'd kill anyone who got close to Declan in the process. By accepting the Williams family's welcome into their home, by taking Luke's and his family's help, Declan had already put them in mortal danger too. As much as he hated the thought, Declan knew beyond any doubt that it had to stop, and he had to stop it, and part of him wished he'd already done so back at the Hotel Monteleone.

"Are you still there, babe?" Megan asked.

"Yeah, I'm still here. Bleeker knows I saw him murder Kevin and he's sending a message. That's why the badge was left there. Bleeker wants me to know that we're not safe anywhere as long as he's alive. None of us and no one we love."

"I'm so sorry, Declan. I really didn't want to tell you this now."

"I know you didn't, but I needed to know. I'm just glad you're safe, and I'm sorry about your family, Megan. This is all my fault."

"No,…" Megan began.

"Yes, it is. All of this is happening because of me. You've lost everything, everyone, because of me. My brother has lost his wife, Will and Charlotte their mom, because of me. My mom is gone and it's my fault. This has to stop. These poor wonderful people who are helping us up here, they're all in grave danger now, because of me, and they don't even realize it. Jessica can't finish school and have a normal life, and that's my fault too."

"Declan, you can't think that way. You didn't cause all of this. You didn't make David Stanton try to kill a church full of people on Christmas Eve, and you didn't pass that stupid gun confiscation law and start all the protests, riots and killing."

"No, I didn't, but I have to put an end to this. I can't leave a wake of suffering in my quest to get home. It's time…it's finally time to put an end to this."

"What do you mean? The only thing you need to do is get to D.C. and get on that plane."

"And I will. I promised you when I left, that I'd make it back home. That's a promise I *will* keep. I will hold you again. I will feel the touch of your lips against my own. I long for that moment like nothing before. It's the thought of that moment, seeing your face again for the first time, that keeps me moving. There's never a moment when you're not on my mind, Megan."

"Or you on mine."

"But I have to stop John Bleeker. I have to put an end to this insanity, or we'll never have any peace. I love you, Megan. I'll be there, in Jerusalem, in a few days. I swear it."

"I know you will. Just promise me that you'll be careful, Declan. Don't take any unnecessary risks."

"Of course not."

"Take care of yourself and get on that plane."

"I will. I love you, Megan."

"And I love you. I'll see you soon. I promise."

"I know you will."

Declan hung up the phone and sat down on one of the steps leading down from the back porch to the pool. He looked up at the darkening sky, at the stars beginning to shine down on the troubled and chaotic world below, and wondered where God was. Why hadn't God decided just to put an end to it all, to all the pain, the evil and the death? Why had He waited so long? Why had He allowed all of the suffering to continue for generation after generation?

Buried in the back of his thoughts, just below

Declan's anger and doubt, he again heard the voice, the voice from the cave which had led him back out into the light. "Trust Me...Trust Me."

Declan looked back up at the stars above, at their multitude and remembered how he'd felt going into the cave that night. How, beyond any logical explanation, he'd known that he was no longer alone, but that God was once again with him. The feeling had been so clear, so unmistakable, and, in spite of the numerous difficulties along the way, Declan still felt it.

"I trust You," he whispered, his eyes on the heavens above. "You're not making it easy, but I trust You."

Chapter 29

"This place is beautiful," Jessica said as she and Luke walked along East Beach amid the growing darkness.

"You should see it at sunrise. It's amazing. You get these gorgeous pinks and oranges out over the ocean. I try to get out here for at least one sunrise a day."

Jessica burst out laughing, "Okay, Phil Dunphy."

"You knew that was from 'Modern Family'?"

"Of course, 'Philsosophies'. I love that episode."

"Me too. Seriously though, it is beautiful."

"Maybe you can show me tomorrow morning."

"I'd like that," Luke replied, making eye contact with Jessica. The two stopped for a second, their bare feet sinking slightly into the sand. Jessica smiled sheepishly, and Luke didn't know what to say or do. He wanted to kiss her, to tell her how he was feeling, but being unsure, he returned her smile and said, "So, I suppose you and Declan will have to leave pretty early tomorrow."

Jessica started walking slowly again, stepping closer to where the tide rolled up across the beach, hoping to get her feet wet. "I suppose."

Luke followed her, edging himself closer to her, "What will you do in Peru? I mean, when you get back there?"

"I don't know. Honestly, at this moment, just walking along the beach with a person like you,...with you...this is the most normal I've felt since before I went to the protests that first night with my brother. I like normal, I miss normal. In truth, I'm not sure I want to go back to Peru."

Luke stopped, the ocean water flowing over his feet. "What would you do?"

Jessica turned and looked at him and smiled again. "Find a place to live and a job. Maybe finish nursing school. Things here, while not like they were before everything went crazy, seem to be getting better. A little better at least. They seem to be getting more normal again. I mean a lot has changed, but I think I'm tired of running. I just want some small measure of peace and joy, and I don't know that I've ever really had either. I want this," she said raising her arms wide toward the ocean.

"Well, I can say, through all this, through everything that's happened, I've been able to hold onto peace and joy, not to mention my sanity, only by looking to, and trusting, God."

"Again, you sound just like Evan."

"I thought that was a good thing."

"It is, but like I've told Evan when he says things like that to me, I just can't trust or believe in a God who would allow all of this to happen. I don't want to trust a God who would allow my parents, both of whom loved Him dearly, to die the way they did. I see it, faith that is, in Evan and in you. I see it in Declan and even Megan, but I just don't have it."

"All I'll say is that we're all capable of faith, even you. Remember, God isn't the one who causes the bad things in our lives. Those things, pain, suffering, sickness, death, they aren't God's doing. God offered us perfection, He gave us everything, He gave us happiness, but our ancestors, Adam and Eve, they chose knowledge of good and evil over happiness, and we, as all humans do, live with the consequences of that choice."

"That doesn't sound fair."

"I agree, but it's life. The thing is though, God loves us so much that He gave us an escape, which is faith. God doesn't cause the bad things. He didn't take your parents' lives and he didn't kill my dad's friend, Edward's family either."

"What happened to Edward's family?"

"His wife and two daughters were killed back in St. Louis, a few days after the protests began. His daughters, Emma and Grace, were the same ages as Hope and I. Hope and Emma had known each other since kindergarten.

Edward and my dad coached their soccer teams together going back to when they were five, and Grace and I were in school together too, often in the same class, until ninth grade."

"How'd they die?"

"When the supply chains dried up, and basic necessities became harder to get, a group of people broke into their house. They broke into a bunch of houses in Kirkwood, where we all lived. Edward wasn't home, but his wife, Anne, and the girls were. They'd both come home for the holidays. I won't go into specifics, but it was pretty brutal. Edward came home and found them."

"That's a tough one," Jessica replied. "I found my parents at home too. They were both lying on the floor in their room, each of them shot."

"I'm sorry, Jessica. I really am. I can't imagine."

"So, see, I have trouble seeing how God would allow that. My parents loved Him, they believed in Him their whole lives, and now they're dead."

"God promises that He is working all things, even the bad and painful ones, for good. When we have faith and we trust Him, God will take those bad things that happen to us all and use them to bring about good, for us and others we may not even know. Look at me. Having cancer as a kid sucked. I had to have a port implanted in my chest, I had to spend a lot of time in the hospital, and I came close to dying once, when I was only four, because one of my chemo treatments caused a serious complication with my liver. All those things were horrible, painful, but look at me now, look at my family. We're super-close and love each other deeply, in large part because of what we went through with cancer. My parents trusted God to bring them through it, to bring me and my sister through it, and God used that experience to forge their faith, our faith, and to show us that you really can be happy and joyful in any circumstance when you know Him. I'm going to be a doctor someday soon and help kids with cancer, hopefully help find a way to completely eradicate it. Without leukemia, without going through what I did, that would never happen. See what I mean? When we trust God, He can take the things that look bad, the things that hurt, and use them for good. We may not always recognize it immediately, or maybe not ever, but He's still doing it. He's doing it right now as we stand here."

"What do you mean?"

"I've been thinking about this. The Feds showing up at the airport, and you having to call off the plane picking you and Declan up, it sucks. It was a bad break, and now you have to hurry to D.C. to try another way out."

"Right."

"But, what would have happened if the plane had been able to pick you guys up last night? You and Declan would be back in Peru now. You and I never would have met, and you'd probably be sitting in Peru only thinking about something you actually have a chance to do now, which is stay here. I see that as God taking something bad and giving you a chance for good to come from it."

Jessica stood silent for a moment, thinking, and looking out over the darkening ocean, listening to the rhythm of the waves cresting against the shore. She thought about her parents and her brother, about being raped by the Homeland trooper after the protests, and about the other Homeland trooper she'd shot. She thought about having to kill Al Rawlings, the old man who'd also tried to violate her before selling her to Homeland troopers for $500.00, and she thought about Evan, her feelings for him, and how much Luke reminded her of him.

Jessica remembered the kindness in Evan's eyes, the gentleness and respect in his words and actions, and she saw the same qualities in Luke. They were so similar, both so sure, so oddly certain, that God would come through no matter what the circumstances, that He would bring about good. Jessica looked at the world around her, at the death and fear, and she saw chaos and tons of good reasons to be afraid and depressed. She saw darkness, not God. But when she looked at Evan, and now Luke, she saw something else, something she didn't quite comprehend, but desperately wanted. In Evan and Luke, Jessica saw light, a pure white light, shining brightly amidst all the darkness around her. The light that shone through them, the gentleness and kindness, the peace, the optimism, and strength of faith, they were all the things she wanted for herself and the only common thread Jessica could find between Evan and Luke was, simply, their faith and trust in a God she didn't trust, but for the first time, wanted to.

Luke held back and gave Jessica her space, until she finally turned from the vast ocean and looked him in the eyes. "I want to stay here," she said with tears streaming from her eyes. "I want a life back, and I want what you and Evan seem to have."

Luke walked toward her. Jessica embraced him, and Luke wrapped his arms around her, thanking God for bringing her into his life. "There's nothing I'd like more," he said. After a few seconds of quiet, Luke said, "So, this is a pretty awesome first date."

Jessica looked up at him and smiled, saying, "I've had a lot worse."

Chapter 30

The Williams' phone rang as Declan sat outside on the back porch, listening to the quiet of the night. When he heard Jessica and Luke come through the front door, Declan got up and headed inside, his mind turning over the various scenarios of what could lay ahead.

"Thank you, Matt. I appreciate the call," Luke's mom said, hanging up the phone.

"Who was that?" Mr. Williams asked.

"It was Matt Hempel. He called to say there were some men at the house in St. Louis."

"What do you mean?"

"He said he saw two men at the house. He asked them what was going on and they showed him FBI credentials, asked if we were home, and told him to go back to his house. A few minutes later, they left."

Jessica looked at Declan, concern showing clearly in her eyes.

"Did he tell them anything?" Mr. Williams asked.

"No, he said that he told them he didn't know where we were."

"It doesn't matter," Declan interjected. "They're looking for me, and if they went to your home in St. Louis, they know, or believe, Luke helped us get out of New Orleans. It also means, if they found that house, they know about this one by now too."

"Wait," Jessica said, looking toward the television. "That's Barbara Lemley."

Luke and Declan turned to see the screen, while Hope turned up the volume. Photos of Barb and Stan were being displayed as a reporter said, "Mr. & Mrs. Lemley were found earlier today at their home. Mrs. Lemley was shot once in the head execution style, and Mr. Lemley shot twice. Police have no suspects at the moment, but an investigation is ongoing."

"Who are they?" Hope asked.

"Barbara Lemley is the woman in New Orleans who helped us last night," Jessica answered, clearly shaken. "She's the woman who helped me get out of the airport and gave us a place to stay for the night."

"This has to stop," Declan said, watching tears begin to stream from Jessica's eyes. "It has to end tonight."

"What should we do?" Jessica asked.

"You need to get everyone out of the house and somewhere safe. Is there somewhere you can go?"

"Yes, we're watching our neighbor's house down the block," Hope answered. "It's a vacation rental and it's empty right now. We can go there."

"What about you?" Luke asked Declan.

"Like I said, it's finally time to finish this. John Bleeker will be down here, likely sometime tonight. I'll be here waiting for him."

"Bleeker," Agent McCall said into his phone, as he crouched low in the darkness within view of the Williams' house. "We have a full house here in St. Simons."

"Is Parker there?"

"I haven't confirmed that, but Jessica Ehlers is here. She was just out on the beach with Luke Williams."

"Sit tight and keep a visual on the house. We're on our way."

Chapter 31

As darkness fell over the island, Declan stood outside on the porch, scanning the block. It was quiet, with no movement. Declan listened to the rhythm of the tide, which could be heard over the light breeze coming down the block from the beach. He knew his time had come. As much as Declan hated the thought of killing, something he had only done once in his life, outside his mom's church on Christmas Eve when David Stanton was ready to massacre everyone inside, he couldn't see any other way out. John Bleeker would be making his way to St. Simons, sooner or later, and if Declan hesitated, even for a second, Bleeker wouldn't. Declan knew what needed to be done and vowed that he'd be ready. He'd be ready to do what he should have done over a month earlier outside his family's lake house and what he should have done that morning when he and John Bleeker had encountered one another at the Hotel Monteleone.

"We're ready," Luke said, stepping out onto the porch.

"Good. Take everyone over to the other house. I'll watch from here to make sure there's nobody following you."

"You think there's someone here already?"

"I'm not sure, but you can't be too careful. When dealing with Bleeker, I assume he's one step ahead of me and I anticipate the worst."

Special Agent McCall watched from the brush across the street as Jessica, Edward Vanek and the Williams' family exited the back of the house and hurried quickly along a dark unpaved alley in the opposite direction. He'd seen Declan out on the front porch earlier and scanned the group for him, but wasn't sure if he saw him. Not wanting to lose the group, McCall hesitantly emerged from his cover and crossed the street, making sure to keep a visual on the others from the shadows.

Declan's eyes followed McCall as he crossed the street after the escaping group. A slight smile formed on his face as Declan whispered to himself, "Gotcha."

McCall maneuvered through the alley, sure to stay in the shadows and keep his distance, but also to maintain a visual. A few seconds later, he heard the sound of a gate opening and watched as the group of refugees filed through. He made his way closer as the gate closed and watched as lights came on inside the rental house.

"I'd better tell Bleeker," he said to himself, reaching into his pocket for his phone. As McCall's hand, still in his pocket, found his phone, he felt the thud of a hard object slam violently onto his back and left shoulder. Immense pain shot through his body as he fell to the ground, his face hitting the sandy pebbled alley.

Still trying to regain his composure, he felt the baseball bat deliver another blow to his back, again followed by an intense searing pain. McCall rolled over, trying his best to get to his feet, as the bat came down hard a third time, delivering yet another blow to his back which drove him forcefully to the ground again.

As he lay on the ground, McCall found it hard to focus. His body ached all over and he began to feel cold. He felt and tasted sand on his lips and his mouth was suddenly as dry as dirt. McCall slowly rolled over onto his back, which sent a violent pain shooting along his spine, causing him to moan aloud. Once on his back, he was unable to move again. Pain coursed like a race horse through his body as McCall lay there helpless, desperately scanning the area for his assailant. Finally, he saw a pair of shoes emerge from the darkness to his left. McCall's eyes travelled from the soles of the shoes, up the legs and finally to the top of the man standing over him. Squinting, he was just able to make out the man's face in the darkness. "Parker," he strained to say.

Before McCall could utter another word, Declan brought the baseball bat down for a final time, connecting squarely with McCall's dusty forehead, and with that fatal blow, the what little light there had been in Special Agent McCall's eyes went out for good.

Declan dropped the bat onto the ground and knelt beside McCall's body. The final battle had begun and there was no turning back. For Declan, and all those who had helped him along the way, the choices came down, simply, to either victory or death. He quickly found McCall's holstered 9mm, two full clips, and a suppressor, and put them all into his own pockets. Then, Declan took the phone out of McCall's pocket, looked up the call log, and hit "Call Back" on the last number dialed.

The phone rang twice and, finally, a familiar voice answered on the other end, saying, "What's the word, McCall?"

"You still want me?"

"Who is this?" Bleeker asked. "Is that you, Parker?"

"If you still want me, come and get me. I'll be waiting right here for you," Declan said flatly, then hung up.

Chapter 32

Evan awoke to see a single ray of sunlight slipping through the window shade next to his fully-reclined leather seat. Rubbing his eyes, Evan looked across to see Will and Charlotte still sleeping, and checked his watch, which was still set to Cusco time. As he sat upright, he saw Megan sitting a few seats ahead, looking out the window.

"I guess I was out for a while," Evan said.

"Yeah, you and the kiddos all fell asleep around the same time. We're only about an hour away from Tel Aviv now."

"That's good news. Were you able to talk to Declan?"

"I did, thank God, and he and Jessica are okay. They got a ride with someone to St. Simon's Island in Georgia, and are staying there for the night."

"That's great. That doesn't leave too much ground to cover to get to D.C. If they leave early in the morning, as soon as the curfew lifts, they should make it easily before sunset. Does Louis know they're coming?"

"I sent an email to his friend, Adam Benjamin, like Louis told me to do. He's sure his email accounts are all still being monitored."

"How did Declan sound?"

"He sounded good. It was wonderful to finally hear his voice again."

"I'm sure," replied Evan.

"How are you doing?" Megan asked.

"About as well as can be expected. It's all still so raw. I suppose I'm still in shock. I just thank God for Michelle and Atau getting my babies out of there. I only wish they could have saved themselves too, or...or that I could have saved them."

"Honestly, Evan, I've been up the whole flight thinking about it and what else we could have done. The only conclusion I can realistically reach is that, if we'd still been there, we'd likely all be dead too. Whoever it was that took our families, they were professionals. They were sent there specifically for that purpose, and they knew what they were doing."

"You're right, I know, but I still can't help thinking that I could have helped. That, maybe, it could have been me instead of Michelle."

A knock sounded against Louis Martino's hotel room door. Louis looked up from his laptop to the clock next to the bed, and saw that it was almost 10:00 P.M. He stopped writing his article on the Israeli Prime Minister's thwarted address to the U.N., and went to the door, looking through the peephole. Seeing his friend, Adam Benjamin, on the other side, Louis quickly opened the door.

"Hey, Adam, what's up?"

"Can I come in?"

"Of course."

Once the door was closed, Adam said, "I got an email from your friend, Megan. She said her husband and Jessica are on their way here. They should be here by early evening tomorrow."

"Okay. Do they know to come here to the hotel?"

"I responded and told them, but there's been a change in circumstances, and the P.M.'s schedule, that could impact our departure time."

"What do you mean?"

"This hasn't been made public yet, so what I'm about to tell you is strictly off the record."

"Absolutely."

"The P.M. spoke with the President not long ago and was informed, informally, that the sanctions resolution had passed the Security Council, unanimously."

"Unanimously, as in the United States didn't abstain, but voted in favor of the resolution?" Louis asked, stunned.

"Sadly, yes. It seems Israel has lost all support of the administration and the American government."

"I can't believe it. I thought, at the very least, the U.S. would abstain from the Security Council vote."

"As did we. In fact, the P.M. was told as much only a few days ago. So, the meeting with the President scheduled for the day after tomorrow has been cancelled."

"By the Prime Minister?"

"No, by the President."

"Amazing."

"The P.M.'s schedule for tomorrow remains unchanged. He's still meeting with a number of legislators, and a number of representatives from various NGO's and foundations. The meetings are scheduled to go into the early evening, so the early word is that we'll fly late tomorrow night, not the following day."

"Thanks for the heads up. Sounds like my friends need to get here quickly."

"There's something else, another reason for leaving sooner. As you're planning on coming back to Israel with us, I thought you should know."

"What?"

"Our intelligence assets are indicating that there's been substantial Russian personnel and equipment movement. The same is true of the Iranians, who, along with Russian troops, have been moving into positions near the Syrian/Jordanian border. There are also reports of Turkish and Russian warships moving south in the Mediterranean, Iranian warships stationed off the coast of Sudan, as well as military movement in Libya and Sudan."

"What's the analysis point to?"

"A four-front assault led by the Russians in the coming weeks or, even days. It seems there's a good chance we'll be at war again very soon, and this time with a much more formidable group of opponents and absolutely no international support."

"What would be the point? What would Russia hope

to gain?"

"For the Iranians, revenge and the realization of their long-stated objective of wiping Israel off the map. For the Russians and Turks, control of the vast natural gas fields in our waters, and the oil fields discovered on the Golan Heights. I thought you should know, in case it altered your plans."

"It doesn't, but thank you."

"I didn't think it would. Look, I'd better get going. I still have a long list of things to do tonight, and we have an early start tomorrow. Keep a look out for your friends and I'll keep you up to speed on our departure time."

"Thanks, Adam. See you tomorrow."

Chapter 33

"I hate just sitting here waiting," Hope said as she paced back and forth through the kitchen of their neighbor's rental house. "I feel like someone should be helping him."

"I agree," said Luke. "Declan doesn't know the neighborhood or the area. He has no idea how many are coming or when. I think we should go back and help."

"Declan knows what he's doing," Jessica replied. "He's a trained FBI Agent."

"Yes, but he could still use help," Hope answered.

"I'll go down there and see what's happening," Edward Vanek offered. "At least get an idea."

"I'm coming too," said Luke, already heading toward the back door.

"Luke, wait…," said his mom.

"Mom, I'll be fine. I'll be fine. Besides, I seriously doubt anyone is here yet. It's only been 30 minutes since we left."

As he dragged McCall's body quietly back toward the Williams' house, Declan heard footsteps coming quickly down the sandy alley path in his direction. He stood upright and, to his great relief, saw Luke and Edward hurrying toward him. When they reached Declan, and saw McCall's body, the shock on their faces was immediately evident.

"What are you two doing out here?"

"We…um…wanted to help," Luke whispered.

"You shouldn't be here, but since you are, help me get him inside the back fence, quietly."

Luke and Edward, reluctantly, each grabbed a leg while Declan picked McCall up under the arms, and they hurriedly carried the corpse through the Williams' privacy fence and left it in a shadowy corner.

"Quick, come inside," Declan ordered. Once back

inside the dark house, he asked, "Are the houses around here occupied?"

"This time of year, mostly not," Luke answered. "Most of the houses in this area, like ours, are vacation homes and most aren't being rented out or used much this time of year. The Michaels, two houses down, live here full-time, but that's pretty much it on the block."

"That's good at least. You two should get back. As you can see, this isn't a game."

"Who is that?" Edward asked.

"An FBI Agent. He's one of John Bleeker's guys. I saw him following you all when you went to the other house."

"So they know you're here?"

"They do, and they're coming, which is why you shouldn't be here."

"Declan, we can help," Luke interjected. "You don't know the area like I do. What's your plan?"

"That's what I'm trying to figure out. I definitely don't like being in this house, or the neighborhood for that matter. If a plane is landing here, a private plane, where would it come in?"

"McKinnon Airport. It's just across the marsh. We passed it when we were coming in, on Demere Road."

"Would an incoming plane be visible in the sky from around here?"

"Absolutely, especially at night."

"What about the marsh you just mentioned? Where's that?"

"It's Bloody Marsh."

"Bloody Marsh?" Declan asked.

"It's named after a battle between the English and Spanish in 1742. It was really more of an ambush by a regiment of Highlanders."

"That's fitting. Where is it?"

"It runs basically down the middle of the island," Luke responded.

"You cross it on East Beach Causeway on your way here," Edward added.

"I remember that now." Declan thought for a moment, trying to formulate a plan. If he could ambush Bleeker's group somewhere away from the house, somewhere they wouldn't expect it, his odds would improve drastically. As he was still thinking, the back door slid open again. Declan, Luke and Edward turned quickly toward the door.

"Luke," someone whispered, not seeing them in the dark.

"Hope, is that you?" Luke asked.

"Yeah, it's me and Jessica. Mom wanted dad and Caroline to stay behind with her, at least for the time being."

"Well let's just make this a party," Declan said.

"We want to help," Hope answered. "We all want to help, and we know the area."

"You and your brother seem to share a knack for persistence and persuasion."

"Trust me, those two traits run through our entire family," Hope replied.

"So, what's the plan?" Jessica asked.

"Hope, what's the Homeland presence on the island like?" Declan asked.

"There is none that I've seen. Mostly just the local police and a handful of National Guard, but they're mostly local boys too. The good thing is that none of them are particularly supportive of the feds, at least privately."

"Do they patrol much around here at night?"

"They'll roll through, but, like I said, they're all pretty cool," Hope answered. "They haven't even really been enforcing curfew on this part of the island. They do more so down in the main part of town, but not so much up here, especially this time of year when not many people are around."

"So could we use a car?"

"Maybe, but that might be pushing it," Luke

answered.

"We have a six-person electric golf cart though," Hope offered. "It's quiet and I bet we can take that out without anyone noticing or caring."

"And all the bikes," Edward added.

"That could work. Can we access the roof here?"

"No, not on this house, but the rental my parents and Caroline are in has a rooftop deck."

"Can you see a plane making its approach into McKinnon from there?"

"Absolutely," Hope responded.

"Okay, I think I have a plan," Declan said to the group. "But, if you all help, you have to agree that I'm the only one to do any fighting. None of you will engage with any of Bleeker's guys or put yourself directly in harm's way. Is that a deal?"

"Deal," they answered together.

Chapter 34

It was an idyllic, sunny morning in Israel as Tom
Langham brought the Gulfstream gently down from amid the
clear blue sky onto the runway at Ben Gurion International
Airport. Megan, Evan and the kids stayed onboard as Tom
ran all the post-flight checks and discussed the plane's care
with the ground crew. Once Tom was finished, the group
met with the Israeli customs official and got a taxi to the
King David Hotel in Jerusalem.

It was the first time any of them, including Evan, had
been to Israel and the sights and sounds of Jerusalem, of the
Holy Land, brought Evan a measure of joy even he hadn't
thought possible given the still raw loss of his wife and
mother. There was something about being in Jerusalem, in
the same city in which Jesus had walked, had spoken, had
given the ultimate gift to the world, which stirred such joy in
Evan that, as they made their way to the hotel, it left no room
for any other emotions.

———————

Paul's iPhone buzzed as the plane began its final
approach into McKinnon Airport on St. Simon's Island. He
looked down at the alert and read the email. "It looks like the
Gulfstream just landed in Israel," Paul said to John Bleeker.

"I wonder why Israel?"

"I don't know, but clearly it isn't headed here to make
another attempt at picking up Parker and Jessica Ehlers."

"That's good, because, after tonight, they'd be
wasting their time. Is our SUV on the ground, ready to go?"

"Yes, sir."

"Is Costello meeting us there?"

"There was some sort of accident on the highway in
Atlanta, which has delayed him getting back to the airport.
He's on the way, but will be about thirty minutes behind us."

"Get another car at McKinnon for him and have him

meet us at the secondary rendezvous point near the house."

"Will do."

"I want to be ready to roll upon his arrival."

Caroline stood on the rooftop patio with her aunt and uncle, peering up at the night sky, looking for signs of a plane. "Look," she said, sighting a set of flashing lights moving in the skies overhead. "That's got to be them."

"I think you're right," Mr. Williams agreed. "There wouldn't be any other planes coming in tonight. Are you texting everyone?"

"Yep, I'm texting them all now."

Hope and Jessica stashed their bikes amid thick bushes in a spot across the street from the airport that afforded a good view of the runway and grounds.

"Caroline just texted," Hope said, looking at her phone. "A plane is inbound."

"I see it, up there," Jessica replied, looking up at the increasingly larger flashing lights. "And over there, it looks like one SUV is waiting at the end of the runway."

"Just one?"

"Yeah, that's all I see."

The plane landed and rolled to a stop within 30 feet of the black SUV at the end of the main runway. John Bleeker led the way out, followed by Paul, Special Agent Neal, and three other trusted agents, Benavidez, Kazan and Sharper. The group hurried to the SUV, hopped in, and the SUV turned around and headed quickly toward the airport exit.

Upon seeing the SUV roll out, Hope quickly texted Luke and the others, "One black SUV, heading east toward you. Couldn't see how many got in."

After hitting send, she said to Jessica, "We'd better get back to the house."

Edward Vanek, hidden in thick brush, watched for headlights coming down Demere Road. As he saw the SUV's lights emerge around the curve and make their way toward the turn for East Beach Causeway, he texted Luke, "SUV Turning onto E.B. Causeway. Be ready."

Declan emptied the grocery bag of screws and nails they'd taken from the Williams' garage across the two-lane causeway and rushed back into the marsh on the north side of the causeway. He pulled out McCall's 9mm, with the suppressor attached, and waited quietly in the dark muck, hidden from view next to Luke. Bloody Marsh was the perfect spot for an ambush, especially at night, and the spot where Declan hoped the SUV would stop, was relatively open and would leave Bleeker and his crew vulnerable and without much nearby cover. The only hole in Declan's intelligence was how many men were with Bleeker, but, given that they were only travelling in one SUV, he guessed it couldn't be too many.

"There," Luke whispered, as the headlights turned onto East Beach Causeway.

Declan readied himself, going over the attack in his mind. "Okay, here we go. Remember, you stay low and out of the way, whatever happens. If something goes wrong, get out of here, alert everyone, and get to the rendezvous point."

Luke remained silent, as the headlights grew closer. His heart was almost beating out of his chest.

"Luke, you promise," Declan said, looking him in the eyes. "If this doesn't work, and Bleeker finds any of you, you're all dead. You have to promise that you'll get them all, including Jessica, to safety. That's your priority."

"I promise," Luke replied, as the black SUV was upon them.

With Luke's promise, Declan raised the 9mm and took aim at the front driver's-side tire of the oncoming SUV.

Chapter 35

"How much further?" John Bleeker asked Paul.

"We're almost there now..."

A loud boom interrupted Paul's response. Agent Neal, who was driving, tried to steady the steering wheel as the SUV veered quickly off the narrow causeway and into the marsh on the side opposite Declan and Luke. Bleeker, Neal, and the others each tried to steady themselves, but when the front of the SUV hit the bottom of the shallow marsh, the jarring impact tossed them around the interior like dice being shaken and thrown.

Agent Neal's head jerked forward, slamming him face-first into the air bag as it deployed. Bleeker's head was thrust forward as well, and he found himself enveloped in the passenger-side airbag. Paul, Agent Benavidez, and Agents Sharper and Kazan, in the far rear, none of whom were wearing seatbelts, were tossed forward, each slamming forcefully into the seats and other parts of the SUV's interior.

Once the SUV came to a complete stop, submerged about half-tire deep in the watery marsh, everyone was silent, still stunned from the unexpected impact.

Declan burst forth from the brush on the opposite side of the causeway, and sprinted across the pavement, McCall's 9mm raised. He swiftly approached the driver's-side window, took aim and fired one round, shattering the glass all over an already injured and stunned Agent Neal. The first round was quickly followed by a second round, which found its intended target, and Agent Neal fell forward into the deflating airbag, dead.

It took John Bleeker a second to realize what was happening, but when he did, when he caught a glimpse of Declan moving from the front driver's-side window to the rear driver's-side window, where Paul had been sitting, he hurried to extricate himself from the bonds of his seatbelt and the nearly deflated airbag.

Not having time to choose his targets with care, Declan took aim at the two men in the middle row of seats, Paul and Benavidez. He fired two rounds, each bursting through the window, and fired three more, the first hitting Paul squarely in the chest and the latter two hitting Benavidez, who was sitting next to Paul.

As Declan moved toward the far rear of the SUV, not sure whether it was occupied, glass from one of the rear windows shot towards him. He felt a couple pieces pierce his torso and left arm, and realizing someone had fired at him from inside the SUV, Declan quickly ducked low, under the window.

Luke watched as best he could from the brush across the causeway, feeling both terrified at what he was witnessing and like he should do more, but not wanting to break his promise to Declan. A few seconds later, he heard steps coming through the brush to his right, and turned. Edward Vanek dropped down beside him.

"You scared me to death," Luke whispered.

"Sorry, I had to check on you guys before going to the rendezvous point. Is that Declan at the back of the SUV?"

"Yeah."

Chapter 36

Hearing the stifled back and forth exchange of silenced gun fire behind him, John Bleeker hurried through the muck, keeping low, toward cover in the form of a large bush. He ducked down low next to the bush, un-holstered his sidearm, and attached the suppressor. Once he was ready, Bleeker peered through the darkness, back toward the SUV, trying to locate Declan, but could only make out dim moving shadows at first.

Declan stayed hunched low, at the back of the SUV. He could hear slight movement inside and waited, hoping to hear a door open. He looked across the causeway and caught sight of Edward Vanek just above the brush, pointing up, above Declan's head. Understanding what Edward was trying to tell him, Declan raised the 9mm and fired three rounds through the back window. As he released the third round, he heard a moan from inside, and what sounded like a door opening.

Declan rose up quickly, finally able to see inside, and saw Agent Kazan, badly injured, still sitting in the back row. Without thinking, Declan fired another round, hitting Kazan squarely in the kill zone. As he caught sight of the open door on the passenger side, a bullet whizzed past his head, and Declan again dropped low behind the SUV.

Bleeker made his way, slowly and quietly, wide around the SUV, working his way toward the causeway, but keeping low in the muck and brush. He'd heard the shattering glass, the moan from inside the SUV, and the muted gunfire, and assumed, rightly, that Declan was taking cover at the back of the SUV. Bleeker hoped that whomever was left could keep Declan busy long enough to give him time to get back to the causeway and outflank him.

Agent Sharper had made his way to the front of the SUV and taken cover. He had no idea if anyone in his group was still alive, or how many attackers were out there, but suspected it was only Declan. He crouched low, looking around the marsh and trying to determine his next move, when a searing pain ripped through his right calf and dropped him to into the watery muddy marsh.

Hearing Sharper splash into the marsh, Declan knew he'd hit him and hurried around the driver's side of the SUV toward the front. Sharper tried to steady himself as he heard Declan moving toward him, but by the time he'd turned around, he felt another bullet rip through his torso, and dropped for the last time into the muddy water.

John Bleeker had made it to the causeway and, looking back toward the SUV, he could finally clearly see Declan standing in the marsh near the front of the vehicle. Declan's back was turned toward Bleeker and he had a clear shot.

Luke and Edward, still watching from the brush on the opposite side of the causeway, saw John Bleeker emerge from the marsh. Realizing that Declan didn't see him, Luke moved as though he was going toward the road, when Edward Vanek pushed him back down and jumped up out of the brush, moving toward the road, shouting, "Declan!"

Hearing Edward's shout behind him startled Bleeker as he pulled the trigger. The bullet missed its mark, going wide-left of Declan. Bleeker and Declan turned toward the causeway at the same time, both spotting Edward Vanek. His finger still on the trigger, Bleeker quickly squeezed off another round, which hit Edward hard in the center of his stomach and dropped him instantly onto the pavement of the causeway, just ten feet or so from where Bleeker stood.

After hitting Edward, Bleeker spun back around to Declan, and as his eyes again settled on Declan, John Bleeker, for the first time in his life, felt the intense heat of a bullet as it raced through his torso. Still not quite comprehending what had happened to him, Bleeker fell back up against a small embankment lining the causeway.

The pain was like nothing he'd ever felt, but, due simply to his body going into shock, not as bad as he'd imagined. Bleeker rolled over slowly, finally lying flat on his back, looking up at the millions of stars glowing against the black canvas above, and realized that was the first time since he was a young boy that he'd taken any time, even a few seconds, to look up at the stars. They were, he thought, quite beautiful.

Declan approached Bleeker as he lay on the ground, and when Bleeker sensed Declan's presence he shifted his gaze down from the stars toward him.

"It would appear you've beaten me, Parker."

"Yes, I suppose it would," Declan answered, feeling an unexpected sense of pity for Bleeker. "Although, I'd honestly hoped it would never come to this."

"This is precisely what it was always coming to, what it had to come to. One way or another, after you'd inserted yourself into the David Stanton matter, it was going to be you or me lying here dying. The only question was simply, which one of us."

"Seems that question has been answered."

"Indeed it has, Parker. Indeed it has." Bleeker looked away from Declan, back up at the stars, taking in a final glimpse of the beauty he'd ignored and hadn't considered for the vast majority of his life. Keeping his eyes on the heavens, the glittering blanket of light above, John Bleeker finally said, "Go ahead and finish it, Parker. I'm ready."

Without saying a word, Declan raised the 9mm and fired one more round, praying it would be the last time he'd ever have to do so.

Chapter 37

Declan, Hope and Luke carefully placed Edward into his bed as Jessica hurried into the kitchen to grab the Williams' first aid kit and some bottled water. After helping get Edward situated, and as comfortable as possible, Luke ran down to the rental house to get his parents and Caroline. Mr. Williams and Edward Vanek had been friends going back years, meeting when Hope and Edward's oldest daughter, Emma, were in the same kindergarten class.

Hope and Jessica worked hard to try and stop the bleeding, but Edward had been shot through the stomach, and was bleeding out.

"Can I get some water?" Edward asked in barely more than a whisper.

Declan went to hand him a bottle, but Edward was too weak to raise his arms, so Declan gently tilted the bottle, holding it so Edward could get in some sips.

"You saved my life tonight," Declan said, with tears beginning to form in his eyes. "I don't deserve it and I can never repay you for what you've done."

"You have a young wife waiting for you in Jerusalem. You have a whole life ahead of you. Hopefully, if you're blessed, children someday. My life has been lived. My family, my wife Anne, and my two beautiful girls have all moved on, and I'm honestly ready to join them."

"You're going to be okay," Hope offered, not fully believing her own words.

"Yes, I am," Edward agreed. "Very soon, I'll be with the people I loved most in this world again, and that's all I can ask for. Declan, you get home now. Get back to your wife, to your family."

Tears streaming down his cheeks, Declan responded, "I will, Edward. I will. Thank you. Thank you for what you've done."

Edward closed his eyes as Chris and Nicole Williams hurried into the room. "We have to get him to a doctor," Mr.

Williams exclaimed.

"No," Edward responded, his eyes still closed. "It's okay. I'm ready."

Chris Williams sat on the bed next to his friend and took his hand. "Edward, we can get you help. There's still time."

"It's too late, Chris. Besides, I'm ready to see Anne and my girls again. Thank you both for your friendship. For helping me when I needed it most, and for showing me the light in this world."

Everyone in the room had begun crying. Chris Williams, tears in his own eyes, simply answered, "You're welcome, my friend. You're welcome."

Edward closed his eyes again and the room was silent, but for his labored breathing. After a few more minutes, Edward's breathing slowed, then slowed again. His eyes still closed, an enormous grin spread across his face, clearly conveying his complete joy and happiness.

Still smiling, Edward Vanek said, "Hi, baby," and took his last breath.

Costello thought it odd that he'd been unable to make radio contact with Bleeker since landing at McKinnon. He drove quickly along Demere Road, making the left turn onto East Beach Causeway and, catching a glimpse of the black SUV stuck in the marsh slammed the car to a stop.

"What the hell?" Costello asked himself as he exited the car with his sidearm raised. He cautiously approached the SUV, his feet slipping into the muck. There was enough moonlight for Costello to make out Neal's body, still slumped in the driver's seat. As he reached the SUV, he also saw Paul and Benavidez dead in the second row and Kazan lying in the far rear.

Costello's pulse began to race as he realized that his compatriots had walked into an ambush. Not seeing Bleeker or Sharper in the vehicle, he hoped one or both had gotten away. That hope was quickly dashed when Costello made his way to the front of the SUV and saw Agent Sharper's body.

He scoured the immediate area for Bleeker, but didn't find him anywhere. Only after broadening the search area, moving closer to the road again, did Costello finally find his longtime boss and occasional friend. Despite knowing Bleeker was already dead, Costello reached down and placed two fingers on his neck, feeling for even the faintest pulse, but there was none. Costello gently closed John Bleeker's still open eyes, got back into his car, and drove to the secondary rendezvous location, not far from the Williams' house.

Evan Parker sat looking out his hotel room window at the city of Jerusalem spread out below. His heart was so full of guilt and remorse. If only he'd stayed back and not gone to the airport, maybe he could have saved Michelle and his mom. If only. Evan missed his wife immensely. He missed watching her wake in the morning, and listening to her map out 36 hours' worth of plans for a 24 hour day. Michelle truly had been the love of his life, the woman God had placed in his life so the two of them could care for and love one another. Evan simply had no idea what he'd do without her, and he began to cry thinking about how difficult it would be to carry on without Michelle.

"Daddy," Charlotte said, coming up behind him, reaching up with her arms. "Hold me."

Evan took his daughter in his arms and brought her up into the chair with him. Charlotte snuggled in close, holding tight to her daddy's hands. Evan kissed her on the top of her head and held every precious ounce of her close to him, knowing that she and Will needed him at his best. Slowly, as he held his baby girl, who reminded him of her mommy in so many ways, Evan's tears subsided and he remembered, as he'd so often been able to do during hard times throughout his life, that God was with him and, because of that, everything would work out for good.

Chapter 38

The sun rising over the ocean reminded Declan of the sunset he'd watched over Lake Pontchartrain only days earlier. The colors, brilliant pinks, oranges, and reds, danced over the rolling waves. As in the Sacred Valley, and on Lake Pontchartrain, Declan could see God's fingerprints on that sunrise.

There was no practical reason for such beauty, he thought to himself. The sun could simply rise and set each day with no great fanfare; however, it generally didn't. Sunrises flourished with colors, radiant colors. They weren't practical, they weren't simply scientific or natural, but artistic and whimsical. Only someone with an eye for beauty, a knowledge as to what touches the spirit and the soul, would think to create such a sunrise.

Declan looked out over the ocean, appreciating the artistry of God's work, the little touches of beauty which, when people took the time to notice, would stir our souls in ways nothing manmade ever could. He stared over the incoming waves, holding his head high in the breeze coming onto shore. Focusing his gaze off to the horizon, Declan imagined Megan standing somewhere in Jerusalem, on a tall building somewhere across the Atlantic Ocean, staring back at him.

"It's time to go home," Declan whispered to himself. "Please, Lord, guide me home this day. Deliver me back to Megan and my family. Deliver me to your Holy Land."

When he turned from the sea, ready to embark on the final leg of his journey, Declan saw Jessica and Luke approaching him, walking together across the sandy beach. For just a second, they reminded him of a photo he'd kept of him and Megan walking on Rosemary Beach years earlier. The fact that Jessica and Luke were becoming friends was easy to see.

"It's time to get on the road," he said as they neared.

"Yep," Luke answered. "My dad and Hope are ready

to go."

"I still don't think they need to drive us up to D.C., but there doesn't appear to be any changing their minds."

"Not usually once they're set," Luke said with a smile. "You'd have about a one percent chance with dad, and even less of a chance at changing Hope's mind."

"Declan," Jessica said. "There's something I need to tell you."

"I think I already know, but go ahead."

"I'm staying here, with Luke and his family."

"I figured you were and, as much as I'll miss you, as much as we'll all miss you, I'm glad to hear it. I'm happy for you."

"I'm just tired of being on the move," Jessica explained. "And, this is a good place, a relatively normal place. Hopefully, I'll get some semblance of my life back."

Declan gave Jessica a hug and said, "Thank you for everything, Jessica. I couldn't have made it this far without you, and I know the same can be said for Evan. You're a good friend. I pray that you'll find joy and happiness that'll last forever."

Turning to Luke, he said, "And you too. I wouldn't be here without either of you. God brought us all together for a reason, and maybe this was it. I pray that I'll see you both again here, but if I don't, you'll both be forever in my heart and in my prayers, and I know we'll meet again in the world to come."

Luke hugged Declan and they both began to shed tears of joy. "God be with you, Declan. I know you'll get back to Megan soon."

"Declan," Jessica said. "Will you explain why I'm staying to Evan for me when you see him?"

"Absolutely."

"And here's the phone Tom gave me. Megan is in contact with Louis Martino, who is with the Prime Minister's entourage. If something changes, if anything comes up, she'll call this phone. You're supposed to meet him at the hotel by tonight, before curfew. They're set to fly tomorrow morning."

"I'll be there," Declan said, taking the cell phone. The three friends walked back across the beach to the Williams' house, where Luke's parents, Hope and Caroline were waiting in the driveway.

Watching from the secondary rendezvous location, Costello took out his secure phone and put in a call to the regional data center. After giving his credentials, Costello ordered an area cell sweep, which picked up on the GPS chips in the various active cell phones within a three block radius. Within a minute, the information downloaded to a sister program on Costello's laptop, and a map popped up on the screen featuring about forty blinking green dots. Costello narrowed in on the five green dots blinking at the Williams' house and waited.

"Are you ready?" Mr. Williams asked.

"I am, thank you."

Nicole Williams stepped toward Declan and gave him a hug, saying, "Thank you, Declan. You're a good man and I know God will lead you home and bring my daughter and my husband back. You take good care of yourself."

"Thank you. You too, and take care of this group."

"Don't worry, I will."

Declan hugged Caroline and Mrs. Williams and exchanged goodbyes. Luke walked him up to the car and said, "I'm gonna miss you, my friend."

"And I you. You've been a miracle in so many ways."

The two hugged once more, and Declan got into the car with Mr. Williams and Hope. Luke's dad fired up the engine, and backed slowly out of the driveway as everyone waved goodbye. Declan looked back at his friends, his saviors, as the car turned left onto Bruce Drive, and they were gone.

Costello sat in his car, watching two blinking green dots as they left the Williams' house and travelled along Bruce Drive. He set the program to lock onto one of those green dots, the one representing Chris Williams' iPhone, and waited a few minutes before moving, so there was no chance that Declan would pick up on the tail. Costello watched the blinking dot on the map as it turned right onto East Beach Causeway. Confident he'd be a safe enough distance behind, he turned on the ignition, put the car in drive, and headed out to follow Declan, wherever he would end up.

Chapter 39

As Louis Martino left the Prime Minister's mid-morning press briefing, he looked over his notes. The P.M. had briefly addressed the rumors concerning Russian and Iranian troop movements, indicating publically that there was no intelligence suggesting cause for concern. He had also given mixed reviews regarding how talks with U.S. senate and congressional leaders had gone earlier, and declined to comment on the President's rebuff with respect to a personal meeting.

Just before Louis reached the elevator, Adam Benjamin caught up with him, saying, "We need to talk. There's been another change of plans."

Louis and Adam stepped away from the crowded elevator bank and found an empty conference room in the hotel. "What's going on?" Louis asked.

"We're leaving tonight, at 7:00."

"Why the change?"

"This is strictly confidential, Louis. You cannot tell a soul, or I could lose my job, or worse."

"I promise, of course."

"The situation with the Russians and Iranians is serious. We received an intelligence report this morning confirming the various troop movements. We've confirmed the presence of Iranian Revolutionary Guard across the border in Jordan, along with a heavy Russian, Iranian and Turkish troop contingent in Syria. There are Russian and Iranian naval vessels positioned in the Red Sea, and Russian and Turkish vessels positioned in the Mediterranean, less than 100 miles off the coast of Tel Aviv."

"That doesn't sound good."

"It's not. Our intelligence points to a four-front attack. We're still battered and recovering from the last round of fighting with Hamas, Hezbollah, ISIS, and the others. It was only by using our nuclear technology that we were able to survive that onslaught, without any significant international support, and the fighting took a major toll. This time, we're totally isolated in the international community, hated even. This morning, the Prime Minister was assured that there will be no assistance from anyone, including the United States. The Russians and their allies know this, and they are taking advantage of the situation to make a move for control over our oil and natural gas fields. The Iranian's motivation is obviously much worse."

"The total destruction of Israel?"

"Just as the mullahs have continuously stated for decades."

"What's the anticipated timeline?"

"Days we think. We're making as many military preparations as possible, but there's realistically no way, without resorting to nuclear technology again, that we can withstand such an attack. We don't have the military capabilities, on our own, to successfully repel a four-front assault led by the Russians. I mean, they'd be a tough matchup for the U.S., let alone Israel."

"The nuclear option wouldn't work either, given the Russian's nuclear arsenal. It would simply ensure Israel's destruction."

"Precisely," Adam agreed. "So, as you can see, without the U.S. or E.U., we're in an impossible position."

"What about negotiations with the Russians? Offer them a share in the natural gas fields."

"Not an option. For one, they already know we're completely alone and can't fight them off. They have absolutely no reason to negotiate. Further, the Iranian regime simply seeks to wipe us completely off the map, and see this as the perfect time to do so. From the Iranian perspective, this is the time to usher in the arrival of the Mahdi and bring about his promised global caliphate. They won't negotiate either."

Louis sat down, feeling a bit dizzy at the prospects facing the Israelis and his good friend.

"I'm telling you this for two reasons," Adam

continued. "First, in order to give you another chance to stay here, Louis. There's a very good chance that, in the next few days, we'll be, at best, engaged in an all-out war we can't win or, at worst, we'll already be gone."

Louis looked up at his friend, saying, "Like I said before, Adam, that's not going to happen. I'm a journalist. I go where the stories are, regardless of the cost, and this is one of the biggest stories of our time, if not all-time. Israel seems to be the center of the universe for some reason at the moment."

"Well, then, the other reason is to get your friends here as soon as possible, provided they still want to go. I emailed Megan a little while ago, but I wasn't sure how quickly the message could be relayed. Here's a new iPhone. This one is under one of our accounts, so it shouldn't be traceable to you. I gave Megan the number, so your friends should be able to communicate with you directly now."

Louis took the phone and put it in his pocket, saying, "Thanks, Adam."

"No problem. The P.M. has a last meeting at 5:45 this afternoon which will likely go for about 45 minutes. He cancelled the meeting which was set for this evening. We're leaving from Reagan National at seven sharp."

"Thanks for the heads up."

Chapter 40

"I wanted to tell you how sorry I am about your friend, Edward," Declan said to Chris Williams as they drove north along Interstate 95 through North Carolina. "I really never wanted for any of you to be hurt or put in harm's way. He literally gave his life for mine."

"Edward was a good man, a good friend. Honestly, he's where he wanted to be, home with Jesus and reunited with his family."

"Jessica mentioned that his family was murdered recently."

"Yes, it was about a week after the Firearms Protection Act passed and things went crazy. If it hadn't been for Edward's faith, I don't know if he'd have made it through."

"I can't imagine what it would be like to lose your children, nor do I want to. Especially like that. How long had you known each other?"

"Oh, since the kids were young, pre-school even. Luke and Grace, their youngest, were in the same pre-school classes and most of the same classes throughout school. We met Edward and Anne through soccer, when Hope and their daughter Emma were on the same team. When did you meet Emma?"

"In kindergarten," Hope answered from the backseat.

"They were good players," Chris Williams continued. "Both went on to play in high school, for one of the top teams in the state."

"Wow, that's impressive."

"Soccer and animals have always been two of my biggest loves," said Hope.

"What position did you play?" asked Declan.

"Midfield mostly. I'd occasionally play forward."

"Yeah, it was all soccer all the time with Hope growing up. Like she said, that and animals. Dolphins and cheetahs especially. About a year after we met Edward and

Anne, Edward's mom passed away unexpectedly. Her death hit him hard, and he was in a dark place for a while, both before and after she died. Ultimately, I think it was one of the things that finally brought him to the Lord."

"God certainly does take bad circumstances and turn them into good outcomes," Declan responded. "I've seen it happen time and again just over the past month or so."

"Yes, He does. Even after all these years, with everything that happened with Luke and leukemia when he was little, and all the good that came out of that, it still amazes me when I see it, when the light finally clicks on and it all makes sense. I know I shouldn't be amazed, because God is simply doing exactly what He tells us He will, but I'm amazed nonetheless."

"I know what you mean. It's hard sometimes, lots of times really, because we don't see things going the way *we* think they should, or we can't see any way forward, or how any good can come from something that seems really really bad. Then, all of a sudden, it clicks and you can see how God's been working all along, how He's been right there the whole way."

"Exactly," replied Chris. "It all comes down to trusting Him to be who He says He is, to do what He promises to do. When a person has that trust, that kind of faith, no set of circumstances is too much or too overwhelming, because we can rest assured God will work it to His good, and our good, in the end. I remember the week before Luke was diagnosed with leukemia. He was only three and he'd been really tired and couldn't shake a strep infection for nearly a month. His mom and I were worried, understandably. When he got a big bruise on his hand, from simply bumping it on a table, my wife knew what it was. She knew in her heart, while I held out hoping it was anything other than cancer. One morning I was driving to work and I remember it so clearly. I was praying and I said to God, 'Please, Lord, don't lay this burden on me, on my family, because I can't handle it. This will break me and

You promise not to give us more than we can handle.' Well, clearly God disagreed because we got the diagnosis that weekend."

"That had to have been tough."

"It was the toughest and scariest moment of my life, without a doubt."

"Definitely," said Hope.

"But, the thing is, we did handle it. We put our trust in God, because we simply had no other choice. We looked to Him for our strength and for peace, and He was right there. That experience, it made our whole family closer. It brought us all closer to God and really taught me, for the first time in my life, what faith really meant. I'd been a Christian for years, many years before that, and had never really understood faith and trust."

"Wow. I think that's a lesson I'm still learning."

"So am I," Mr. Williams replied, with a smile. "It's a lesson I hope to continue learning each and every day, because as soon as I think I know the Lord, He opens my eyes to something new about Him and I'm amazed all over again."

Declan sat for a second, thinking about that, thinking about all the things, the new sides of Himself, that God had revealed over the past month. He thought about how much Mr. Williams reminded him of his own dad, and how wonderful it would be to see his parents again one day.

As the two sat silently, the cell phone Jessica had given Declan began to ring. It took Declan a second to realize it was his phone, and once he did, he hurried to answer it, saying, "Hello."

"Declan, it's me," Megan replied. "Where are you?"

"In North Carolina, but I'm not sure exactly where. Hold on," Declan said, looking for an indication. "Hold on, there's a sign coming up…It says we're about fifteen miles away from Fayetteville."

"Where's that?"

"I think we're about five or so hours from D.C.

What's going on?"

"You have to hurry. Adam Benjamin emailed me again, and the Prime Minister's travel plans have changed. They are departing tonight at 7:00, instead of tomorrow morning."

"Why the change?"

"I'm not sure. Adam didn't say, but there are rumors going around here about a possible attack by Russia, Iran and Turkey, among others. I suspect that has something to do with the change in travel plans."

"You're kidding?"

"No, but I wish I were."

"Is everything okay there now?"

"Yeah, things are fine. People are making preparations and taking precautions, but everything is calm. It's a beautiful city."

"I can't wait to get there."

"That makes two of us, so make sure you hurry and get up to D.C. I don't want you to take any chances on missing the flight and who knows if they'll leave even earlier."

"Okay. It's only about noon here, so we should be okay, but I'll hurry. Am I still meeting Louis at the hotel?"

"No, go straight to the private terminals at Reagan National. Louis will be waiting for you beginning at 5:00, and he has passports and press credentials for you and Jessica."

"She's not with me."

"What happened? Is she okay?"

"Yeah, she's good. She wanted to stay behind on St. Simons. She's with a really good family there and she's happy."

"That's good to hear. I'll let Evan and Adam know."

"Okay."

"Declan, please hurry. If this plane leaves without…"

"Don't worry, my love," Declan interrupted. "I'll be on that plane. There's nothing that will stand in my way."

"Okay, good. I have a new cell number for Louis. Adam gave it to me. Call Louis when you get close."

"Will do."

"I'll text you the number in a second. Just let me know that it came across."

"I will."

"And be careful, Declan. I love you."

"And I love you. I'll see you in the morning."

Chapter 41

Louis Martino sat alone outside one of the briefing rooms, finishing the update to his running blog post regarding the Prime Minister's various visits in D.C. when Adam Benjamin approached, saying, "Louis, the vans taking the press corps to Reagan National will be outside in ten minutes."

"Thanks," Louis replied. "Any further changes to the departure schedule?"

"None at this point, but the situation is fluid, so to speak."

"What about the other situation? Any news there?"

"We have a much clearer picture," Adam responded.

"And?"

"It's not good."

———————————

Costello pulled over to the side of the highway as he saw the green dot take an exit about 10 miles ahead on his laptop screen. It was only the second stop the car had made since leaving St. Simons and Costello figured, correctly, that Declan's car had stopped to get gas. Deciding it was a good opportunity to stretch his legs, Costello stepped outside his car and walked a few feet into the tall grass on the side of the road to relieve himself.

———————————

"Are we all set to go?" Chris asked as Declan and Hope emerged from a tiny convenient store just outside Petersburg, Virginia.

Hope was about to answer when she spotted a Homeland vehicle pull up and park directly behind their car. Instead of saying anything, she motioned subtly to her dad, who turned to see two Homeland troopers stepping out of their vehicle. One of the troopers approached Mr. Williams, asking, "Is this your vehicle?"

"Yes, it is. Is there a problem?"

"Are you traveling together?" the trooper asked, directing his question to Hope and Declan, both of whom nodded affirmatively.

"We'll need to see everyone's identification."

Having learned that it was better not to ask too many questions, the three complied, Chris and Hope offering their driver's licenses and Declan offering the passport Megan had obtained before they went to Peru, which listed his name as William McKean. The trooper took the ID's and got back into the cruiser to run each through the various Homeland databases.

The other trooper, who'd been looking into the car, pulled out Declan's backpack from the passenger seat, and asked, "Whose is this?"

"Mine," Declan answered with some hesitation.

As the trooper set the backpack on the hood of the car and began to unzip it, Declan grew uneasy, knowing the 9mm his dad had given him, "The Lone Ranger" was tucked deep inside, wrapped in his extra shirt, which was tucked beneath his Bible and a couple of full water bottles. Declan's mind began to run through various scenarios, but, except for the trooper not finding the gun, none seemed desirable.

As the trooper rummaged through the backpack, Declan began to sweat slightly, not wanting to put Hope and Mr. Williams in danger, but unwilling to miss his flight due to being arrested by two random Homeland troopers. The other trooper stepped out of the cruiser, looked at Chris Williams, and taking him by the arm, said, "You're going to have to come with us."

"Why?" Hope exclaimed loudly, moving quickly toward her dad and the trooper. "He hasn't done anything."

Seeing Hope's sudden movement, the trooper who'd been looking through Declan's backpack quickly set it aside and raised his weapon, stating loudly, "Step back! Step back now!"

"But he hasn't done anything," Hope yelled again, still moving toward her father, who had his hands raised above his head.

"I said move away!" the second trooper repeated, his weapon spotted on the center of Hope's torso. "Step back or I will shoot you!"

"Hope," Declan said, moving toward her and placing his hand firmly on her shoulder in an effort to calm her down.

Realizing the second trooper was on the verge of killing her, Hope stepped back, still seething, and said, "My dad didn't do anything. What reason could you possibly have for taking him in? You're both nothing but a couple of idiots who hide behind their guns when no one else has any."

"It's okay, Hope," Chris said, sensing the growing tension. "Calm down."

"Your father checked out positive on one of our domestic terror databases," the first trooper advised flatly, forcefully pulling Chris Williams's hand down and placing handcuffs tightly on them.

"That's ridiculous!" Hope yelled.

"I've had enough of your mouth, sweetheart. Put your hands on your head and get down on your knees!" the second trooper yelled to Hope and Declan, still pointing his weapon at Hope. "Both of you."

"Let's just calm down," Declan replied. "She doesn't want any trouble. She's understandably upset and just wants a reasonable explanation about why you're taking her father into custody."

"What are you, a lawyer? I said get down! Both of you, on your knees now!"

While Declan was pleased the second trooper's attention had shifted from rummaging through his backpack, he could see the anxiety and tension in the second trooper's eyes. It was something he'd seen before in the Academy and during his short time in the FBI, and he knew that jumpy, over-excited, and armed was never a good combination. The situation had the potential to turn ugly quickly, and if that happened, there was a high likelihood of someone getting killed.

"Fine," Declan replied calmly, putting his hands on his head and moving slowly to his knees. "We're not a threat to you guys, so you can lower your weapon, trooper. We're getting on our knees."

Hope reluctantly followed suit, though Declan and her father could still see the venom in her eyes as she stared down the second trooper, who began to relax a bit as they went down on their knees, but still kept his weapon on them.

"Is this better?" Declan asked the trooper calmly. "Are you good?"

"Just shut up," the second trooper responded. "I don't want to hear another word from either of you, or I'll take you in along with him."

Costello had been back in his car, watching the green dot simply sitting in place, for nearly five minutes when he decided to proceed along the highway and see what was taking so long. As he approached the exit where he could see the motionless green dot flashing, he caught sight of the Homeland cruiser at the gas station, and knew what was happening.

"Damn it," he said aloud, exiting the highway and heading in the opposite direction of the gas station. "Damn it."

A few seconds later, Costello pulled to a stop and whipped out his phone. He quickly dialed the direct line of a high-ranking friend at Homeland. When his friend answered, he said, "It's Costello. I need a big favor and I need it ten minutes ago."

The first trooper had placed a still-handcuffed Chris Williams securely in the backseat of the cruiser and was talking quietly with his partner, as Declan and Hope remained kneeling on the pavement with their hands above their heads. Declan's backpack was still on the hood of Chris Williams' car, only about five feet away.

As the troopers talked, Declan assessed how quickly he'd be able to get to the backpack and get his 9mm out. It was an unrealistic thought. The second he moved toward the car, the troopers would open fire on both of them, and Declan knew it. Unsure what else to do, Declan began to pray silently, asking the Lord to somehow deliver him from yet another mess he'd found himself in. He didn't know it of course, but Hope and Chris Williams had been silently saying that exact prayer themselves.

A call came over the first trooper's radio. He stepped away from the group for a moment, and when he came back, he simply said, "Get up. You all can go."

Stunned, Hope and Declan looked at one another, not knowing whether or not to believe him. Their doubts subsided as the first trooper pulled Chris Williams out of the cruiser and un-cuffed him. He then handed their ID's back, and the troopers got into their cruiser and pulled out of the parking lot.

"What just happened?" Declan asked as he, Hope and Chris stood looking at one another, dumbfounded.

"God just answered our prayers," Hope replied.

"No doubt," Declan said, but privately he still wondered why the troopers had just let them go. Clearly, someone had contacted them over the radio and said something which had prompted the troopers to free them. Declan had no clue who had called, or what had been said, but while he was ecstatic to be free, the situation left him with a slightly uneasy feeling.

Watching Chris Williams' car get back on the highway, and the green dot begin to proceed north again, Costello reached down, gently rubbing the scar on his leg where Declan had shot him outside the lake house more than a month earlier.

"You're not getting off that easily, Parker," he said to himself. "Wherever you go, I'm going to be right there with you waiting to pay you back."

Chapter 42

Louis stood outside the private terminal at Reagan National from which the Prime Minister's plane was set to fly. He looked again at his watch, which read 4:51 P.M., and looked up nervously scanning for an approaching vehicle, when his iPhone buzzed in his pocket. He took the phone out and saw a text from Adam Benjamin. The text read, "Conditions worsening at home. The P.M. is leaving his meeting early and we're taking off immediately upon his arrival at Reagan. Expect wheels to go up at 6:30."

"Great," Louis said aloud. "This just keeps getting worse and worse. C'mon, Declan. Where are you?"

———————————

"We're less than an hour away from D.C.," Mr. Williams said as the car raced north along Interstate 95. "If traffic's not bad, we should be at Reagan by six."

"Good," Declan responded. "I'd better call and tell Louis."

Declan took out the cell phone and dialed Louis, who answered, "This is Louis Martino."

"Hi, Louis. I'm within an hour."

Knowing it was Declan, Louis replied, "Get here as fast as you can, Declan. The departure time just got moved up again. Now, we're expected to fly at 6:30, and the way things are going, I wouldn't be surprised if it gets moved up again."

"Why the rush?"

"There have been reports of military movements by the Russians, Iranians, Turks, and others. The intel points to an imminent attack."

"Megan and Evan are already in Jerusalem. Do they know?"

"No, nobody outside the Prime Minister's circle knows, other than you now. I shouldn't even know. That's why you've got to hurry. The Prime Minister and his staff are pushing to get out of here as soon as possible. Basically, we're wheels up once the P.M. hits the tarmac."

"I understand. I'll be there."

Declan hung up the phone and Mr. Williams could see the look of concern on his face. "Problems?" he asked.

"Always. They've pushed the departure time up to 6:30, maybe sooner. Israeli intelligence is apparently anticipating an attack from Russia, Iran, Turkey and others, and my wife, brother, and niece and nephew are currently sitting at a hotel in Jerusalem with no idea."

Mr. Williams pressed a bit harder on the accelerator and said, "Don't worry. We're going to get you on that plane."

"That's right," said Hope. "God has brought us too far for you to miss this chance. We'll make it."

Declan took a deep nervous breath and replied, "I hope. It just seems like the obstacles keep getting higher and higher."

"Maybe for you and me, but not for God. Keep your faith, especially when the obstacles seem insurmountable. Look at what just happened to us. Did you see that coming?"

"You mean the troopers just letting us go like that?"

"Exactly."

"No, I sure didn't."

"Neither did I, but however it happened, whatever caused them to change their minds, God saw it all along."

Chapter 43

The blinking green dot finally exited Interstate 95 just outside Washington, D.C., and began heading east on the Pocahontas Parkway. Costello continued to follow, only about five minutes behind, and the dot left the parkway and proceeded north along Airport Drive, finally coming to a stop at Reagan National. Correctly surmising that Declan's final destination was Reagan National, Costello sped up, racing along the Pocahontas Parkway toward the exit for Airport Drive, only a few minutes behind.

Adam Benjamin's text flashed onto Louis' phone screen. He looked down and read, "We're on our way now. ETA 7 minutes, wheels up at 6:15."

"Dammit," Louis exclaimed as he paced back and forth outside the private terminal, looking up the road again for a car. He nervously checked his watch again, seeing that it was 6:01 P.M., and looked again up the road. Finally, he spotted a car coming toward the terminal.

"God, I hope this is you, Declan," Louis said to himself, doing his best to peer ahead to the passenger and driver.

The car came closer, finally coming to a stop in front of the terminal, and Louis immediately recognized Declan in the passenger seat. He hurried toward the car, saying, "You really like to cut it close. We're taking off in less than fifteen minutes."

"I thought it was 6:30?"

"It was. No matter, now that you're here. We'd better hurry and get through the security checkpoint. Here are your passport and press credentials," Louis offered, handing them to Declan through the open window. They're all legit, so there shouldn't be any issues."

"Thanks," Declan replied. "I appreciate it."

Declan turned to Chris Williams and said, "Thank you, Chris. I couldn't have done this without you and your family. You all are truly a blessing."

"We're happy to help get you home. Now, you'd better get moving."

Declan opened his backpack and took out The Lone Ranger, wrapped in a shirt. "I won't be able to take this with me. It was my dad's. He gave it to me before he died, and as much as I hate to leave it behind, I'd like you to have it."

"I'd be honored," Mr. Williams replied, tucking the handgun beneath the driver's seat. "I'll take good care of it. Now, get going and God speed."

The two men shook hands, and Declan stepped out of the car, saying, "God bless you, Chris. You and your family."

Hope had gotten out of the car and she gave Declan a big hug. "Take care of yourself," she said.

"You do the same. And take care of that brother of yours."

"Don't worry. I will."

Hope hopped into the passenger seat and waved to Declan. Chris Williams put the car in drive, turned it around, and drove back toward the airport exit, as Declan and Louis watched. Louis looked at his watch again, which read 6:05 and said, "C'mon, we'd better get going."

Costello didn't bother to look at the car to his left as he and Chris Williams passed one another. He could see Declan up ahead, going into the private terminal and his focus remained locked in on his target. A few seconds later, Costello parked outside the terminal building and hurried toward the entrance. He had to get Declan somewhere in private, someplace where he'd have time to put an end to this affair once and for all, without attracting attention.

Declan and Louis showed the security personnel at the initial checkpoint their credentials and were moved through after being scanned without any issues. The Prime Minister's security team had set up a secondary checkpoint outside the terminal, just before entry to the plane, which they'd also have to clear.

After the first checkpoint, they stepped to the side to put their shoes and belts back on. With his shoes back on, Louis looked again at his watch and asked, "Are you ready?"

"Yep," Declan replied, as he finished tying his second shoe. "I'm good to go. Let's get on that plane."

———————

Costello flashed his FBI credentials to the American security personnel, who waived him through the initial checkpoint. He already had his 9mm out and concealed beneath his coat as he approached Declan and Louis from behind. His pace was quick and his heartrate normal as he neared his target.

———————

As he began to walk, Declan suddenly felt a hand firmly grip his left shoulder, immediately followed by the unmistakable feeling of a metal gun barrel digging into his lower back. He froze as Louis turned to him to see why he'd stopped walking.

"Don't make any sudden moves, Parker," Costello whispered. "Both of you, see that restroom over there? Walk toward it."

Declan immediately recognized the voice as Costello's and reluctantly began to move slowly in the direction of the restroom, with Louis, looking again at his watch, walking in front of him.

Chapter 44

As the three entered the otherwise empty restroom, Declan's mind was racing. He tried desperately to overcome the surprise of encountering Costello, just when he thought he was finally in the clear, and focus his thoughts on a way out of the situation. His eyes scanned the entire restroom, anxious for a solution, any solution, and his mind dashed uncontrollably between rage, panic and disappointment as he thought of the plane taking off without them in a matter of minutes, and Megan waiting in Jerusalem for a husband she'd never see again.

Still trying to regain some level of composure, Declan felt a stinging blow come down on the center of his back and he stumbled forward, falling into Louis. They both fell forward, slamming into one of the tiled walls near a row of three sinks. Raising his muffled 9mm, Costello looked into Declan's eyes as he turned around a few feet away and said, "It's time for you to join your family, Parker. Did you know I'm the one who killed them?"

As the words came forth from Costello's lips, oddly enough, Declan remembered the look of peace that had come across his dad's face when he finally succumbed to cancer when Declan was just a boy. The look had seemed, to him then, ethereal and surreal and, what he remembered being most surprised by was how, in the midst of the greatest grief he'd ever known, amid the tempest of emotions he'd felt as his dad was dying, the peace on his father's face had somehow transplanted itself into Declan's own heart and mind in those few final seconds. Contrary to all expectations, to all desire, for the few seconds when his dad had left this world for the next, Declan experienced a peace unlike any he'd felt before or since. It was, quite simply, he began to realize as he found himself staring back at Costello, the touch of God.

Declan's thoughts crystallized around the pure unblemished memory of his dad in his mind's eye, and he was able to clearly see his dad's face again. Declan watched as his dad spoke one simple word to him, "Fight."

Finally, clarity filled Declan's senses, pushing out all confusion and doubt. Even as the realization hit him that he may very well meet his end in that airport restroom, Declan leapt with all of his strength toward Costello as Costello's finger squeezed off a muffled round. The bullet whizzed to the right of Declan and Louis, shattering two panes of the white ceramic tile on the wall, dropping dust and tile fragments into Louis's hair. The two men hurled onto the floor as Costello tried to squeeze off a second round, but by that point Declan had thrust himself forcefully into Costello's torso and the round fired up and further to the right, again missing everything but the restroom ceiling.

As the combatants hit the hard cold restroom floor, Declan hammered his shoulder into Costello's abdomen, knocking the air from Costello as his head slammed in conjunction against the floor. The 9mm flew from Costello's hand and slid into an adjacent bathroom stall. Declan raised up and brought his fist down hard against Costello's mouth, which was already gasping desperately for air.

Louis rushed toward Declan, pulling him away, saying, "C'mon, we've got to go now or we're going to miss the plane."

"Okay," Declan replied, with heavy breathes and a racing pulse. He grabbed Costello by the legs and dragged him into the closest bathroom stall. "Here, help me sit him up on the toilet."

Louis and Declan placed the badly injured and barely conscious man on the toilet seat. Costello slumped over, still gasping for air.

"Okay, let's go. They won't hold the plane," Louis pleaded. "If we miss it, we're stuck here."

"Go outside. I'll be out in five seconds."

Hesitantly, Louis headed for the door, as his iPhone vibrated again with another text from Adam saying, "Where are U? Hurry, we're leaving now."

Declan hurriedly unrolled some toilet paper, wrapped it around his hand and picked up the 9mm from the floor. With little hesitation and much remorse, he took the only course of action he could to ensure the safety of Jessica and the Williams family. Stepping to one side while pressing the 9mm against Costello's slumped head, Declan pulled a trigger for what would be the last time in his life. The job finished, once and for all, Declan placed the 9mm in Costello's limp hand, locked the stall door from the inside, and slid stealthily underneath into an adjacent stall.

As he exited the bathroom, he and Louis sprinted to the next security checkpoint, where Adam Benjamin was waving them through. The three dashed through the checkpoint, out onto the tarmac and up the stairs into the plane as the ground crew stood waiting to roll the stairs away.

"You just made it," an attendant advised as he closed and secured the door behind them.

Declan leaned over, his hands on his knees, sweat dripping from every part of his body. He was panting and his body was still pulsing with adrenaline. So many times before he thought he'd never find himself standing onboard that plane. So many obstacles he'd had to overcome.

"Please, gentlemen, hurry and take your seats," the attendant said. "We're rolling."

"I'll come see you after we get underway," Adam said. "I'm glad you both made it. Man, you guys like to cut it close."

"That's what I said," Louis replied, as he led Declan back to where the press corps sat and found two open seats. The plane began to roll forward toward the runway as they buckled themselves in, and Declan looked out the window watching the asphalt begin to roll beneath the plane.

The captain came on the intercom and said simply, "We're clear." The wheels rolled faster and faster, picking up speed until, seconds later, Declan felt the wheels leave the runway and the plane take flight. As the plane climbed, it banked slightly for a moment, and Declan watched the United States grow smaller and smaller below. The plane straightened, facing due east toward Israel, and Declan leaned back in his plush seat, unable to control the tears which poured from within him like a burst water pipe as he could, at long last, see Megan standing on the near horizon.

PART III

"[7]Ask and it will be given to you; seek and you will find; knock and the door will be opened to you. [8] For everyone who asks receives; the one who seeks finds; and to the one who knocks, the door will be opened."

Matthew 7:7-8

Chapter 45

Megan was awash with anticipation since she'd received a text from Louis indicating that he and Declan were safely onboard the Prime Minister's plane and on their way to Israel. Wanting to be well-rested, she'd tried to sleep, only to lie awake in her suite at the King David Hotel from about 4:00 A.M. on. When the sun finally rose, she threw on her exercise gear and went for a seven mile run in and around the Old City, taking in the sights, scents, and sounds of the ancient streets as they slowly came to life.

After a quick shower, Megan realized she still had way too much nervous energy just to sit in her room alone, so she called Tom and Evan's suites to see if they were up and asked if they wanted to meet for breakfast. They agreed to meet her downstairs for the breakfast buffet thirty minutes later. Unable to wait, Megan headed downstairs after getting off the phone with Evan and took a stroll around the hotel grounds.

Finally, she headed to the restaurant, where she found Tom standing at the entrance waiting for her. "Good morning," he greeted her, with a gentle hug.

"Good morning."

The two headed inside and were seated at a table for five. "So, this is a big day," Tom said as they waited for coffee.

"I can't believe he's finally on his way, Tom. It feels like it's been forever."

"Did you sleep at all?"

"No, not really. I got Louis's text around 1:30 and slept off and on until four or so. After that, I was up for good, and I haven't been able to sit still since."

"That's understandable. You and Declan have waited a long time for this day."

"And there were a few times recently when I wasn't sure it would ever get here."

Their waitress brought coffee and water to the table

as Evan arrived with Will and Charlotte, saying, "Sorry we're late."

"No worries," Megan replied. "How are my wonderful niece and nephew this morning?"

"Good," the kids replied.

"Are you excited about seeing your uncle today?"

"Yes," Will answered. "I can't wait to hear all about his trip."

"Me too," said Charlotte.

"Can I get you anything to drink?" the waitress asked Evan and the kids.

"Please," Evan answered. "I'd like a large orange juice and two waters for the kiddos please."

"Of course, sir."

Evan and the kids sat down at the table, and he took out two coloring books and crayons he'd picked up for them in a nearby bookstore earlier. "Here you go guys," he said, handing them the coloring books and crayons. As the kids began looking for pages to color, Evan asked Megan and Tom, "Have you seen the news this morning?"

"I've been keeping track," replied Tom. "They're passing out gas masks for anyone who doesn't have them."

"Yeah, it's looking like this is for real."

"I'm wondering if we should try and head back to Peru tomorrow morning," Megan said. "Last I heard, if an attack is coming, they expect it in the next few days. We may want to try and get out before then, and get back to Uncle Ignacio's."

"As painful as going back there will be in some ways, I think that's a good idea," Evan replied. "Although, there's still a question of safety. They found us there once, and they may come back to finish the job."

"The text I got from Louis this morning said Declan had asked him to let me know that it was over for good."

"They've stopped looking for him?"

"Louis didn't go into detail," Megan answered. "But, from what he did say, it sounded like there isn't anyone chasing him, or us, any longer."

"Well," Tom said, "If that's true, given the circumstances here, I think the sooner we get off the ground, the better. I would prefer not to be stuck here in the middle of a war."

"I agree," said Evan. "If this is what I believe it is, this isn't going to be just any war. I believe, based upon what we're seeing, that this is going to be the battle described by the prophet Ezekiel. If that's the case, we don't want to be in the middle of it."

"What does he say, Evan?" Megan asked.

"In Ezekiel 38 and 39, he prophesizes a battle, an attack really, by Russia. It's called the Battle of Gog/Magog, Magog being the biblical name for the lands that are now known as Russia. Ezekiel says that Russia, along with Iran, Turkey, Sudan, Libya, and some Balkan states, will attack Israel, seeking to plunder her. The Israeli's won't be strong enough to repel this attack and will appear doomed, but God will step in and defeat the invading armies. This is the battle that most Bible and prophecy scholars believe will finally turn secular Israel toward God again, and turn God's full attention from the Church, back to Israel."

"You really think that's what this is?" Tom asked.

"Based on Ezekiel's words and what we're seeing, I think there's a strong chance."

"Well, either way, I think the sooner we can get up in the air, the better," Tom replied. "Again, I'd prefer not to be here during any war, Biblical or not."

"I agree," Evan replied.

"That's fine with me," Megan said. "Let's plan on flying tomorrow morning."

"Good, it's settled then. I'll call the airport and have them get the plane fueled up and ready to go for a 7:00 A.M. departure," said Tom. "We'll have a car here at 5:30, ready to drive us."

"Perfect. Louis said the Prime Minister's plane is supposed to land at Ben Gurion at 1:45 this afternoon. I told

Louis I'd meet them at the terminal with a car, so they don't have to mess with finding a cab or a shuttle."

"Sounds like we have a plan," Evan responded. "Why don't you give us a call after you and Declan have had some alone time together, and we can get together so the kids can see him."

"That works. Shall we eat? I'm famished."

Chapter 46

Declan woke from a deep sleep, the deepest and most refreshing he'd had since leaving Peru, and saw Louis sitting across from him, typing on his laptop. Although he'd had a very good dream, Declan couldn't remember the details. All he knew was that he felt revived, rested, and, much to his surprise, peaceful.

"Where are we?" he asked Louis.

"Over the Mediterranean," Louis answered, looking up from his laptop. "I think we're about an hour or so away from Israel."

"Sorry, were you working on something?"

"No, actually I was just responding to a few emails. I texted Megan earlier and she said she'll meet us at the airport with a car."

"Awesome. I can't wait to see her. It's been way too long."

"I never got to congratulate you two on the wedding, by the way. I know it's been a crazy couple of months, but you guys have earned some happiness."

"I'm not sure we've earned it, but I'm definitely looking forward to it. Any updates on the Russian situation?"

"I spoke with Adam a little while ago. The Prime Minister has been in contact with the Russian President, but nothing came of it. They're denying everything, even while their navy ships move closer to the Israeli coast and their ground troops and artillery units are massing along the eastern and northern borders."

"That doesn't sound good."

"No, it doesn't. An attack of some sort seems imminent, like within the next 24 hours."

"I guess we're jumping from one fire into another fire."

"Yeah, but this fire feels even hotter than the one we just left."

"Well, at this point, after the past few days, I think I may have finally learned just to trust God to take care of things and go with it," Declan replied. "There have been so many times along this road when I couldn't understand why things were happening the way they were, why something didn't go as I thought or hoped it would. But, ultimately, God got me through it and here. If He's leading me to Israel just as it's about to be embroiled in war, I may not like it or understand why, but I just have to go with it and keep trusting Him."

"I'm envious," Louis responded. "I wish I was able to do that, but I've just never been able to grasp the whole God thing. It seems like having someone bigger than me, bigger than all of us, to trust in would be awesome, but even after what I saw happen with Damascus, or maybe because of what I saw there, I just can't believe there is such a God."

"It's interesting that you mention Damascus, because that was actually the turning point for me finding God again, for finding faith again."

"How so?"

"My mom and brother, Evan, had talked about the destruction of Damascus overnight for years. They pointed to its continued existence throughout history and to a Bible prophecy in the Old Testament. I think it was Daniel 17. They said Daniel foretold the destruction of Damascus overnight. I honestly thought they were mostly crazy or just really gullible, but just before Christmas, as I was tracking David Stanton and beginning to feel as though there was more going on in the world than I was aware of, I met a really interesting Jewish man at the airport. His name was Joseph Steinman and I met him while waiting for Megan's plane to arrive. He also talked about the prophecy in Daniel and all the other prophecies that were given in the Old Testament pointing to Jesus being the Jewish Messiah."

"That's interesting, because just before the bomb hit Damascus, Sgt. Ya'alon, my IDF liaison, said something to the effect that people had been waiting for what was about to happen for over 3,000 years," Louis replied. "I asked him about it and he also talked about the Daniel prophecy. I meant to look it up, but never did. I frankly can't get the vision out of my head."

"Did you see it in person?" Declan asked.

"I did, from a school rooftop in Nazareth."

"I didn't know that. That must have been intense."

"I don't really know how to describe it," Louis replied, his face somber. "I remember actually being excited to see it before it happened. Can you imagine that? It makes me sick to think about it now, but I was actually looking forward to seeing, live and in-person, such total destruction. When it happened, there was this intense flash of light, the brightest whitest light I've ever seen, pure unadulterated energy. Then, the cloud began to form, in the shape of a mushroom, just like I'd always heard. Once it finally happened, once I saw the cloud rising so far off in the distance, that was the first time the enormity of the destruction dawned on me."

Louis paused and leaned forward in his seat. He began rubbing his chin gently as he looked down at the floor. "I felt so ashamed, so ashamed to have actually wanted to see that. All I could think of were the people. So many people, just immediately vaporized in that flash of light and those that weren't, but were within the blast zone, probably wishing they had been vaporized as they died a slow agonizing death. Sgt. Ya'alon was next to me, standing at first, but after the blast, I looked over and saw him on his knees, like he was praying. I never did ask him. I wanted to pray too, to ask someone, anyone, for answers as to why we people make such a disaster of things, why we destroy one another, but I had nobody to pray to, so I just crumbled down against the wall on the rooftop and cried."

"I'm sorry, Louis. I really am. I can't imagine the emotions you must have felt, actually witnessing something like that."

"I don't blame the Israelis, I don't. I experienced

first-hand what was happening to them. It literally was a last resort to save their nation, their people. But, I just don't know why people have to constantly destroy. From one perspective, it makes me sick to even be part of the human race, but then I look at my own actions, my own sensationalized, almost gleeful, anticipation of having a front-row seat to widespread death and suffering and I know that I'm no better than anyone else. I'm just as bad."

"We all are, Louis. I felt in a similar way for most of my life, since I was eleven and my dad died. I'd known God, I'd believed in Him and in Jesus, and I'd loved them with all my heart. But, when my dad got cancer and died in his prime, I hated God, and I despised myself for hating Him. I thought, if God could take a man like my dad, a man who loved God with a passion deeper than almost anyone I'd ever known, then what was the point? I felt like my dad deserved more, that I deserved more, but I finally realized that deserve has nothing to do with it. We all fall well short of God's standards. We simply can't achieve them, and for that we all deserve the worst, but God, because of His grace and His love, gives us an option to have the best."

"I can certainly see how *I* deserve the worst."

"But that's the beautiful thing, Louis. God doesn't want to give us what we deserve, He gives us a chance to accept what He wants us to have, which is His unending love."

Chapter 47

Megan sat in the backseat of the small passenger van as its driver sped along Sderot Chaim Weizmann toward where it changed to Sderot Ben Gurion. She gazed out the window at the clear blue skies and the sun shining down upon the stunning landscape surrounding her. Megan's heart beat quickly with anticipation as she could think of nothing but leaping into Declan's arms. Their reunion, finally, was less than an hour away.

As she pictured her husband again, pictured him as he'd looked when he'd left Peru to go back to the United States and rescue his family over month earlier, the sudden burst of air raid sirens shattered the peacefulness around her. Simultaneously, Megan and her driver looked up, and caught a dark speck streaking across the sky above.

"What is it?" she asked.

"Missiles," the driver replied. "We've got to get off the road."

As the driver took a hard left onto Giv'at Shaul, an explosion rocked the air around the van and shook the ground beneath them. The driver tried to maintain control, but the van swerved back and forth, finally tumbling off the road toward a small open space. Megan held tightly to a handhold near the ceiling, trying to keep herself from slamming to and fro as the van flipped sideways. Glass shattered all around her and she bounced sideways, slamming hard into the back of the driver's seat.

The van rolled twice more, again tossing Megan and the driver with it, until finally coming to a stop in the dirt. It had landed flat on the driver's side, and Megan's head lay against the dirt through the shattered window opening.

She stayed still for a moment, trying to gain control of her thoughts and assess whether there were any serious injuries, as the air filled with another loud boom and the ground rumbled beneath her yet again. Despite being thrown around during the crash, she didn't feel like anything was broken. She was sore, for sure, but her arms and legs, hands and feet, all felt okay. Instinctively, Megan felt her belly, which also felt fine, and prayed that the tiny child growing inside was okay too.

Megan unbuckled the seatbelt, and stood up inside the sideways van. The air raid sirens were still blasting, and she could hear shouts and screams off in the distance.

"Are you okay?" she asked the driver, but was met with silence. Looking into the front seat, Megan could see the driver still in his seat, but he wasn't breathing.

"Oh, God," she said aloud. She reached forward and placed two of her fingers against his neck, searching for a pulse, but felt nothing. As she pulled her hand away, another explosion rocked the immediate area, again shaking the ground and the van.

"That one sounded close," Megan said to herself. "I'd better get to cover somewhere."

She wiped a relatively small amount of blood from her temple, and felt the sore spot where she thought it had come from. After a quick self-examination, Megan had some cuts and bruises but, all things considered, was in pretty good condition. She reached up to the passenger side window opening and slowly pulled herself up and through, trying very hard not to cut herself on any of the broken glass. Once on top of the van, Megan dropped down to the ground and scanned the area, looking for somewhere that looked safe.

———————

The sirens began to blare as Evan and the kids were swimming in the pool at the King David Hotel. The hotel staff were running about, urging everyone out of the pool and inside the hotel. Evan scooped up Will and Charlotte and hurried inside, still dripping wet. They fell in line with a large group heading downstairs toward safety shelters.

"What's going on, dad?" Will asked.

"I'm not sure, honey, but everything is going to be

alright," Evan answered, wrapping towels around the shivering kids as they hurried along. "Don't worry, we're okay."

An explosion rocked the area outside. The stairwell vibrated slightly and everyone's pace picked up substantially as they hurried toward the underground shelters.

"I'm scared, daddy," Charlotte said, tears beginning to form in her eyes."

"I know, but don't worry, Pumpkin. God is watching over us and He's going to protect us all and keep us safe."

Activity aboard the Prime Minister's plane became frenetic, with staff people and aides constantly moving through the plane. The captain had put on the seatbelt light and Declan and Louis sat, buckled in, looking out the windows as the plane began its final approach into Ben Gurion Airport. From the plane, they could see the missile fire coming from the armada of Russian, Turkish and Iranian war ships in the waters off Israel's coast, and the fighter jets launching from the Russian aircraft carriers.

"Look," Louis exclaimed. "We've picked up an escort."

Declan looked out to see three IAF jets flying close to the plane outside his window. He looked across to the windows on the other side and saw at least three more. "They're over there too," he replied.

"This is bad," Louis exclaimed. "Really bad."

Three more Israeli F-15's streaked by the plane and Declan and Louis watched as they engaged with two Russian MiG's. The plane shook and rattled as anti-aircraft guns and missiles were fired from the Mediterranean Sea below.

"We're in the middle of a fire fight," Declan said. "The attack has begun."

Chapter 48

Once out of the van, Megan ran for cover amid a cluster of trees nearby. Fighter jets streaked through the skies overhead, firing on the city below from all directions. Megan knelt low among the trees and felt relatively safe. She took out her iPhone, intending to call Louis or Declan, but it couldn't pick up a signal. Putting the phone away, Megan scanned the area, looking for a place that may be safer than the cluster of trees she'd taken refuge beneath.

Probably two hundred yards or so in the distance, she saw groups of people running toward a large building and disappearing inside once they reached it. Megan guessed there was some kind of bomb shelter within the building and decided to make a run for it. She looked up to the blue streaked sky to see if there were any incoming fighters or missiles and, seeing nothing for the moment, dashed out of the trees and back toward the road.

Megan ran as fast as she could, calling ahead to what appeared to be an Israeli family of four making their way to the building. A father was carrying one small child in each arm, the mother following with a backpack over one shoulder and a small bag in her left hand. As Megan neared the family, she heard the increasingly familiar sound of a jet behind her, and turned to see the plane streaking toward her, firing its guns at everything on the ground in its path.

Realizing she was within about 30 feet of the building, Megan ran faster, hoping to outrun the plane, but the sound of its engines grew louder, as did the sound of bullets slamming into concrete and metal behind her. Megan looked back once more and decided there was no way she'd make the building, so as the fighter jet sprayed rounds all along the street, she ducked at the last minute behind a parked car. Ducking as low as she could, and tucking herself into a ball, Megan heard the bullets from the jet whizz around her and repeatedly pelt the car. Glass shattered to her left and right and bullets pierced the metal body, but within seconds, the jet had blown past, directing its fire on the building Megan had been running towards and beyond.

Once the coast was again clear, Megan jumped up and bolted for the building. A man and woman, each looking like they were in their early-fifties, emerged from behind another parked car, and reached the building entrance at the same time as Megan.

"Is this a shelter?" Megan asked the couple.

"Yes," the woman replied. "Hurry, follow us."

Megan followed the couple as they hurried inside the building. All the lights were off inside, and it was somewhat dark, but Megan followed the couple down two flights of stairs, to a narrow hallway below-ground. At the end of the hallway was a steel door, which was still open. The couple rushed to the door and, just before going inside, the woman turned to Megan to make sure she was still following them and said, "In here, we'll be safe in here."

Megan entered the crowded underground shelter and looked around, seeing numerous Israeli families settling in. She was surprised by the range of emotions on their faces. Some appeared fearful and nervous, which was how she felt. Others however, seemed almost calm, as if they were just in the shelter waiting for a bad storm to pass through.

"Here," the woman said, motioning for Megan to follow her. "Please, sit with us."

"Thank you," Megan replied, taking a seat next to the woman on a long wooden bench that ran the length of the wall.

"Are you American?" the woman asked.

"Yes, I am staying at the King David."

"What brought you out here?"

"I was on my way to the airport to meet my husband and a friend. They were flying in on the Prime Minister's plane from the United States."

"I heard on the radio that the plane had come under fire," a young man nearby interjected.

Megan's face went white as she turned toward the

young man, who could see immediately that he had terrified her. "I'm sorry," he said. "I believe they were able to land at Ben Gurion safely though."

"Thank, God," Megan replied, as some of the color returned to her face.

"I'm sure your husband is fine," the woman offered assuredly.

"Thank you. I am too," Megan responded.

"You stay here until it's safe to go out. If your husband is traveling with the Prime Minister, he'll be well protected."

Chapter 49

The plane bounced from side to side and Declan, Louis, and the other passengers held tight in their seats, trying not to be rocked around. As the runway at Ben Gurion grew closer and closer, Declan watched through the window as the Israeli Air Force F-15's continuously engaged the Russian MiG's and Sukhoi's. It was an all-out air war, akin to something Declan had only seen in the movies.

The plane descended lower, the ground getting closer. Declan looked down at the ground below and said to Louis, "It looks like we're almost there."

Louis looked out the window and saw a Sukhoi flying straight toward the side of the plane. "Whoa!" he exclaimed.

Declan looked up from the nearing earth and saw the plane. Its guns fired and Declan yelled, "Get down!"

Within seconds of its guns firing, a surface to air missile hit the Sukhoi, knocking it out of the air with a great fury as the rounds it had fired just before going down pounded against the side of the plane. The plane vibrated and shook and suddenly took a hard dive. Declan clenched his armrests and closed his eyes to pray as he could feel the plane picking up speed and downward momentum. Louis, also clenching his seat like it was the only thing protecting him from a free-fall, began sweating, fearing the plane was going down hard.

A few seconds later, one engine smoking, the captain was able to level the large plane out and bring it down with a hard but rolling landing onto the runway. The thud that accompanied hitting the asphalt jolted everyone forward, then backward. The flaps went full-out and with no shortage of skill, the captain finally gained full control, slowed the plane down and rolled it right up to an armored convoy awaiting the Prime Minister.

Members of the Prime Minister's security team hurried into the main cabin and commanded that everyone stay seated, as other members hurried the P.M. out of the plane, down the awaiting stairs and into the convoy, which immediately began to roll. Once the P.M. was safely off the plane, Sgt. Ya'alon, came into the press section and advised the press corps that vehicles were awaiting them outside, one group heading to Tel Aviv and the other to Jerusalem.

Louis hurried over to Ya'alon, saying, "We need to get to Jerusalem."

"You and your friend ride with me, Louis. Come, let's go."

Declan and Louis grabbed their bags and hurried after Ya'alon to the plane's exit. A Humvee was waiting at the base of the stairs and the three rushed down and hopped into it, where a driver was waiting. Once inside, the driver put the Humvee into gear, and began to roll.

"Where do you need to be, Louis?" Ya'alon asked.

"We're supposed to go to the King David."

"Louis," Declan interjected. "Wasn't Megan supposed to meet us here?"

"The roads from Jerusalem here have been shut down to all but military traffic," Ya'alon replied. "If someone was supposed to meet you here, she will have had to turn back to Jerusalem."

"Okay, let's go to the King David then," Declan responded, still concerned that Megan may have tried to make the trip.

The explosions and ground-shaking rumblings could still be heard overhead as Evan and Tom huddled close with Will and Charlotte in one of the King David's underground shelters.

"Where do you think Megan is?" Tom asked.

"I don't know. I looked for her a little earlier, thinking she may have turned around and come back, but I didn't see her anywhere in here."

"I hope she didn't get caught out in this."

"Me too," Evan answered.

"I never should have let her go alone."

"Nobody could have known it would start today, Tom, and so suddenly. She'll be okay, no matter where she is."

"I hope so." Tom sat silently for a moment, looking at the hundreds of faces in the shelter, most of which wore fear and worry with no pretexts. "At breakfast this morning, you said this was some kind of biblical war."

"Yes," Evan replied. "The battle foretold in Ezekiel 38 and 39."

"I thought you said that God was going to show Himself or something. That He would come and defeat Israel's enemies."

"That's right. The prophecy states that God will summon a sword against Gog, the name for the leader of Magog, or Russia. God says each man's sword will turn against his brother, in other words, they'll begin to fight themselves, and that He'll pour down torrents of rain, hailstones and burning sulfur on the troops. God says that He will show His greatness and holiness, make Himself known in the sight of many nations, the people of which will tremble at His presence. He says, on that day, 'Then they will know that I am the Lord.'"

"If that's true, I sure wish He'd hurry up and get it over with," Tom said, as another explosion shook the entire shelter.

Evan smiled, and said, "No need to worry, Tom. You won't be disappointed."

Chapter 50

Megan tried numerous times to call and text Declan and Louis, but the service was either down or overloaded and she couldn't get her iPhone to do much of anything. Someone in the shelter had a radio, and kept changing and adjusting the dials, trying to pick up any news as to what was happening outside, but the signal was spotty at best, and the shelter's inhabitants were essentially blind and deaf inside. They knew by the rattling thud that accompanied each explosion and the occasional ground shaking, that the attack was still underway, but that was about the extent of their collective knowledge.

Growing anxious, and worried about Declan and the others, Megan paced through the shelter, winding her way around the roughly hundred Israelis inside. Many would smile as she passed, either calmly or trying to appear calm, but Megan quickly began to realize she couldn't stay down in the shelter without knowing where or how Declan was indefinitely. For all she knew, the attack could last for days, if not weeks. The more she paced, the more anxious she grew, until she finally felt confined and constrained.

She began to sweat and an overpowering urge to see the sun and to feel the wind wrap itself around her enveloped Megan. "I've got to get myself under control," she whispered to herself. "I've got to get back to the King David."

Sgt. Ya'alon's driver pushed the Humvee at high speeds along the mostly empty Highway 1 toward Jerusalem, every so often slowing down to maneuver around abandoned or damaged vehicles. The only other traffic were military transports. Ya'alon listened to military communications in his earpiece, staying up to speed on the assault and the IDF's countermeasures.

"I can't get anything," Declan said to Louis, after trying to call Megan again.

"Neither can I," Louis replied. "There's no service."

"I'm worried about her, Louis. If she said she was going to meet us at the airport, she'd have at least been on her way when the airstrikes began."

"True, but once the strikes started, she'd have turned around and headed back to the hotel. She's got to be there."

"I don't know. I'm not so sure."

"There've been no ground movements," Ya'alon interjected. "So far, the attack has been limited to airstrikes and missiles and other heavy artillery fired from the ships in the Mediterranean and from mobile launching stations near the Golan Heights."

"Do you think they're trying to hammer away with air and artillery strikes before moving the ground troops in?" Louis asked. "I mean, we know ground troops are already stationed along the Heights and the eastern border."

"That appears to be the strategy. To this point, we've done a reasonably good job in the air and we've hit a couple of the war ships, but without outside assistance, the consensus is that we'll be overrun within the next twenty-four hours. We just don't have the resources or firepower to stand toe-to-toe with the Russians alone, much less the alliance they've formed."

Declan sat back and whispered a prayer. "Lord," he said, "you've brought me this far, all the way to your Holy Land, to Jerusalem. You've brought my family here too, and I know that you have a plan in mind, not just for our good, but the good of Your people. Please, Lord, please see me back to my wife and family, wherever they may be right now."

Chapter 51

Megan tried to sit, tried to calm her anxiety, but within seconds of sitting down, she was up pacing the shelter again. She had to know where Declan was, whether the plane had landed safely. The battery on her iPhone was nearly drained, showing only about 10% and absolutely no signal. It was useless. The radio someone kept messing with, trying to pick up a signal, offered mostly static, white-noise, with an occasional incoherent word or two.

Nobody inside the shelter knew anything about what was happening outside, and, after she'd paced the outside perimeter of the shelter for the fiftieth time, Megan finally reached her breaking point. The total lack of knowledge and action became too much for her to bear. Regardless of what could happen outside, she had to be with her husband and family again, with Tom, and to know what exactly was going on. Come what may, she was going back to the King David.

Her decision made, Megan made a beeline for the exit door. As her hand reached to turn the lever, an older Israeli man sitting next to the door said to her, "No, you can't. It's too dangerous."

Her hand pushing down on the lever, Megan looked at him and replied, "I have to. I can't stay here any longer. I have to get back to the hotel. I have to know where my husband is."

"Wait…," the man began, but Megan was already through the heavy door and sprinting up the stairs toward street level. Upon reaching the top of the stairs, she turned left into the main hallway and slowly made her way toward the building's main exit. Broken glass from the shattered windows crunched beneath her running shoes as she moved cautiously down the hall.

As she reached the main exit, the ear-jarring screech of a MiG whizzed overhead, and, seconds later, the sound of a nearby blast reached her ears and the building rocked again, knocking Megan into one of the inner walls. She waited and steadied herself, then moved again to the exit and, spotting an abandoned car about 50 feet away, ran as fast as she could toward it.

Megan was shocked by the heat she felt all around her. When she reached the car, she knelt low and looked around. She could see the open space, a park maybe, and the overturned van she'd been in when the attack started. Always a planner, Megan had studied the route from the King David Hotel to Ben Gurion Airport before leaving, and she knew the route back. If she could make it back to Sderot Chaim Weizmann, she reasoned, then she could make her way back to the hotel from there. She could run parallel to the road, which would provide some cover from the Russian planes.

She looked up as three more jets burst across the skies and then looked ahead, toward the overturned van.

"It's now or never," she said to herself, and bolted from the car toward the open space and, finally reached the van where she'd started.

The dead driver was still inside, strapped into his seat. Megan looked away from the van and ahead to a patch of trees next to Sderot Chaim Weizmann. Again running as fast as she could, she reached the cover of the trees about twelve seconds later, and was finally able to look up the road, back in the direction from which she'd come earlier that day. The road was littered with bombed out and abandoned vehicles, but it was passable on foot and, she thought, the cars could actually be useful for cover along the way. Moreover, there may be some food or water inside some of them that she could use.

"Okay," she said to herself. "King David, here I come."

"When will the banging stop, daddy?" Charlotte asked as Evan held her tightly. Will had fallen asleep, his head on one of Evan's legs.

"Soon, honey. Everything should stop soon. Try and take a nap like your brother, and I bet it'll all be over when you wake up." Charlotte laid her head down on Evan's other leg and stretched out as best as she could in the crowded shelter. She closed her eyes, hoping to fall asleep, but instead laid there hoping her dad was right and that all the thumping and loud noises above would end soon. Evan ran his hand gently through the little girl's still damp hair, doing everything he could to comfort her.

"Can I ask you a question?" Tom asked.

"Sure," Evan replied, happy for any topic of conversation capable of taking his mind off of the bombs and explosions continuing above.

"I've always admired your calm. You seem to have a sense of peace about all these things taking place that most of us, including me, just don't. Even with the deaths of your wife and mom. I can honestly say that you've handled that with a sort of grace that's surprised me."

"Thank you, I appreciate you saying that, Tom."

"I've been considering the things about you, your qualities that set you apart from most of the people I've known, and from what I can tell, what I believe, is that you really do live your faith."

"I try."

"Well, you're one of the few people I've known in my life who have called themselves Christians I can say that about. Honestly, it's one of the things that has always turned me off to Christianity. It always seemed to me that Christians were great at talking about how to live and how I should live, but they seemed pretty awful at living that way themselves. So, and I guess this is my question, what makes you so different? Where does your peace, your grace, come from?"

"It comes from God, from Jesus and the Holy Spirit living inside me. I don't know how other Christians you've seen have behaved or, honestly, whether those people really were Christians. But I can say that what you've described, what you've hit upon is the entire reason for our faith, for Jesus, in the first place."

"How do you mean?"

"When I talk about God, about Jesus, one of the things I hear regularly from people is, 'Christians are such hypocrites, they tell everyone how to live, but they can't do it themselves', like you've described."

"I've seen it myself and it turns me off. I mean, if a person can't live up to their own beliefs, then why should I bother looking at their beliefs."

"That's a valid question, Tom, and the answer is quite simply, that none of us can live up to the standards God has set for salvation. It's impossible."

"Then what's the point?"

"The point is that we don't have to. According to the Bible, we're all born sinful with a sin nature. Thus, our natural human inclination is toward sin, which is, in many ways, really selfishness. God, being perfect, can't be in the presence of sin, and a price has to be paid for sin, and that price is death. One sinful thought is all it takes, so you see, nobody, other than Jesus, has, could, or ever will live even a few days, much less their entire life, without sinning. It's not possible, but that's the point of Jesus' death on the cross and His resurrection. He paid the price for us and once we accept Him as our Savior, our sins have been forever paid for by God's grace and God views us as sinless."

"So, why do so many Christians fail to live up to what they preach?"

"Because they're human. Like me, like you, like the Apostle Paul, they can't. I still sin, even though I don't want to. When my wife was alive, I'd sometimes still look at other women I found attractive, and think about them sexually. Or, I'd get upset and curse the man or woman who cut me off on the road. We all do things like that because, even once we're saved by God's grace, we're still not perfect. We still have our sin nature. As you grow as a Christian, you recognize sin, but you often still do it, even when you don't want to. Other times, many times, you don't. I strive not to sin, but to live my life in a way pleasing to God in thanks for the sacrifice of His Son, who literally gave His life for mine. Sadly, I'm not always successful, but I'm saved."

"Well, Evan, I'll say that you've opened my eyes a bit. The way I see you live, as much as your words, it impresses me."

"I appreciate that. Even though we're far from perfect, Jesus calls His followers to spread the gospel of grace and salvation. Personally, I feel that's best accomplished by staying as focused as I can on trying to live my life in a way that, in my best moments, reflects Jesus. The rest is up to God."

"Well, if God really does stop this attack in some supernatural way, like you said the Bible says He will, then He may have Himself another believer."

"I'll be praying for exactly that, Tom."

Chapter 52

Declan looked around, nervous and full of anticipation, as the Humvee raced along the road toward Jerusalem's Old City. He silently repeated the same prayer, a constant petition to God that he would find Megan unharmed and safe at the King David Hotel. However, as Declan took in the growing destruction and debris on all sides of the speeding Humvee, even with his growing faith and knowledge of God's goodness, he feared the worst for Megan, Evan and the others.

"We're getting close," Louis said, looking over to Declan. "We'll be there soo…."

"Get down!" Ya'alon yelled, as a Sukhoi swooped down from the skies, raining a barrage of bullets on the Humvee. The rounds pummeled the vehicle as the driver did his best to maintain control. Declan and Louis tucked as low as they could in their seats, heads down and unable to see as the Humvee careened off the road and slammed head on into an abandoned car on the roadside. The collision threw the men violently forward, jolting the driver into the steering wheel and tossing Ya'alon, Declan and Louis about the inside of the vehicle as if each weighed a mere ten or fifteen pounds.

The Sukhoi darted off and climbed again. Ya'alon tried to shake the cobwebs out of his sore and bleeding head. Looking toward the driver, he immediately saw the man's bleeding head and slumped body. Ya'alon felt for a pulse, but found none. He stepped out of the badly damaged Humvee and looked up to the sky. Once his eyes settled on the screaming Sukhoi, which appeared to making a quick turn for another run, he opened the door and yelled inside to Louis and Declan, "Hurry, we have to get to cover! It's making another run at us!"

"My leg's hurt," Louis said.

"Here," Declan replied, as he reached over and helped to maneuver Louis out of the Humvee. Ya'alon, still dizzy, wrapped Louis's left arm around his shoulder and, once out of the vehicle, Declan took Louis's right arm and the three hobbled together toward a nearby building.

The Sukhoi, having made its turn, shot toward the street again. "C'mon," Declan said, catching sight of it. "He's almost on top of us again."

Ya'alon and Declan picked up the pace, basically dragging Louis with them. As they were within about ten feet of the building, and cover, the pilot in the Sukhoi opened fire, and rounds began to whistle through the sky and pelt the nearby buildings and abandoned vehicles. With only seconds before they were in range of the barrage, Declan pushed Louis through the open doorway, and he and Ya'alon jumped inside behind him. The Sukhoi's fire pummeled the building's outer façade, as the three men lay low inside, waiting for the assault to end.

Hearing the plane ascend again and fly off behind them, Ya'alon stepped outside and looked up, trying to discern whether the pilot was making any attempt to circle back for a third pass. After a minute of clear skies, he stepped back inside and said, "It doesn't look like he's coming back. How are you both?"

"I'm sore, but generally okay," Declan replied.

"I think my ankle is broken, or really badly sprained," Louis answered. "What about you? Your head doesn't look good."

"I'm okay," Ya'alon answered, not mentioning the ribs he suspected could be broken.

"What about the driver?" Louis asked.

"Dead," Ya'alon replied.

"Do you have any idea where we are?" Declan asked Ya'alon.

"We're not far from Giv'at Shaul. Just about a block off."

"Are we close enough to make it to the King David on foot?"

"It would be a long walk under normal conditions.

There's a bomb shelter nearby, maybe a block and a half from here. We should try and get there and regroup. The sky is clear at the moment, so I think we have a good window."

"That's fine with me," Louis answered. "That is, if you guys don't mind dragging me there."

"Let's go," Declan replied.

Ya'alon and Declan each helped to lift Louis up and wrapped one of his arms around their respective shoulders. The skies still clear of planes, the three left the cover of the building and made their way as quickly as possible over to Giv'at Shaul and toward the shelter Ya'alon had suggested.

"There, it's just ahead," Ya'alon advised. "Inside that building."

The three hobbled to the building and quickly made their way inside. Ya'alon and Declan helped Louis down the stairs as they heard more planes overhead. As they reached the lower steps, an explosion in a building across the street rocked the area.

"That one was close," Louis said.

"Yes, it's a good thing we were already inside," Ya'alon answered. "Here, I'll get the door."

Ya'alon knocked firmly against the metal door and, a few seconds later, the door began to creep open. A man inside looked the trio over and said in Hebrew, "Please, come inside."

Seeing Ya'alon's IDF uniform and Louis's injured leg, a group inside made some room for Ya'alon and Declan to gently place Louis in a chair near one of the walls. Once Louis was seated, people began peppering Ya'alon with questions in Hebrew. He was quickly surrounded and did his best to answer, offering up what information he had. Declan took a seat on the floor next to the chair Louis was in and tried to catch his breath. An older Israeli couple were seated next to him, speaking softly to one another in English.

Declan closed his eyes for a second, hoping the darkness would stop the throbbing in his head. As he lay there, he overheard the woman next to him say to her husband, "I hope that American girl is okay."

Her husband replied, "So do I. I still can't believe she ran outside like that. I pray that God is with her."

Declan opened his eyes and sat up. "Excuse me," he said to the couple, "but did you just say there was an American girl in here earlier?"

"Yes," the woman replied. "She came into the shelter with us when the attack started. She was worried about someone, her husband coming into the airport on the Prime Minister's plane."

Declan shot to his feet and reached quickly into his pocket, taking out his wallet. His fingers moved nimbly inside the wallet and he pulled out a photo of Megan, one of the photos Ignacio's friend had taken on their wedding day in Cusco.

"Is this the girl?" Declan asked, showing the woman the photo.

"Yes," the woman replied. "That is her. Are you her husband?"

"Where did she go?"

"I don't know. She suddenly ran out of here and back outside."

"When? When did she leave?" Declan asked frantically.

"Maybe twenty minutes ago."

"Did she say where she was going?"

Having overheard the conversation, another man, the one who had tried to stop Megan from leaving came over. "She said she had to get back to the hotel," the man told Declan. "That she had to see if her husband was okay."

Turning to the man, Declan asked, "She said 'the hotel'?"

"Yes, I'm sure of it."

"Which direction is the King David Hotel from here?"

"It's about 2 miles southwest of here, just before you

reach the Old City."

Without another word, Declan ran to the shelter door, threw it open and sprinted up the stairs. Ya'alon, who had heard the latter portion of the exchange, looked over to Louis, who said quickly, "Go ahead. He'll never get there on his own. I'm fine here."

With that, Ya'alon rushed out of the shelter in pursuit of Declan.

Chapter 53

After having taken cover from building to building along the roadway, Megan ran quickly from Sderot Ben Tsvi, into the northern end of Sacher Park near Kraft Stadium. She remembered seeing the park and football pitch on her way to the airport earlier that day, and felt a slight sense of relief that she had, in fact, been moving in the right direction. By Megan's mental calculations, the King David Hotel had to be within a mile to the east.

Hearing the whistling and booming of jets getting closer, she ducked down in a patch of trees near Kraft Stadium and looked up to see two IAF fighters engaging a Russian MiG overhead. From the ground, she could clearly see the planes deftly maneuvering around one another, as the trio of jets streaked through the sky, climbing, then descending, then banking sharply and shooting back up as if racing toward the outer atmosphere.

For a moment, Megan found herself enraptured by the aerial display. There was an ironic sense of beauty in the planes' movements. A few seconds later, one of the Israeli F-15's locked onto the MiG, and Megan watched as its missile streaked across the blue background. A loud boom and great flash of light and fire lit up the sky as the missile found its target and the MiG exploded, almost like a burst of fireworks, in the sky.

The explosion brought Megan back to the reality surrounding her, and she shuddered as she looked at all the burning buildings across the street from the park. Buildings that had once been people's homes had, she knew, in many cases become their graves. Despite the earlier aerial display, there was no beauty in war Megan thought, and with the skies temporarily clear, she hurried across the park toward another patch of cover.

As Megan made her way south through the park, sticking close to Sderot Ben Tsvi, she repeated the word, "Ramban." It was one of the streets she remembered taking from the hotel and, she thought, it would be visible from the park as long as she stayed near Sderot Ben Tsvi.

The numerous damaged and burned out buildings along Sderot Ben Tsvi served as a constant reminder of the danger she faced and spurred Megan forward as fast as her legs would carry her. After a few minutes, a playground, deeper in Sacher Park, caught Megan's attention and the irony of the scene caused her to stop for a second. On her left were bombed buildings, many still burning, but to her right, tucked away in the seeming peacefulness of Sacher Park, sat a children's playground.

The playground was unharmed, somehow untouched by the chaos and destruction teeming throughout the rest of Jerusalem. The swings swayed gently in the breeze, the play scape, monkey bars and slides silently waiting for smiling kids to assail them. The playground was like a small innocent oasis tucked behind green foliage and hidden away from the rest of the decaying world. Megan thought of the tiny developing baby in her womb and wondered whether she and Declan would ever see their little one hurdling down the slide or swinging carelessly across the monkey bars. Maybe, just maybe, she thought.

Another plane jetted directly overhead and jolted Megan back to reality. She resumed her journey, darting from cover to cover, and staying out of sight when she'd hear planes or rockets streaking through the skies overhead. As she neared the center of Sacher Park, a large missile suddenly roared in from the east, followed almost immediately by another. Before she could react, the missiles struck the large building just west of her that housed the Supreme Court of Israel. The explosions, one after the other, shook the entire park and bordering buildings, knocking Megan off her feet.

From the ground she looked up to see smoke rising from the Supreme Court building in the distance. Stunned, but not injured, Megan stood up and began to make her way further south, when another missile screeched through the sky and slammed into one of a group of sand-colored high-rise apartment buildings lining Sderot Ben Tsvi. The missile hit the apartment building squarely, and the energy wave from the explosion rushed outwardly from the building into the park, lifting Megan off her feet and slamming her forcefully onto the ground. Megan could hear nothing but a loud ringing and, looking up from the ground, could see nothing but blurred shapes and outlines.

"Declan," she whispered softly, then everything went black.

Chapter 54

"What's the best way back to the King David?" Declan asked Sgt. Ya'alon as the two stopped running for a second in Max Fisher Square. "I mean, which way do you think someone who doesn't know the area well would go?"

"My guess is that she'd try and stay near roads she may have taken and may remember, but there are numerous routes one could have taken from the Kind David. They could have traveled up Ben Tsvi, along the park, or they could have taken Agripas. Those two are the most likely routes, but by no means the only ones."

"I think we should split up."

"I agree. Can I have her photo?"

Declan took Megan's picture out of his pocket and handed it to Ya'alon, saying, "This was taken about a month ago."

Ya'alon took a good look at Megan's face and put the photo in his pocket. "I'll go this way and follow the Agripas route. I can also scan the various side streets. If you follow this street, the one just over there, Heikhal ha-Mishpat, that'll take you into Sacher Park, which is bordered by Sderot Ben Tsvi. There's good cover in the park, so she may have gone through there, but follow Ben Tsvi until you reach Giv'at Klor Garden, which is where Ramban Street is. That's the most direct route from the hotel. When you get to Ramban, go left and follow it until you reach Tsarfat Square. From there, go right and look for Abraham Lincoln Street. That'll take you to King David."

"Okay, I'll meet you at the King David. If neither of us sees her along the way, and she's not there, we can backtrack on another route."

"Agreed," Ya'alon answered. "God go with you, my friend."

"And with you."

Sgt. Ya'alon darted off from the square in the direction of Agripas Street. Declan found the street Ya'alon had pointed to and ran as fast as he could. Not long after, he ran through New York Square and across an open parking lot, ending up on Ha-Aluf David She'alti'el Street. Declan scanned the area, trying to get his bearings. Directly in front of him was a basketball court, and beyond that he could see what looked like a soccer field. Determining that both must be part of, or at least in the vicinity of the park Ya'alon had mentioned, Declan ran around a chain-link fence and hurried toward the soccer field, keeping his eyes out for Megan as he ran.

A minute or so later, Declan reached the soccer field, Kraft Stadium, and quickly scanned the area, calling out as loud as he could, "Megan! Megan!"

Looking to his left, he spotted what appeared to be a large street and ran in that direction, bounding through a small garden and quickly jumping a metal fence. Once over the fence, Declan found himself on the sidewalk adjacent to Sacher Park on his right, and Sderot Ben Tsvi on his left. He ran south along the sidewalk, scanning the park and the street and again calling Megan's name as he ran. After passing a bombed-out gas station on his left, which was still burning, the expanse of Sacher Park opened up again on his right. Keeping the Sderot Ben Tsvi in view, Declan headed off into the park, hoping to gain better cover from the fighter jets that had appeared in the skies overhead.

Gunfire began to rain down from the fighter jets into a building opposite the park, so Declan delved further in to the park, continuing south under the cover of the various trees and bushes along the way. He fell into a pattern of running 40 or 50 feet, stopping to scan the area, and calling out Megan's name. He knew he wasn't making the fastest time, but something kept telling Declan, as it had since he and Louis had landed in Israel, that Megan wasn't at the hotel. He continued to pray silently for wisdom and discernment, and believed whole-heartedly that God had heard his prayers.

As Declan's path through the park passed over Sderot

Yitshak Rabin, he began to notice large buildings burning on both sides of the park. Up ahead, he wasn't sure how far, he saw a row of tall light-colored building on fire, and on the opposite side, off to his right, was another large blaze. Emergency vehicles rushed by on the Sderot Ben Tsvi occasionally, and Declan realized for the first time just how damaging the on-going attack was. Jerusalem was in tatters, and getting worse.

Declan continued through the park, heading further south, when he ran upon the playground Megan had seen earlier. He didn't stop as she had, but the playground struck him with a vague sense of familiarity, although he couldn't understand why.

"Megan," he called out again. "Megan, are you out there?"

Hearing nothing but another explosion off in the distance, Declan hurried forward.

Chapter 55

Sgt. Ya'alon quickly approached the intersection of Agripas Street and King George Street, and turned to head south on King George Street. Moving at a medium running speed, he caught sight of an IDF jeep parked outside a bombed-out store in the once-bustling shopping area. There appeared to be someone in the driver's seat, and Ya'alon called out to him as he approached, but got no response. Once he'd reached the jeep, Ya'alon discovered a dead male soldier slumped over in a shot-up, but still running, jeep.

Acknowledging the increased risk of driving the roads, Ya'alon decided the risk was worth the reward as he could make much better time and cover more ground in the jeep. He gently and respectfully moved his deceased colleague to the back, hopped in and drove quickly south along King George Street, keeping his eyes and ears on the alert for any signs of Megan as well as incoming missiles and jets.

The rumblings in the immediate area around the King David Hotel had been silent for nearly five minutes, which to those who had taken refuge in the shelter, seemed almost like a lifetime. Conversations began to bubble up around Evan and Tom in numerous languages, that maybe the attack was over, maybe the Israelis had successfully fought off the aggressors.

"Please, everyone stay calm," one of the senior hotel staff advised. "I'll go up and see if there's any news."

Tom Langham looked to Evan and said, "I'm going up too. I need to see what's happening out there and get some fresh air."

"Are you sure?" Evan asked.

"Yep, I'm sure. If there's any sign of danger, I'll head straight back down. At the very least, maybe I can get a snippet of info as to what's happening. We're basically blind and deaf down here."

"Be careful."

"Will do," Tom replied as he hurried to follow the hotel staffer.

Declan continued running south through Sacher Park, following a tree-lined and well-covered sidewalk which ran almost parallel to Sderot Ben Tsvi.

"Megan," he called out as loud as he could. "Megan, are you out there somewhere?"

"How long do you think you'll stay?" Megan's dad asked her, as she stared off into the horizon far beyond the waves rolling over her feet and toes. The sun was rising over the ocean, announcing its return with an explosion of color. The pinks, oranges, and yellows rolled ashore with the waves, blanketing Megan in a pure and radiant warmth.

A smile prominently spread across her face, and Megan replied, "I could stay here forever, daddy. I always loved this place. I loved coming here with you and mom, Timmy and John."

"I loved it too, pumpkin, but this place doesn't exist anymore. This is just a dream."

"But I want it to be real, daddy. I want us to be back here again."

"No you don't, not really. Listen, Megan. Listen closely to the sound coming over the water."

Megan looked past the beach, past the rolling waves, and out onto the ocean beyond. She focused her senses, forcing out the gentle wash of the surf as it crashed against the sand, and listened for a sound coming from beyond the surf, a sound coming from the far horizon. It took a few seconds, but just as her dad had said, she did hear something out there.

The sound was garbled at first, far-off in the distance, but as each wave came ashore, the sound grew stronger, as though it were riding the tide toward the beach. Megan closed her eyes and focused harder on the sound, blocking out every stimuli her other senses could pick up. She directed all her energy to the sound and, finally, all at once, she heard it clearly, "Megan."

It was her name being called out over the ocean. "Megan…Megan…Megan," and the voice calling it was, unmistakably, Declan's.

"Megan, are you out there?" he called. "Megan!"

Without hesitating, she answered, "Declan, I'm here. I'm here," and as she answered, his voice grew louder, even more clear than before. The waves died down, the sand slipped from beneath her feet, and the ocean began to disappear from her view.

"Declan, I'm here," she called out again, and as Megan slowly opened her eyes, so was he.

Seeing Declan's tear-stained face just inches above her own, Megan lunged toward him, wrapping him so tightly in her arms that she vowed never to let him go again. The two had finally found themselves in the one place they'd longed to be since their last night together at the hacienda in Urubamba, the night before Declan had left to return to the U.S. and rescue his family. They kissed one another more passionately than they ever had before, and each found that their love for one another, in its purest form, pulsed throughout their bodies as they held each other in an unbreakable embrace.

"Thank God you're okay," he said. "I thought I might have lost you."

"I knew this moment would finally come," she replied, not even bothering to hold back her tears. "I love you so much. Oh, how I love you."

"And I love you," he replied, his own eyes filled with

tears. "I love, love, love you."

Declan and Megan held one another tighter than ever before. Tears poured forth from their eyes and neither wanted to let go of the other.

"There were so many times when a small part of me doubted this moment would come," Declan whispered, still clutching his wife in his arms. "It was the thought of hearing your voice again, of feeling your touch again, of looking into those sparkling green eyes of yours again, that, in spite of everything, kept me moving forward."

Not knowing how much time they'd actually have together, and not wanting to waste any of it, Megan said, "I have something to tell you."

"What?"

Megan hesitated, not knowing exactly how she wanted to tell Declan about the baby she was carrying. She'd thought of twenty different ways to give him the news, none of which had involved bullets and bombs exploding all around them.

"What is it?" Declan asked again.

An enormous smile filled Megan's face, and, her eyes looking coyly down toward her belly, she replied, "Nothing. The *three* of us had better get moving."

Her comment didn't immediately register with Declan, but a couple seconds later, his eyes wide, he asked, "Did you just say, 'The *three* of us'?"

"I sure did."

Declan looked into his wife's eyes, which glittered even more dazzlingly than ever before and couldn't contain his excitement and joy. He was overcome with gratitude, wrapping Megan, and the small baby growing inside her, securely in his arms again. Bombs exploding all around, Declan and Megan simply held one another and laughed joyously, celebrating, even if for just a moment, their new family and forgetting entirely about everything happening in the world around them.

When they finally separated, they stared into one

another's eyes and smiled widely. Each had imagined that moment, and what it would be like to see one another again, to hold one another again, and to simply *have* one another again. Even with fighter jets streaking through the skies above them, and the city of Jerusalem burning around them, the actual moment, surpassed their best imaginary moments by all the miles it would take to get up to Heaven and back.

Chapter 56

Seeing no sign of Megan anywhere, Ya'alon made his way to the King David Hotel, which, to his surprise, was still in comparatively good condition. Ya'alon wasn't sure whether such an important target had simply been missed, or, more likely, whether it had been intentionally spared given the large number of foreigners typically found there, but whatever the reason, aside from some stray bullet and shrapnel damage, and some broken windows, the King David was mostly unscathed.

Ya'alon parked the jeep outside, which was nearly desolate but for a random hotel employee or two and hurried inside. He immediately found a group of hotel employees standing near one of the stairwells and rushed toward them, Megan's photo in hand. "Have you seen this woman?" he asked in Hebrew.

The hotel staffers looked at the photo carefully, but none recognized Megan.

"Is there a shelter here?" Ya'alon asked.

"Yes, this way," one of the staff replied. "I'll show you."

Ya'alon followed the young hotel employee down a hall toward another stairwell. Just before reaching the stairwell, they encountered another staff member, being followed by a tall gray-haired man who appeared to be in his late-fifties to early-sixties. Ya'alon stopped the staffer and showed him the photo, again asking in Hebrew if he had seen the woman.

As the staffer looked at the photo, Tom Langham, who was standing behind him caught sight of Megan and Declan in the picture and said, "I know her. That's Megan Parker and her husband, Declan. Where'd you get that picture?"

"You know them?" Ya'alon asked, turning his full attention to Tom. "You know this woman?"

"Yes, I flew her here with Declan's brother Evan and

his niece and nephew."

"Is she here? Is she in the shelter?"

"No," Tom answered. "She left before the attack to meet Declan and Louis Martino at the airport. That's the last time we saw her. I don't know where she is. Who are you?"

"I'm Sgt. Ya'alon, of the IDF. I flew in with Louis and Declan. Declan and I have been out searching for Megan. She was apparently at a shelter off Giv'at Shaul, but left in an attempt to get back here. You're sure she isn't here?"

"Positive."

"Thank you. I have to go back out and try to find her," Ya'alon said, turning toward the exit.

"Wait," Tom said. "I'm coming with you."

"I can't let you do that. It's too dangerous."

"You can't stop me. Two sets of eyes is better than one."

"Fine, let's go, Mr.?"

"Langham. My name is Tom Langham."

Ya'alon and Tom hurried back outside to the jeep and hopped in. "Declan was looking for Megan in Sacher Park, along the Ben Tsvi. We'll drive back in that direction first and see whether we can find him."

"Sounds good," Tom replied.

Ya'alon put the jeep into gear and rushed away from the King David toward Sacher Park, as a squadron of MiG's streaked overhead. The jeep hadn't gone fifty feet, when a barrage of gunfire rained down along the road. Ya'alon weaved and aimed the jeep for cover next to a nearby building. Tom ducked low in the passenger seat as the jeep screeched to a halt.

"Hurry, over there," Ya'alon yelled, pointing to an enclosed area.

The two men sprinted for the safety of the enclosure, each making it just as more gunfire pelted the jeep behind them, and it erupted into a large ball of flames.

"The jet presence seems to be picking up again," Declan said.

"I know. What should we do?"

Declan looked around and assessed their position. They were well hidden in a plush wooded spot in Giv'at Klor Garden, just about ten or fifteen feet off Derech Ruppin Road. In that spot, they were protected from the view of any Russian pilots and, presumably, there was no tactical reason to bomb the garden. Declan could see the intersection with Ramban Street about 100 yards ahead, and knew from Ya'alon's instructions that was the road to take back to the King David.

"Well, we're in a good spot here. We can either stay here and wait it out, or make a run for Ramban up ahead. If we make Ramban, we'll have to use the buildings for cover, but I don't have any idea how far it is back to the hotel."

"I don't know exactly, but I do know it's less than a mile," Megan replied.

"Well, counselor, what do you think?" Declan asked.

"We can't stay here forever and who knows when we'll get a good break."

"True," Declan agreed.

"So, we're in agreement that we should make a run for it?"

"Absolutely. God's brought us back together again. To me, that's all that matters. If we're supposed to make it back to the King David, we will. If not, then at least we'll die together. I've been blessed beyond anything I could ever deserve just having you as my wife and sharing even five minutes of my life with you, so I can live with that."

"I can too."

"I love you, Megan."

"And I love you."

Declan took his wife's hand as the two peered up through the trees, looking for an opening. Two MiG's streaked by, each shooting a missile at targets off in the distance, northeast of where they stood. Megan and Declan locked eyes and she said, "On three."

Declan kissed her and nodded affirmatively.

"One…two…three!"

Chapter 57

Evan Parker held his two young children close to him as the ground began to shake and rumble around them in the shelter beneath the King David Hotel. The relative expressions of comfort and relief that had made their way onto the faces of so many in the shelter just moments earlier had vanished. Instead, with each rattle and thud, with the clearly audible sound of each and every explosion seemingly directly above them, the faces of most people were awash with fear and anxiety.

"It's okay," Evan said to Will and Charlotte. "Don't be afraid. We're going to be just fine."

"How do you know, daddy?" Will asked.

"Because God told me. A long time ago, well before any of us were born, God spoke to a man who lived here in Israel named Ezekiel."

"What did God say to him?"

"God told Ezekiel about everything that is happening outside right now. He told Ezekiel about this attack, about the people and nations who would try and hurt Israel and its people."

"But, daddy, if God told Ezekiel all this stuff before I was born, before you were born, how did He know it would happen?"

"Because God knows the end from the beginning. He knows the end of the story already."

"So, He skipped to the last page of the book and looked at the picture," little Charlotte said. "Just like I like to do."

"Sort of," Evan answered, giving his daughter a kiss on top of her head and marveling at just how much, even at such a young age, she reminded him of his wife, Michelle. "But, do you want to know what else God told Ezekiel?"

"What?" both children responded.

"God told Ezekiel that, when the time was right, God Himself would come to protect Israel and would defeat the people trying to hurt her."

"So God's going to get rid of the bombs outside?" Will asked.

"He is."

"How's He going to do that?"

"He's going to shake the ground, turn the bad soldiers against each other, and pour down rain, hailstones and burning fire from the skies, which will knock the planes and bombs out of the sky and send the bad guys running away."

"He won't get us with that stuff, will he, daddy?" Will asked.

"No, we're safe in here. So, see, there's no need to be scared. We just have to sit tight and trust that God will do exactly what He said He'd do."

"When will God do all that stuff?"

"Hopefully, soon," Evan replied, as another explosion rocked the surface, and the ground shook hard around them. "Very soon."

Ya'alon and Tom Langham found themselves pinned down inside the standing remnants of a bombed-out building not far from the King David. The air and missile assault had moved into higher, more intense, gear, and the bombing was relentless. A swarm of MiG's swept down from the sky, flying low, just above the buildings and inflicting a barrage of heavy damage. Tom watched as two MiG's raced by, firing missiles at a wing of the previously unscathed King David Hotel. The missiles ripped through part of the hotel, delivering a direct blow and setting a section of the upper floors ablaze.

"The attack is intensifying," Tom said. "They aren't leaving anything unscathed this time around."

From what Ya'alon could see, the skies over Jerusalem were replete with Russian bombers and MiG's, with little to no IAF presence. The few IAF F-15's he did see were being shot out of the sky or were courageously engaged in outnumbered and unwinnable skirmishes. Based on his military training and knowledge, Ya'alon suspected the Russian attack coalition was engaged in a last round of pummeling the city with air strikes and heavy-artillery in order to soften the defenses as much as possible for an impending ground invasion.

"It can't be much longer now," he said to himself.

"What?" Tom asked, having heard him.

"I think they're readying for a ground invasion. This is the heaviest air assault we've seen yet, and it appears to be working. From the looks of things down here, the Russians have achieved air superiority."

"I was just thinking the same thing," Tom agreed, as another missile streaked overhead and blasted into the side of a nearby building. "It looks like you and I aren't going anywhere soon."

"No, unfortunately, I agree. We're stuck here."

"I hope Declan and Megan are okay out there. I hope that, somehow, they found one another and got themselves to somewhere safe."

"As do I, Tom," Ya'alon said. "It looks like Declan and Megan are on their own out there. Wherever they are, may the God of Abraham be with them."

Chapter 58

Declan and Megan ran hand-in-hand, making good time, east along Ramban Street, toward the King David. They crouched and ducked into cover when necessary, and ran as quickly as they could during the few seconds when the skies were relatively clear. Amid all the chaos, the burning buildings, the diving planes, the destruction, and death, each had an ironic sense of peace. They were, finally, back together, and because of that one fact, something so insignificant to the rest of the world, the couple firmly believed they could handle anything that was thrown their way.

Upon reaching the intersection of Ramban and Keren Hayesod streets, Megan noticed a small fountain to her right that she remembered seeing on the way to Ben Gurion Airport earlier that day.

"Wait," she said to Declan. "I know this place. We need to take a right here. The hotel isn't much further."

"Okay," Declan replied. "Let's go."

The pair ran across the rather exposed intersection, looking up to the sky for any incoming MiG's or projectiles, when Declan noticed, for the first time, what appeared to be an oncoming storm moving in very quickly from the west.

"Look," he said, pointing to an ominous charcoal-colored sky racing toward Jerusalem over the horizon. Megan stopped for a second to look up and, upon seeing the oncoming storm, said, "We'd better get moving."

"Or get to cover. I don't think we're going to outrun it. I've never seen clouds move that fast. It's almost surreal."

Within seconds, rain began to pour down, light at first, then increasingly heavy as the tempestuous storm clouds raced closer, practically swarming the city. Before Megan and Declan could move, the sun had completely disappeared from sight, taking its light with it, and the sky became black, as though it had instantly switched from day to night, except there were no stars to see above. There was nothing but empty blackness, lit up by the occasional flash of lightning.

"What just happened?" Declan asked as the rain began to dump, as if from buckets.

"I don't know, but we have to get off the street."

Out of nowhere, the pair heard the shriek of a missile streaking through the sky, but just as quickly, a bolt of lightning burst forth from the black clouds and hit the missile head-on in mid-flight, causing it to explode high in the sky. A few seconds later, another bolt of lightning shot forth from the clouds and hit a MiG flying off to the east. Like the missile, the plane exploded in mid-air, lighting up the sky with a ball of fire which could be seen and felt for blocks.

"What's going on?" Megan said.

"I have no idea, but it seems to be helping. Let's keep moving. The debris is going to start littering the ground. We need to get to cover."

The rain continued to wash down on Jerusalem, literally flooding the streets with water, some of which streamed into the makeshift shelter Ya'alon and Tom Langham had found themselves in. Tom watched with amazement as successive lightning bolts shot from the tumultuous darkness above. What had transfixed Tom was the precise nature of the strikes. What he was witnessing was no ordinary storm. There was no randomness to it. Each and every lightning bolt struck, with otherworldly precision, a particular target streaking through the sky, each time knocking a missile or a Russian plane right out of the air. As Tom watched the display, he remembered Evan's words regarding Ezekiel's prophecy and a bewildered smile spread across his face.

"It's happening," he said, recalling exactly what Evan had told him about Ezekiel's prophecy concerning the battle of Gog/Magog. "I'll be a monkey's uncle, it's actually happening."

"What?" Ya'alon asked.

"The prophecy. The Ezekiel prophecy about God Himself coming and defeating your enemies."

Just as the words came out of Tom's mouth, the two men caught sight of an enormous ball of fire hurling, like an asteroid entering the atmosphere, out of the black clouds that had descended and settled upon the Holy City. The fire ball collided with a streaking Russian jet, causing another violent explosion in the sky. As Ya'alon and Tom looked out from the bombed-out building, they were stunned to see what appeared to be thousands of similar fire balls lighting up the darkness.

Witnessing the fire balls pour forth from the heavens, each destroying Israel's enemies, Ya'alon fell to his knees, praising God Almighty, saying, "Oh-deh ehl shah-dai, oh-deh ehl shah-dai,..."

Tom Langham was overcome with a feeling he'd never known before. He knew beyond any doubt that what he was witnessing was exactly what Evan had described and that God, the creator of the universe and everyone in it, was, in fact, showing Himself in an unmistakable fashion to the world. He was coming to the defense of His people as only He could. Tom was witnessing the power and force of God.

Remembering his words to Evan earlier, and no longer able to deny his Creator, no longer able to ignore the truth, Tom fell to his knees, bowed his head, and whispered, "Dear God, I finally see you. After all these years, I finally see you. Please God, please save me. I believe in You, in Your Son, Jesus. I believe that He died for my sins, and I believe, with all of my heart, finally, that the only way to heaven is through Your Son. Please God, come into my heart and be my Savior."

Tears poured from Tom's eyes as he opened them to see, as promised to Ezekiel so many thousands of years earlier, the one true God, the God of Abraham and Isaac, and now Tom's God, rescuing Israel from destruction, as He'd promised He would.

Chapter 59

The blackened, yet living, sky burst forth with shots of lightning and an army of enormous fire balls, as Declan and Megan looked up through the pouring rain. The ground began to shake beneath their feet, rocking them from side to side. Declan clung to Megan, each trying to maintain their balance.

What neither of them knew, what they couldn't know or see, was that the earth was shaking from beneath the Mediterranean all the way to Israel's eastern border, where the various Russian, Iranian, Turkish, and Sudanese ground troops who had gathered in advance of the ground invasion, were also being rocked violently. Many of the troops had begun to fight amongst themselves, confused by the ethereal darkness and the barrage of fireballs which had rained down upon them. The ground opened up in places where the troops were staged, creating chaos and gaps in the earth so sudden and large that they swallowed up men and equipment without warning.

Neither Declan nor Megan knew exactly what they were looking at, or what was happening throughout Israel, but each knew, without a doubt, that what they were witnessing was supernatural. As Tom had observed, the lightning strikes and fire balls were precise, specifically targeted at the invaders. Each strike accurately hit every enemy plane and missile over Jerusalem, destroying them on contact, with none straying or hitting anything on the ground or any of the IAF planes in the sky.

If Declan, Megan, Ya'alon, or any of the others on the ground in Jerusalem had had the ability to see for miles around, they'd have seen the same phenomenon over Tel Aviv, over the Russian, Turkish and Iranian ships in the Mediterranean, and over the enemy ground troops massed for invasion on each of Israel's borders.

Lightning and large balls of burning Sulphur poured down from the heavens on Israel's attackers, stopping the onslaught in its tracks. After a mere thirty minutes of the storm, the charcoal sky began to lighten again and the rain slowed down. The storm dissipated nearly as quickly as it had arrived.

"I think it's over," Declan said.

A strong wind swept across the open intersection near where Declan and Megan had taken cover. The rain completely ceased falling as a chilly gust of wind wrapped itself around them. As the wind passed, the dark clouds totally disappeared from view, not really moving off as much as simply disappearing. Clear blue skies returned to Jerusalem and with them, warm rays of sunlight which reached down, illuminating the Holy Land and its inhabitants. As promised thousands of years earlier, the lightning and fire from God's storm had soundly defeated Israel's enemies and the heavy rain had extinguished many of the fires on the ground.

"What just happened?" Declan asked, taking in the suddenly quiet and peaceful skies over the city. "That was incredible."

"I think we just witnessed God," Megan answered. "Evan talked about this happening at breakfast this morning. About this possibly being the attack that would prompt God to show Himself and to defeat Israel's enemies. That has to be what we just saw. It's the only rational explanation."

Declan wrapped his arms around his wife and smiled. "I believe it," he said. "I believe it wholeheartedly. After everything we've been through, after all that we've seen, I absolutely believe God is truly capable of anything."

"I don't think there's any doubt about that. I don't know how anyone who witnessed what just happened could ever deny Him."

"Neither do I," Declan replied, still smiling.

"We should get back to the hotel and see how the others are," Megan suggested. "Where's Louis, anyway?"

"He's back at the shelter where you were earlier. He hurt his leg when we crashed. We'll see if we can find a car and go back and get him."

The pair made their way along Keren Hayesod Street toward the King David, the sun shining down on their every step. With each passing minute, more and more people began to emerge from hiding. Many burst out onto the street and fell to their knees, calling out their thanks to Heaven and to a God many assumed had forgotten about them. Declan and Megan were amazed at the outpouring of emotion and thanks they witnessed among the Israelis as they began to realize what had just taken place, and Who had just delivered them and their nation from certain destruction.

Chapter 60

"I'm really not sure what has happened," the veteran reporter said, stumbling to find the right words, as Luke, Hope, Jessica and the rest of the Williams family watched the events unfolding in Israel on television. "It's all clear now, but as I reported earlier, a vicious storm moved into the area. It was unlike anything I've seen before, even with what, crazily enough, looked like fire falling from the sky. Here, roll back the video."

The T.V. screen switched to video the cameraman had taken earlier, during the storm. The reporter's voice began over the video, "Here, as you can see, there was a heavy downpour of rain and lightning everywhere. See, right there, there were like six lightning bolts at once, followed by different explosions in the sky. And here come what looked like fireballs, but that really doesn't make any sense, so I'm wondering if what we're seeing are more explosions. There were hundreds of fighter planes and missiles in the sky as the storm moved in when the attack was in full swing, and now they're all gone. I've been told the Russian naval ships in the Mediterranean were all severely damaged or destroyed as well."

"What do you think, dad?" Hope asked. "I can't see any explanation other than the fulfillment of Ezekiel 38."

"I agree," Chris Williams replied. "I still can't believe we're here to witness it, but I absolutely agree."

The reporter continued, as the camera went back to a live view, "As you can see now, the skies are clear and, from what I can see, the attack is over. People are filling the streets, many falling on their knees in what appears to be prayer, and there's a definite celebratory feel to the scene. I'm not sure I'll ever fully understand what took place, or where that storm came from, but, amazingly, it appears to have stopped the assault by the Russian-led alliance."

"Yes, Dan," the news anchor interrupted. "We're getting reports confirming that the storms apparently destroyed the warships in the Mediterranean and the Gulf of Aqaba, and killed or scattered the troops which had been massed along Israel's northern and eastern borders."

Jessica, who had been standing near the front door, watching the coverage, turned and stepped outside onto the large front porch, unable any longer to acknowledge death and destruction, pain and suffering, and evil. She leaned against the porch railing, where she could just get a glimpse of the nearby beach, and let the purifying breeze washing in from the ocean curl around and bathe her face. Jessica thought of Evan, Megan and the others, and hoped they were okay. She hoped Declan and Louis had actually made it to Israel safely, and, with a certain level of conflict and guilt, she felt relieved about her decision to stay on St. Simon's Island with the Williams family.

As Jessica stood, looking out toward the beach, she began to embrace an emotion that had been somewhat foreign since everything around her had begun to fall apart after that first night in the protests: happiness. Tears began to trickle from her eyes as she thought of her brother, Aiden, and, for the first time in her life, she *prayed* that if he wasn't still alive somewhere, he was at least at peace. She had no idea yet if God could, or would, hear her small prayer, but she said it silently anyway. She remembered her parents and the last words she'd ever heard them speak to her the night she'd gone out to the protests, "We love you."

Jessica remembered meeting Louis, and her awful ordeal with the Homeland trooper, and more tears flowed. She thought again of Evan, of his seemingly endless kindness and grace, and she missed him dearly. Jessica thought of what she'd loved and respected most about Evan, which was the way he didn't just talk faith, but he *lived* his faith, and, despite remaining reluctant to fully acknowledge God, she finally hoped and prayed that, someday, she could fully believe and that someone would think the same thing about her.

"Are you okay?" a familiar voice asked.

Jessica turned to see Luke standing a few feet away. She looked into his eyes and saw the same grace and kindness she'd seen in Evan, and she rushed toward him, wrapping herself in the warmth of his arms.

"What's wrong?" Luke asked.

Jessica looked up and kissed Luke, taking in every essence of him as her lips pressed against his. When their lips separated, she answered, "Nothing, absolutely nothing is wrong. I'm happy, Luke. For the first time in a long time, I'm happy. I…,"

Jessica stopped herself, unsure of the emotions bubbling to the surface of the often-tormented cauldron inside her. Part of her wanted to tell Luke what she thought her heart wanted her to say. To tell him that she was in love with him. Yet, even as the words were on the tip of her tongue, doubt raced to slam her mouth closed. Jessica thought of all the pain she'd witnessed, all the pain she'd felt, since the protests had begun. She still felt the weight of that young Homeland trooper on top of her, allowing her to "earn her freedom" after being arrested that first night of the protests, and felt her capacity for loving another person begin to shrivel into nothing.

She looked into Luke's eyes, which were fixated on her, as though he almost knew what she'd stopped herself from saying, and she felt the kindness exuding from them. Luke was nothing like that Homeland trooper or Al Rawlings, or any of the other disgusting individuals she'd encountered in the world; however, even so, Jessica just couldn't let herself acknowledge that she may love him. What if she did? What if she let herself feel again? Everyone she'd loved had either died or was missing. Jessica couldn't bear losing Luke and, at that moment, while she wanted to love him, to tell him that she loved him, strange as it seemed, to love Luke was, in her mind, to lose Luke. Whether that day or another.

"Are you sure you're okay?" Luke asked, sincerity emanating from his eyes.

"Yes, I'm fine," she replied, embracing Luke and holding him tightly. "I'm just starting to feel happiness again, and that kind of scares me."

"I understand," Luke whispered, as he stroked her hair gently. "I promise, I'm not going anywhere."

Chapter 61

"Thank you again," Louis Martino said as he hobbled out of an IDF Humvee in front of the King David Hotel. "I really appreciate you guys giving me a lift."

"Happy to help," replied the young Israeli soldier in the driver's seat.

Louis turned, with some difficulty, and hopped on his one good leg toward the main doors, when a young man approached him, saying, "Here, let me help you. Lean on my shoulder."

"Thank you," Louis replied, doing just that.

The scene at the King David was practically festive, as it was throughout much of Israel. The small nation had, undoubtedly, suffered severe damage and many lives had been lost; however, Israel had survived and the general consensus among Israelis, and Jews the world over, was that its survival was due solely to supernatural intervention. The God of Abraham, Isaac and Jacob had, after thousands of years, appeared and literally delivered His people from their enemies yet again.

"Where can I help you go?" the man asked Louis.

"I'm not entirely sure. I'm looking for my friends. Maybe if you can just help me inside to the lobby."

A second later, Louis heard a voice behind him call out, "Louis! Louis!" With the man's help, he turned to see Declan and Megan hurrying toward him. Megan practically threw herself at him, wrapping her arms around her longtime friend, and nearly knocking him off balance.

"You're okay. I'm so glad that you're okay," she said.

"How'd you get here?" Declan asked. "We were going to try and find a car to come get you."

"A group of IDF soldiers stopped at the shelter for a moment, and I caught a ride with them. Thank goodness you're both safe. Where did you find each other?"

"In a big park a mile or so away," Declan answered.

"Here, let me take over."

Shifting his weight from the man's shoulder to Declan's, Louis told the man, "Thank you for your help. I appreciate it."

"I'm just happy to see that you found your friends. Bless you all," the man replied, and turned to leave.

"And you," Declan responded.

"So, do you know where Ya'alon is?" Louis asked. "Or your brother and the others?"

"No, Ya'alon and I split up and we were supposed to meet back here. I hope that he made it."

"We should try and find them," Megan suggested.

The three headed slowly into the hotel, looking around for Ya'alon, Tom, or Evan and the kids. After a few minutes, Declan spotted Ya'alon and Tom on the opposite side of the lobby. "There," he said. "I see Ya'alon and Tom over there."

Calling for their friends, the group began to make their way across the crowded floor. Hearing his name, Tom turned. As his eyes fell upon Megan, he immediately burst into joyful tears and hurried over to her. When they met, Tom and Megan silently embraced, with tears flowing.

As Tom and Megan expressed their joy at being reunited, Ya'alon hugged Louis and Declan while praising God for keeping them all safe and bringing them back together. The only ones missing were Evan and the children, and, just as Tom was getting ready to lead Declan downstairs to the shelter, they emerged from the stairwell.

Declan rushed over to his big brother, tears in his eyes, saying, "I'm so sorry, Ev. I'm so sorry."

"It's okay, Declan. Michelle and mom are home and it's okay."

"I just feel like everything is my fault."

"It's not, and don't think that. None of us have any control over anything that's happening. I'm just happy to see you again. I hated leaving you behind that day. I wanted to stay with you. If anything had happened to you...," Evan broke off, trying to get a hold of his emotions.

"It's okay. We're back together now, and that's what matters.

Chapter 62

Three days passed since the attack, and, while still in tatters, Jerusalem slowly resumed a sense of something resembling normalcy. Makeshift tent camps had popped up throughout the city, and throughout Israel more generally. The people in Jerusalem and Tel Aviv, which had also suffered greatly, began to clean up, to move rubble and debris from the streets and open them up to trickles of traffic. Stores and businesses which hadn't been too damaged, began to open again, and people's spirits, despite everything they had been through, were joyful.

Tom Langham had made his way, with some difficulty, to Ben Gurion Airport to check on the Gulfstream. To his amazement, the plane itself hadn't been damaged, but the airport was gradually getting back on its feet and Tom had been advised that it would be a few more days before any flights, private or otherwise, could get out.

A few hours before dawn on the fifth day after the attack, Declan and Evan met in the lobby of the King David and walked in the early-morning darkness to the Mount of Olives. Once there, they sat atop the Mount of Olives, looking out over the thousands of grave stones covering the sacred hillside toward the Old City, as the day's first light appeared with a blast of color on the eastern horizon. The Old City was bathed with a subtle golden hue, prompting Declan to say, "Nature's first green is gold."

"What?" Evan asked.

"This scene just brings to mind that Robert Frost poem, 'Nothing Gold Can Stay'."

"I remember that one. Dad taught it to me."

"Me too."

"I hadn't thought about that in years. Nature's first green is gold, Her hardest hue to hold."

"Her early leaf's a flower," Declan continued. "But only for an hour."

"Then leaf subsides to leaf," they recited together. "So Eden sank to grief. So dawn goes down to day, Nothing gold can stay."

The brothers looked at one another and laughed.

"I never really understood that poem when I was a kid," Declan admitted. "In fact, I don't think I ever truly understood it until now, looking out over this city. Even in this condition, with all the damage, it's more beautiful than I ever imagined. As incredible as it sounded when dad would talk about it."

"I still miss him," Evan said, referring to their dad.

"So do I. Every single day. It's amazing because, in body, he's been out of our lives for so long, but, in a way, he never left. So much of me, of who I am, is because of him. I so desperately wanted to please him, even after he was dead."

"Me too. I always envisioned dad watching over me, over all of us, as we went through each day. Sometimes I'd even look around for him, hoping to just catch a glimpse of him somewhere, some flash of a second where he'd show himself."

"It was his voice I could always hear," Declan said. "I still do. I wish he and mom were here with us now."

"He always wanted to come here, to Jerusalem, to the Mount of Olives. I remember looking at photos of this place with him. 'To be able to sit where Jesus and the Apostles sat,' he'd say. 'To look upon the same ground Jesus looked upon.'"

"He was a good man," Declan replied. "The best I've ever known, except maybe for you."

"No, I'm nowhere near the man dad was. He always seemed to have the right words at the right time. I'm struggling right now to find any words at all. Every time I think about Michelle, I just want to break down and cry. I miss her so much and I don't know that I can do it without her. I almost feel lost with the kids at times. I don't know all the things they like to eat, I can't do everything for them that Michelle did, the way she did, and I fear I won't be, that I can't be, the parent they need, the parent they deserve, even though I'm the only parent they have now."

"You're an amazing father, Evan. I don't say that lightly, or just to make you feel better. You're the kind of dad I hope, I pray, to be. After dad died, obviously mom did everything she could, and she did an amazing job, but, just like you can never fully be what Michelle was, she couldn't exactly be a father. She could never take dad's place, just as he could never have taken hers. For me at least, you kind of picked up where dad left off. I don't know that I've ever told you how much I looked up to you growing up. *You* were always there with the right words at the right time for me, and I know you'll do the same for Will and Charlotte. Don't try to be their mom, just be who you already are, and Will and Charlotte will be just fine. Don't doubt yourself, and don't doubt God. You're the one who has always said He can take the bad and use it to bring about good, and, as I've finally come to learn during the course of this adventure, that's absolutely true."

"Thank you, Declan. I needed your words of encouragement, probably more than you know. And, I couldn't be happier that you've found your faith again. Truly, that is an answered prayer."

"Well, like you, I've seen it first-hand. There were so many times, getting here, that my path looked hopeless or impossible, but I kept my faith and trust in God and, not surprisingly, time and again, He got me through. He brought me here and back to you and to Megan, and to someone I didn't even know was waiting for me."

"Who?" Evan asked.

Declan smiled. "Megan's pregnant."

"Declan, that's amazing news. What wonderful news. I'm so happy for you two."

"She told me when we found each other in Sacher Park. I still can't believe it."

"You're going to make wonderful parents."

"And you'll make an amazing uncle, Ev. Also, I wanted to ask you something. For a favor."

"Of course."

"Would you be the baby's Godfather?"

"I'd be honored. Thank you, Declan."

"Thank you, for everything, Evan. I know I haven't always been easy, but you've always been there for me."

"This truly is a blessed day. I'm really glad we did this," Evan said, looking out over the softly gleaming Old City. "It's been a long time since we've been able to just sit down and talk. Way too long, and I've definitely missed it."

"So have I, brother. So have I."

Chapter 63

"President Firenze," a reporter said as Raffaele Firenze and his team made their way to board his plane for the flight from Brussels to Tel Aviv. The reporter's voice was one of many firing questions at him; however, she'd somehow gotten Firenze's attention and he stopped in front of her, offering a look which, while still patient, seemed to indicate she should hurry and ask her question.

"In light of the unofficial reports that the harsh sanctions resolution against Israel was unanimously passed by the U.N. Security Council, do you fear a trip to Israel now could send the wrong message?" the reporter asked quickly.

Firenze, a relatively-young, disarmingly-handsome, Italian with rare green eyes, didn't answer immediately, choosing instead to flash a smile at the camera while looking down thoughtfully. After a slight pause, he began, "On the contrary, I firmly believe a visit to Israel today sends the right message. Many of my colleagues disagree, and while I respect their positions, I feel, more strongly than ever, that the pending resolution is ill-advised."

"But," the reporter interrupted, "they used a nuclear…"

Firenze cut her off, politely, stating, "I understand the rationale behind the resolution and I understand and join in the world's rightful anger in response to Israel's utter destruction of Damascus. However, where has the path of conflict and aggression brought us? The issues plaguing Israel and her neighbors have been festering almost since the moment of Israel's inception back in 1948. Multiple attempts, however feeble, have been made at fostering peace, yet all have ended in violence. The U.N. resolution will simply lead to more pain and anger, which will ultimately lead to more violence. That is why I consider it ill-advised and, to a large degree, reactionary and reckless. In less than two months, we've had chemical weapons used in the region, a nuclear weapon used and an entire ancient city destroyed, and, five days ago, the region was yet again thrown into turmoil because of a vicious, not to mention illegal, coalition attack against Israel led by Russia and Iran. What has any of the violence and fighting solved? Please, tell me, what?"

"I, uh…I don't know," the reporter sputtered.

"It's solved absolutely nothing," Firenze continued. "The results have consistently been death, destruction and instability in a region where stability is of the utmost importance to the global community as a whole. I'm traveling to Israel today to meet personally with its Prime Minister because it's time, finally, to find a solution to the issues which have plagued the region for far too long. It's time to finally bring a lasting peace to Israel and the entire Middle East. I firmly believe, and I do not say this lightly, that the future of humanity, of the global community, depends entirely on bringing about such peace, and true peace cannot be reached without a genuine and sincere dialogue."

President Firenze smiled again to the cameras, and walked briskly to his plane.

Chapter 64

"How's the ankle feeling?" Declan asked as he and Megan joined Louis for lunch.

"It's better. I'm still gimping around a bit, but keeping off of it for the past few days has helped a lot."

"Where'd you disappear to this morning?" Megan asked.

"Evan and I went up to the Mount of Olives to watch the sunrise and chat. It had been a while. Too long, really."

"Good," Megan replied. "You two needed some time alone."

"So, when are you guys heading out?" Louis asked.

"Hopefully tomorrow," Megan replied. "Tom went out to the airport again early this morning to make sure that everything is cool and that the plane is ready to fly. From what he said, they're close to having two fully operating runways out there, so I think we might finally be good to go."

A waitress came and took everyone's orders, and Louis sat back in his chair, sipping a steaming cup of coffee. "So, it's back to Peru for you all then?"

"It is," Declan replied. "What about you? You know you're more than welcome to come with us."

"Declan's right," Megan added. "It's beautiful down there and there's plenty of room."

"I appreciate it, but I plan to stay here for a while. Adam Benjamin is coming in about an hour to drive me over for the Prime Minister's address and his meeting with Raffaele Firenze. The inside, off-the-record, word is, in light of what most Israeli's believe about their God delivering them from the Russian alliance, that the P.M. is going to call for the Jewish Temple to be rebuilt. That's going to be huge news. That and Firenze's remarks this morning about finally bringing peace to the region. "

"Yeah, but I still can't imagine the prospect of a temple in Jerusalem will be too popular with the rest of the world. Particularly if it's on the Temple Mount."

"No, it can't imagine it will," Louis replied. "Nothing Israel does these days seems to sit well with the rest of the world."

"And yet, they persevere," Declan said.

"How true. Who knows, maybe there is something to them being God's people," Louis responded. "I think of you two as friends. You're intelligent, well-read, rational people, and I trust you both. I value your thoughts and perspectives on things. So, let me ask you guys, honestly, what do you think about what happened? I mean, you saw it with your own eyes, while I was hunkered down in a shelter. Do you think it was some sort of divine intervention?"

"Absolutely," Megan said, answering without hesitation. "There's not a doubt in my mind."

"Same for me," offered Declan. "Like you said, we witnessed it first-hand, out on the street, and it was unlike anything I'd ever seen."

"Well, maybe if I'd seen it with my own eyes I'd be totally convinced too, but I guess it really doesn't matter much what I think. It was what it was. I just wish I'd seen it. I still can't believe I was stuck, immobile and underground while one of the largest stories in recent memory was unfolding above. The footage they keep running on the news…well, it leaves the questions open for debate."

"Trust me, Louis," Megan replied. "The footage on the news doesn't come close to doing justice to what actually happened. If you'd seen it, if you'd felt the power behind it, you'd know, without a doubt, that it was God. There's no debate."

The trio finished their lunch, each happy to have time to simply eat, talk and enjoy their friendship. When Declan would look at his wife and his friend, and think about everything that had happened to get to that point, he silently gave the Lord thanks. His path hadn't been straight, nor had it been easy, but God, as Declan's dad had said so many times when he was alive, is forever faithful to His promises. God had, in fact, had a plan for Declan, a plan for him to prosper and for him to have hope, as evidenced by the baby slowly growing within Megan, and a future by her side. Declan's only wish, his only regret, was that his mom and dad weren't there with him, but he knew where they were and that he'd see them again.

After breakfast, they walked together to the lobby of the King David. "Here's Adam," Louis said as he caught sight of his friend entering the lobby. "Are you going to watch the Prime Minister's address?"

"We'll try," Declan answered. "Evan was taking the kids over to Sacher Park to get them out and let them burn off some energy and let loose a bit before we're in the air for ten or so hours tomorrow. We're going to walk over and meet them there."

"Cool," Louis replied. "Promise me you won't leave before we get to say a proper goodbye. I know Ya'alon is planning to come by at some point before the day is done and say goodbye too. Let's all get together tonight. I've got a little going-away gift, and we need to send you guys back to Peru with a proper toast or two."

"Perfect," Megan answered.

"Louis, I just wanted to say…," Declan paused. "Give Him a chance."

"Who?" Louis asked.

"God. Just give Him a chance and I know He'll surprise you. He sure surprised me."

"I will say that my curiosity is certainly piqued. We'll see. There's plenty of time. I'd better get going. I'll see you guys tonight."

Chapter 65

Luke shined a flashlight on the ground ahead, illuminating a path over the white sands of East Beach to where the waves fell rhythmically against the shore. When he, Hope, Caroline and Jessica reached a spot just close enough for the waves to tickle their toes, Luke handed Jessica the flashlight and spread two soft red blankets out over the sand.

"This should be perfect," he said. "Please, after you."

"Why, thank you," Jessica replied, sitting on one of the blankets, her bare feet stretching past its borders into the water.

"This was a great idea, Hope," Luke said, sitting next to Jessica. "Thanks for getting everyone up."

"No worries," his sister replied. "I love watching the sunrise over the ocean. Next to watching the dolphins out there, it's probably my favorite thing in the world."

"Our ancient prophets spoke of such a time as this, a time when the God of Abraham would again shine His light on His people. A time when He would deliver them from their enemies and set His people up among the world. I say, resolutely, that time has come, and with it, the time for a new temple, a third temple standing proudly and solemnly in the midst of a rebuilt and revived Jerusalem for all the world to see."

The room erupted into applause as the Israeli Prime Minister concluded his speech, calling, as many had anticipated, for the building of a new temple for the Israeli people. Louis had stopped scribbling notes and found himself standing, applauding with the others, overwhelmed by an odd, and unexpected, sense of excitement and pride.

"It's a miracle day," a familiar voice said exuberantly behind him, and Louis turned to see Ya'alon.

"It certainly feels that way, my friend," Louis replied. "It certainly feels that way."

Declan looked to Megan as Sderot Ben Tsvi exploded into celebration around them. Israelis were pouring out of their badly-damaged homes and makeshift tent-colonies, onto the street, waving flags and holding high the Star of David.

"Everyone must have liked the speech," Declan said as he and Megan crossed the street and entered Sacher Park, which, for whatever reason, had mostly escaped the Russian attack without significant damage. Debris still littered the park here and there, but, for the most part, it was almost like an oasis of normalcy amid the otherwise battered, but energetic, city.

"Clearly. Do you think the Prime Minister called for a new temple, like Louis said he might?"

"I guess so."

"That'll be an amazing thing to see."

"Yeah, it sure will. It almost makes me sad that we'll be in Urubamba and won't get to see it firsthand."

"Not me," Megan replied. "I'm ready to get back home."

"That's why I said *almost*. I've been missing the smell of eucalyptus in the air and the morning light dancing on the river ever since I left."

"I like the imagery. When did you get to be so poetic, Declan Parker?"

"I suppose I'm a lot of things I wasn't before," Declan answered with a smile.

"I agree, and I love them all."

"Isn't the playground just up ahead?"

"It's just up that way," Megan replied, pointing across the park. "I remember that clearly."

"Cool. Evan just texted and said that's where he and the kiddos are. He said Tom was on his way there too."

Declan and Megan walked hand-in-hand over the grass, slowly nearing the playground, which was set off behind some greenery in the distance. As they got closer, Declan could see his nephew, Will, running atop a metal play structure, then disappearing down what Declan suspected was a slide. A few seconds later, he saw Charlotte do the same.

"Wow, Tom beat us here," Megan said as they came even closer.

"He must have had the driver drop him off here. I can't wait to find out if everything is set with the plane."

"Neither can I. I'm ready to get back to Urubamba and Uncle Ignacio."

Finally entering the small playground, Declan was suddenly overcome with a strange sense of deja-vu. He stopped, looking all around the playground, as Megan walked over and gave Tom and Evan each a hug. Declan couldn't figure out where he'd seen the playground before, but he was positive he had. The swings, the slides, the green metal benches, Charlotte and Will running along the play-structure among all the other kids of different ages: it was, down to the smallest detail, all eerily familiar.

The strange feeling Declan experienced was apparently so evident on his face, that, having noticed it, Evan called over from where he was standing next to one of the benches, "Declan, are you okay?"

Still looking around, Declan didn't immediately answer. Instead, a thought, a memory, that had been tucked away in the deepest corner of his mind, slowly began to emerge as he looked over to Evan standing next to one of the green benches. He focused his gaze on Megan, and the glow radiating from her as she lightly touched her belly, and thought of the tiny baby growing inside.

The thought continued to emerge and develop as he looked up to the top of the slide and saw Will and Charlotte waving at him. By the time Declan looked back over to the bench, where Evan, Megan and Tom were all looking back at him with concerned faces, the thought had finally manifested itself completely, and, in his mind's eye, Declan saw his mom and Michelle sitting on the bench next to them. His mom was smiling at him from across the playground. She had the same look on her face, the same love and thoughtfulness in her eyes, which he'd always been able to count on.

Seeing his mom smiling at him from the bench, Declan finally knew precisely where he was. He knew beyond any doubt what would come next, and a sense of peace unlike anything he'd ever experienced filled his entire body as a tear fell from his eye and he smiled back at his mom.

Out of nowhere, the ethereal shout the Apostle Paul spoke of in First Thessalonians echoed over the ocean and across the beach as Luke, Hope, Caroline and Jessica took in the day's first wisps of sunlight dancing on the water. The shout however, filled their senses and each looked to the other, and then looked around trying to find the source.

"What was that?" Louis asked Ya'alon, listening as the all-encompassing shout quickly gave way to a trumpet blast which, itself, filled the air and everyone's senses.

"It's a shofar," Ya'alon answered hesitantly. "But why?"

The sound of the blasting shofar resonated throughout the playground and, like the shout, completely filled everyone's senses as all in the playground, save Declan, looked up into the sky, trying to figure out where it was coming from. Declan remained still and silent, knowing full-well what would come next, and he was stunned to be alive and part of one of the most anticipated moments in human history.

Megan ran toward Declan, asking, "What's going on? What is this?"

Declan smiled at her and said simply, "It's okay, my love. We're good. Look up."

———————————

"Dear, God," Hope whispered as she looked into the sky over the vast Atlantic Ocean and saw the even more vast face of the Son of Man, the King of Kings, above them. Jessica gasped, stunned by the genuine love in His eyes. A feeling of intense peace filled her, then in a flash, before anyone could say anything, His face had vanished and Jessica found herself sitting alone on the two red blankets, the rising waves washing gently over her solitary toes.

———————————

Louis, dazed and not understanding what was happening, turned back to where Ya'alon was standing, only to find him looking as perplexed as everyone else who remained. They both looked around the room, slowly realizing close to half the people who had been in the room a second earlier had simply vanished. A few seconds later, Adam Benjamin appeared, his face ashen, and said simply, "The Prime Minister is gone. I was talking to him and…he vanished. All that's left are his clothes in a pile on the floor."

"What in the world?" Louis asked as he and those who remained looked at one another hoping someone had an explanation.

At Sacher Park, where seconds earlier children had been running around by the dozens, only a handful of adults remained. Once they'd regained their senses, those who were left began to look frantically for their children, all of whom had vanished before their eyes, leaving only small piles of clothes, shoes and toys on the ground where they had previously stood.

As the blanket of unblemished white light slowly faded from his view, Declan found himself looking into the pure, wise, endlessly-loving eyes he'd seen in the sky above Sacher Park seconds earlier, but he was no longer in the park. He was no longer on the Earth. The peace and pure goodness in Jesus' eyes flowed freely into Declan and the billions of others he stood amongst, and, without a word, He assured them, as only He could, that pain, suffering, sickness, and death were all things of the past. Such things no longer existed for them. Declan touched his arm, searching for the bullet wound, only to find there was none. His body was, in appearance, recognizable, but felt so very different. He couldn't remember what fatigue felt like, what pain or soreness had felt like.

Megan stepped next to him, taking hold of his hand, and Declan looked to her. Standing next to Megan, holding her hand, was their daughter, as beautiful as Declan had imagined she would be. He looked slowly into the crowd of faces that surrounded him and saw so many he knew: Michelle, Evan, Charlotte and Will; Luke, Hope, and Caroline; Edward Vanek, who stood among his wife and two daughters; Chris and Nicole Williams; Atau and Ignacio; Tom Langham; Declan's mom.

As Declan took in the scene of complete joy and celebration in front of him, the triumph, as promised by God from the beginning, of life over death, of light over darkness, a familiar hand fell gently on his shoulder. He knew the hand simply from its touch, and tears of total joy began to flow from his eyes. Turning to find his dad smiling and crying behind him, Declan knew beyond any doubt that he was finally, and forever, Home.

Epilogue

A cool breeze swept through the open windows into the Williams' house in East Beach. The temperature was roughly 20 degrees cooler than usual, and Jessica had put on one of Luke's sweaters she'd found in his closet. It was a heather-gray, wool, cable-knit sweater she'd seen him wear once, when they'd taken a late-night walk along the beach. Every so often, Jessica would catch a subtle hint of Luke's scent in the sweater, which, while it broke her heart, brought a smile to her face.

Tucked up comfortably on a soft leather loveseat that was by one of the open windows, Jessica looked down again at the handwritten letter in her hands. The letter was from Evan, and it had fallen out of one of the books in her backpack a few days earlier. Evan had snuck it into the book before she'd left Peru for New Orleans.

Jessica read the letter again, for the fifth or sixth time. It read:

"Jessica,

I know I've said this before, and that, given the circumstances, it just isn't possible, but I do wish I had gone back to the states, and that you hadn't had to. I'm not sure when you'll find this letter, but there are a few things I feel must be said. I know your thoughts on God, on Jesus, and I understand them. I really do understand your reluctance. This world doesn't make it easy to believe anymore, not that it ever did.

Regardless, I pray every day that God will call you to Him, and that your heart and mind will be open to Him, to His love, and to salvation through His Son. I pray this happens soon, very soon.

There's something else, something I've mentioned before, but never really discussed in depth. I always thought there'd be time to do so, but with you leaving, I'm not so sure. The Bible describes what is commonly known as "The Rapture". While the word, rapture, isn't specifically mentioned, this event is described by the Apostle Paul in a number of instances and by the Apostle John in Revelation.

In essence, at some point, when the time is at hand, Jesus will take His church home. The living and the dead. Anyone who is or was saved. Paul says in 1 Thessalonians that there will be a loud shout, the shout of the archangel Michael, followed by a trumpet blast, and then Jesus will appear in the clouds. In a flash, in an instant, the dead in Christ will rise, followed by those who are still alive, and they will meet Jesus in the air, and go to be with him forever.

Paul also describes this event in 1 Corinthians 15:51-53, saying [51]Listen, I tell you a mystery: We will not all sleep, but we will all be changed— [52] in a flash, in the twinkling of an eye, at the last trumpet. For the trumpet will sound, the dead will be raised imperishable, and we will be changed'.

I'm not saying this will happen before you get back, as no one knows the timing, but it could. As I said, nobody knows when this will happen, but given the events taking place, particularly the destruction of Damascus, I strongly feel it could be any day now, and I want you to be aware, just in case. I want you to know why, if it happens and you remain here, that millions, if not billions, of people simply vanished. I pray that you're among them, among us, but if you aren't, if you haven't accepted Jesus as your Savior at that point, you'll be left behind.

If you're left behind, the world is very quickly going to go nuts (for lack of a better word). As

bad as things seem now, they will be 100 times
worse then, quickly devolving into chaos. It's all
described in Revelation, and it's chilling.

Jessica, I want you to know that I love you. I
love you as if you're of my own blood, which is
how I view you. You are a true friend. You're
family. I pray for your quick return and that
when you get back here to Peru, if you've read
this letter, we can talk.

With Love,

Evan"

Jessica looked up, tears in her eyes and caught
another hint of Luke's scent rise up from his sweater with the
breeze. She thought of him and Evan, finally meeting one
another in Heaven. Would they be able to see the
similarities, the same loving and thoughtful qualities, in one
another that she'd seen in them? She tried to picture Luke
meeting her mom and dad up there, and hoped they'd like
him as much as she did.

Evan had been right. In the days after an estimated
billion people had simply disappeared from the face of the
Earth, chaos had ensued. Jessica had spent nearly 48 hours
glued to the news coverage, trying to get an idea what had
happened. Rafaelle Firenze and the other world leaders had
appeared on the news, each offering their explanation and
urging calm, but the entire globe was in a tailspin. It was, as
Evan had warned, 100 times worse than before, and Jessica
expected things to get even worse still.

Yet, as crazy as the world had become outside, that
morning, East Beach was quiet. A cool breeze whispered
through the house and Jessica, finally, had peace. It may not
last long, and difficult times were surely on the horizon, but
in that moment, Jessica had everything she needed. She took
a sip from a cup of steaming green tea sitting next to her,

picked up Luke's Bible, and tucked Evan's letter inside the back.

"Thank you, God," she whispered. "Thank you for Luke and for Evan. Thank you for my parents. Thank you, Lord, for finally opening my eyes to You and my heart to Your love."

Jessica's prayer rose into the cool breeze and danced through the air, rising higher and higher toward the heavens as she opened Luke's Bible and, for the first time in her life, read and believed, "In the beginning God created the heavens and the earth…"